GW01388480

DAVID M. SINDALL

SNATCHED

Copyright © 2016 David Sindall

The moral right of the author has been asserted.

Apart from any fair dealing for the purposes of research or private study,
or criticism or review, as permitted under the Copyright, Designs and Patents
Act 1988, this publication may only be reproduced, stored or transmitted, in
any form or by any means, with the prior permission in writing of the
publishers, or in the case of reprographic reproduction in accordance with
the terms of licences issued by the Copyright Licensing Agency. Enquiries
concerning reproduction outside those terms should be sent to the publishers.

This is a work of fiction. Names, characters, businesses, places, events
and incidents are either the products of the author's imagination
or used in a fictitious manner. Any resemblance to actual persons,
living or dead, or actual events is purely coincidental.

Matador
9 Priory Business Park,
Wistow Road, Kibworth Beauchamp,
Leicestershire. LE8 0RX
Tel: 0116 279 2299
Email: books@troubador.co.uk
Web: www.troubador.co.uk/matador
Twitter: @matadorbooks

ISBN 978 1785893 087

British Library Cataloguing in Publication Data.
A catalogue record for this book is available from the British Library.

Printed and bound in the UK by TJ International, Padstow, Cornwall
Typeset in 11pt StempelGaramond Roman by Troubador Publishing Ltd, Leicester, UK

Matador is an imprint of Troubador Publishing Ltd

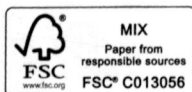

MIX
Paper from
responsible sources
FSC
www.fsc.org   FSC® C013056

'One is not called noble who harms living beings. By not harming living beings one is called noble.'
The Buddha

PART ONE

Many people would probably despise what I do for a living. I don't care. No job is morally neutral. Priests absolve people of disgusting things; nurses take part in abortions; firefighters call in sick. People ignore all of that shit so they can feel better about their own lives. Think about what you do each day and ask yourself, do you really make a living in such a pure way? I'm pretty sure that when you think about it, there's a deal you know about that you want to keep quiet, something you would rather not mention over a beer with your buddies. The guy who got fired who you didn't stand up for, the expenses claim that was a bit iffy, the elected official who is suspect, but you keep quiet about. I know that you know. You just don't want to be honest with yourself.

I can sleep soundly at night and I make good money. I pay all my taxes; I even vote for progressive parties of the centre left. Last year I gave over 200K to children's charities and not as some poxy tax loophole on the advice of my accountant. I always tip well too, just as the waitress who is approaching my table knows.

She says something to me that I pretend I don't understand.

'English,' I say and she smiles.

'Would you like another beer?' she says, as the smile lingers on her face.

'*Ja*,' I say, 'but you'll have to fill in the rest for yourself because I don't speak German.'

This is a lie, but it's a useful lie. I speak reasonable German; it just suits my purpose that people think I am a clumsy English businessman.

'Hey, no worries,' she says, flashing me a perfect smile. 'I like to speak English. You here for long?'

'Unfortunately not,' I say. 'I have a meeting in London tomorrow.'

'You'll need to get to Tegel then?'

I shake my head, showing disagreement.

'I hate flying. Why fly when you have Deutsche Bahn?'

She looks at me, interested. I know that look. If I were staying in Berlin tonight I reckon I could meet her later, buy her dinner and end up back at her place. Another time.

She smiles. 'Back soon with your beer, OK?'

I let her go; it is pointless flirting with her and I want time to reflect.

I look across to the Reichstag. I love the building – the shape of it and the sense of it being a phoenix rising from the ashes. A city divided is a city united. Berlin has everything. Great people, great buildings and an amazing history. What's not to like? My clients like it here too. They can blend in, they don't get too much attention and they can come here without raising suspicion.

In my job, blending in is important. I am never rude and never overfamiliar with people. I do nothing to draw attention to myself. You've got to be a bit of a prick not to blend in, so the first rule is not to do anything that makes you seem difficult, showy or memorable in anyway whatsoever. I dress business casual. Not Armani or anything flash, just Marks and Spencer. If I wear jeans they're Levi's; my watch is cheap – not a Rolex; my phone and my laptop are never the latest kit. I just have a way of presenting myself that says, 'nothing memorable'.

Sometimes my clients are initially shocked. The deal I closed this morning was worth twelve million euros. I think some of the people I work for would be happier if I arrived in a Porsche and big Prada shades, looking like some movie star. If I did, I could guarantee every fucker everywhere would notice me. I don't want to be noticed. This extends to everything else too. I have a modest house in St Albans. I have another apartment in central London, but my neighbours there think I'm an IT specialist, renting on a company let. The only luxury I afford myself is the occasional First Class ticket on Eurostar. Everything else about me is inoffensive and understated.

There is one exception – I have a place in Biarritz. A project I started about five years ago; an old, enormous château. Rooms everywhere. It is my hideaway, my refuge and the nearest I have to a real base. The chateau is so private I don't have to worry. The one thing I like about the French – and let's face it, with their arrogant wines, snotty waiters and useless cars there isn't much to actually like – is that they respect your privacy, they keep their distance.

The waitress brings my beer back. In a few weeks' time I will be drinking in Rome, meeting my client from this morning at the Champions League final. We will have good seats; it will fit with the deception of my job. Officially, I run a ticket agency where I specialise in hard-to-get sports tickets. Mostly in Europe, but sometimes, particularly if the client is North American, it might be cricket in the Caribbean or basketball in NYC. The important thing is that the deception is maintained. We'll go through the whole charade. Go to the match together, be seen enjoying each other's company, so that the story absolutely fits. Luckily, it's football, so I might enjoy it. If it were rugby or, God forbid, golf, I'd be in for a tedious 'day at the office'. Then, at the end of the match, he'll go back to Moscow, I'll take a train to London and life will go on. The deal isn't due for completion until the group stages of next year's competition. Doubtless, we will end up in the Nou Camp to sort out the final details. I look after my clients; there'll be no complications.

If people knew what I did, I suspect they'd wonder how I got into this line of work. I wish I had a complex answer, but there isn't much to explain. I'm the son of a London Underground ticket collector. I did a degree in Psychology and specialised in Child Psychology. Unlike all the other losers who ended up in the public sector, I wanted to make some real money. To begin with, though, I never knew how; I stumbled on this lark when I was reading the colour supplements one Sunday. The rest is history, albeit not very nice history.

Time is passing. I am twenty minutes from the Hauptbahnhof. I need to get Anna moving back in London.

Anna
Hanger Lane
London
18:00
April 17th

So now he has called. He has told me the approximate target and I have to do the rest. I made it clear. This is my only job. I want to go back to Bielsko after this. I have had enough of England. The weather is useless, the food is tedious and the people here are ugly. That is why so many Polish people fit in here – their face fits. Eventually, like me, they come to realise home is better. Here they pay you well and that is all there is. There is nothing to like or love here, nothing about this beer-swilling nation of badly dressed people that I will miss.

Everything is expensive too. From food to sanitary wear, everything is three or four times more than it costs in Poland and the stupid people do not complain. Instead, they read their ridiculous newspapers, watch stupid soaps and get excited about cookery programmes and dancing shows on TV. I wonder how the British managed to have an empire on which the sun never set. Maybe the world was more stupid then, or maybe they just got lucky?

Tomorrow, I have to go to Chiswick. Apparently, the 'w' is not a 'v', it is silent. Stupid language. If the letter is silent, why have it? I have an interview for a job as a nanny. I have to dress like a frumpy old maid. At least I can wear some sexy underwear underneath. The family are wealthy. Maybe the husband will try it on with me. This has happened before. But this time I will not let this happen. I have to spend time concentrating on the little boy, Thomas. I have to build a relationship with him.

The agency have confirmed my appointment for an interview with the family in the afternoon. He is a doctor, she is in publishing. That is the other stupid thing about this country, there is more red tape than Poland under the Communists. Does anyone follow it? No! They should have done police checks on me, but the woman at the agency, an African woman who smiled a lot but was not competent, lied that they had done all the checks. Later, when she put the phone down, she told me that I looked trustworthy and they had never had any trouble with 'your type' in the past. I do not know what she meant by 'your type'. I told her I was Slovakian, but I could have been Martian, for all she cared. Profit and money, red tape means nothing here. She didn't even check my passport. So now I am Anna from Bratislava.

I look out of the window. It is raining. I have to dye my hair tonight and then tomorrow I will be a redhead. Before this is finished, I will become a raven head and then go back to blonde.

Will they ever know the true me? They won't even know my real name.

I am heading for Paris and I am in my cabin on the overnight sleeper. This is total privacy, very secure. I prefer Paris to Brussels for my return journey. The temptation to stay overnight is hard to resist, but suppose all this unravels? What sort of businessman takes a Thursday night break in Paris? At least the rail travel is convincing; the official version is that 'I don't like flying', but in practice, more people would recognise you on a plane. There is a bigger churn on a railway journey, passengers leaving and joining, whereas on a plane you are stuck around the same people for several hours. They notice you.

I realised, when I was younger, that I am a meticulous planner. I might even be on the OCD scale. Used to annoy the hell out of people at university. 'Fancy a pint, Kieran?' 'Where?' I'd ask and then the whole planning stuff would cut in. Sometimes, I knew they were doing it to take the pee, but usually I was too preoccupied with planning and organising to notice. Yet, in my experience, successful people are able to turn their flaws into strengths. So that's what I did.

Unsuccessful criminals are badly organised and make bad judgements. So being well organised meant I was halfway to having the necessary vocational aptitude to succeed. Judgement? A hard one. In my early days, I was very self- reliant, so there was no need to trust anyone else. The summer I graduated, I creamed five grand from nicking other students' benefit giros.

In my opinion, it was a victimless crime. Benefits offices readily replaced the missing cheques and most of the recipients were middle-class kids anyway. Their parents would cover the cost of a missing dole payment after one call home.

That money gave me breathing space. I took off for a month's island-hopping around Greece. I meant to cover them all, but ended up shacking up with a Finnish girl on Hydra for two weeks. All either of us wanted was sex and someone to talk to. At the end, we didn't even swap phone numbers. It was pointless – we both knew we wanted different things from life. She wanted a career in corporate life, a family, a Volvo and a summer house on a lake near Helsinki. I was not remotely interested in this pastiche. We could have fooled ourselves and pretended, but we both understood that this was an interlude. So we said goodbye on our final morning and walked away. This gave me another clear insight. I discovered then that I am more than capable of emotional detachment. Not everything or everyone matters to me.

And when I came back, I enrolled for my postgrad in Child Psychology. I had an idea for my future, which ultimately is why I am now enjoying the womb-like quality of my sleeping compartment. I am being gently rocked to sleep by the clicking of the train across the tracks, as if my mother is wearing high heels whilst she walks with me in her belly.

Anna
Chiswick High Road
18th April
14:30

I quite like being a redhead. Men seem to notice me more. Maybe the red lipstick is what is causing the glances.

She was OK. Cathy. Not stuck-up and very friendly. I played the bright, excited child enthusiast, getting down on all fours to interface with little Thomas. She loved it, said I 'had a natural rapport' with kids. I felt like telling her, 'I'd have a natural rapport with a toad for the money I'm being paid,' but, instead, I smiled sweetly and told her I would like kids of my own one day. Not a lie exactly, but politics is politics and I was telling her what she wanted to hear.

The house is big! Enormous really; they must be loaded. Anyway, after meeting Thomas, we sat in this huge kitchen drinking coffee. It seemed like chitchat, but I did my best to be agreeable. After about fifteen minutes, she said, 'Oh, to hell with this, Anna. Give me a moment.' She flicked open her expensive-looking mobile and called the agency.

'Look, don't send anyone else,' she told them, 'Anna is perfect.' And, as she did this, she wrinkled her nose at me. I thought this was a bit spooky actually; she made me think of a weird witch. Still, I played the game, feigned shock and pleasant surprise, stuck both thumbs up and went through an act like all my life I had been waiting for this moment to happen. People are dumb – if they thought about it for one minute what would really be so great about looking after a kid?

Now I am waiting for him to call and to confirm what the timetable is. Sometimes we take as long as twelve weeks, but with this one, I think it might be a little longer. He hasn't said, but past experience hints that nothing will be resolved until August. We shall see.

August. A million euros in my account and then I will be free.

Anna took some photos of the kid on her mobile. I have e-mailed them to the client, just to confirm he is happy. He is very pleased. Says that he thinks they can even pass him off as having the family look. We agreed to a longer game on this one which will take us through to August.

Anna has said she wants out and I'll honour my promise to her. She's been reliable, but I only ever use them for two jobs. Polish girls are good. I tried to get a Kiwi interested once, but she turned out to be indignant, religious and a blabbermouth. She also drank shit loads, so just wasn't suitable. She shagged around too. So I just passed it off as a wind-up and dropped her from my contact list. Such a doughnut; she never even could get my name right, so not much fear there.

I got Anna through an ad in a newsagent's window in Hammersmith. A plumber I know is Polish; he wrote it out and, of course, I got loads of people calling me. Most were thrown when I told them to speak in English. Not Anna. She switched instantly. Impressive.

I need reliability too. How do I test it? I ask them to meet me at specific times in particular places. I'll say meet me outside 391 King St at 14:07. I will park nearby, so that if they turn up early, I know they're not suitable. Needless to say, they can't be late. Anna was always on the money. Three times I arranged to meet with her, three times she showed up, minute perfect. Final time I met her, I gave her precise details. In a text message, I said: *Meet in 2 days, Coach K, London Newcastle service, 5 mins after we leave Peterborough.* Not only did she show, but she turned up with the cheapest ticket for the First Class carriage we were in. She was excellent.

I gradually introduced her to the business proposition. For the first eight weeks I paid her 2K a month for doing nothing. It was a final test. If she was unsuitable, she would've been texting me every five minutes, asking what was going on. Not Anna. She waited. Now, in the movies, you'd imagine in a job like mine, you would tell your accomplice some cock and bull story and then compromise them. Hollywood always gives you a compromising factor, sexual or, say, drug-related. Yet, in my line of work, I wanted to recruit somebody who could not be compromised. Compromised people make compromises, whereas solid people don't. Once I told her the setup, I said she could walk away, but she didn't. I upped her retainer from 2K to 8K a month and explained how she needed to bank the money, ideally outside of the EU, but if not, in an offshore account. Her inexperience made her say, 'You mean Switzerland?' which made me smile. So I explained all the places other than Switzerland where she could put her money and she settled for an account in Guernsey.

Then, at York, I left the train. I told her to go on to Newcastle and then fly back to London. She needed to buy the ticket herself. She didn't need a receipt for the fare, but I had checked and knew it should cost her no more than £400. She needed to pay cash and get used to doing so. Again, she didn't object, just did as I said. Her compliance was total and, on that basis alone, I knew I could work with her. I asked her to text me at the exact time she arrived at Heathrow. Sure enough, two minutes after her flight arrived, I got a message, one word: *Landed.* She was perfect and has remained so ever since. Part of the kick I get from this job is knowing that Anna will not have to worry for many years to come. She will not be super rich, but will have enough money to be more than comfortable. She has earned her success, illegally, the hard way.

I am unable to sleep tonight. I don't know why. Some nights I lie awake and wonder.

I know some of what is happening, but not all of it. Little Thomas will not grow up in Chiswick, will soon have new friends and will eventually not be an English speaker. He has told me all I need to know, not much more. His justification is that there isn't one job that is guilt-free. I understand. Yet he doesn't see that being brought up a Catholic, I was indoctrinated with guilt from an early age. We all sin and our sins are absolved through confession. The trouble is, I am never convinced by this. Just telling a priest does not remove the stain of guilt, it just means you've told a guy in a frock coat who is probably buggering his little choir boys. The thing is that I do not yet know what this sinful act is. All I know is it is sinful. Nobody will die, I think, but maybe lives will be wrecked. Yet fate may have transpired for the lives to be wrecked anyway. If Thomas ran in front of a car whilst I was minding him, wouldn't his mother and father feel guilty? I think so. At least this way he gets to live. These are the thoughts that keep me tossing and turning at night. They are not good thoughts, but I know this is not good. Guilt is like a cancer that weakens the soul. Whilst I have so much money, I also feel bankrupt. Spiritually, I am not with Jesus, not with Moses and not with Allah. I am with the Devil. The fact that I know this also keeps me awake.

Maybe it is not guilt? Tomorrow, I move from here into the attic room in the house in Chiswick. I will live with a doctor and his wife who is a literary agent. I do not know what that means, but it seems she spends a great deal of time on the telephone, talking loudly and drinking white wine. Perhaps, when I get back to Poland, I will consider this as a career choice. The wine I like and I could learn to talk loudly.

Kieran
Kew Gardens
1st May
14:00

I've just finished with Anna and advised that she needs to dig in for the long haul. We need the right opportunity, so I have asked her to keep me advised of developments. I want to know about weekend trips, family holidays, that kind of thing. She mentioned that they are planning a trip to the Algarve in September. I asked her to check if she would be going, but she doesn't think she is invited. This is great because it means we can do the lift with her being back in London to all intents and purposes. The additional passports I got for her might be useful, but I've not mentioned them.

She says she is quite liking Chiswick. I explained it is a ghetto. She was confused. 'Ghettos are where black people live,' she said with a puzzled expression. So I explained that Chiswick was a middle-class ghetto that excluded anyone not prepared to pay £4 for a decent coffee. She seemed to like this and smiled, the first time I had seen her smile for a long time.

Sunday is her day off, so we walked through Kew Gardens. I explained that we needed to hold hands and pretend we were at least very good friends. She reached out her hand for mine at this point and leaned across to whisper something into my ear: 'I will hold your hand, but keep your fucking cock in your trousers, OK?' I laughed very loudly and dirtily and then pulled her close for an embrace.

'Don't flatter yourself, this is just a front,' I told her. She slowly pulled away but nodded, a very sweet-looking smile on her face. Anybody looking at us would've thought we were just a couple fooling around on a date and that is exactly the impression we both wanted to give.

One of the problems with this job is that you don't judge things at face value. If I see a couple looking into each other's eyes lovingly, I think it is a big act. If I come across two guys in the street arguing, I am more likely to suspect it is a con, not a fight. The message I give myself all the time is that nothing is what it seems, everything is false.

So Anna and I walked through Kew Gardens and then down along the river to Richmond. We said goodbye at the Tube station. I gave her a kiss and a big hug. Just as I was walking away, she ran after me, tapped me on the shoulder and then when I turned around gave me a massive snog. A group of rugby fans on their way to Twickenham gave us a big round of applause and Anna, like the Oscar-winning actress she is, bowed to them – almost showing too much tit. I smiled as she then ran off, jumping on an overground train, heading towards Chiswick.

She's not at all my type, but she's perfect for what I need in this job.

Anna
Chiswick
1st May
19:00

Today was funny! He made me play this game so that we would blend in. It was funny because I have no desires for him, so flirting had no risk. I even managed to impersonate Keira Knightley in *Love Actually* and run after him to give him a kiss. I liked it when the rugby guys gave me a big cheer. It left me with a big smile on my face.

I am still a bit sad though. He has said that this will be a 'lean burn' job. I am not sure if I have to persuade Cathy to take me on the family holiday to Portugal. I don't think so. He mentioned that I needed to start a story about my sick grandmother in Poland. Mention how she is very ill, that I miss her and that kind of thing. He didn't say why, I just understand it as something I have to do. I do actually have a picture of my gran in my purse. On the way home, I stopped in a cheap charity shop and bought a frame. She looks nice. She is as fit as a fiddle though, on account of drinking at least two glasses of plum brandy a day!

As luck would have it, Cathy has just come into my room to talk about plans for the week. She sometimes seems such a lonely woman. She noticed Gran's picture and decided she would say something. 'Is that your mum?' she asked.

Well, I wanted to hit her! If that was my mother, she would have got pregnant at sixty-one! So I had to make a joke. 'No, it is my little sister,' I told her.

She looked blank for a moment until I said I was joking. That it was my gran.

'Aw,' she said. 'She looks sweet!'

This gave me the chance to explain that she was in my prayers often as she was quite ill.

'Ooh,' Cathy asked, 'is it serious?'

So I explained that it was bad and even managed to get a few tears to flow. Cathy came across and gave me a hug which would have been sweet from a friend, but was weird in the circumstances. I didn't think we were on hugging terms. Then she started rambling about how her mum died when she was sixteen and you never get over the death of a close relative. So depressing! No wonder she is sad. Then, after a few more minutes of this, she asks me if I want to come to the gym with her, to the sauna. I think, *Does she fancy me?* because a sauna is quite an intimate place. I suppose, in fact I know, she is like all other English women and probably wears a rain coat and wellington boots to go into a steam room. Still, if it is a sign she trusts me this is a good thing, no? So I make like I am a puppy dog, that going to a sauna with this mad bitch would be the best thing that has happened in my life. So then she squeezes my hand, gives me a strange half-smile and says she will see what can be done. Why does she make it feel like it was my idea now?

There are things I love about London. Parks, the way people on the Tube are so distant, the view from Primrose Hill. At the same time, there are things I don't like about here. Litter, noisy children and English women. Tonight, this Cathy woman reminded me of that last one.

Kieran
St Albans
3rd May
08:00

Home. I keep asking myself what home means. When I was a kid, home meant my mum and dad arguing day after day, shouting and cursing each other whilst I sat in my bedroom wishing the world could be different. By the time I was eleven or twelve, I realised it couldn't be. I decided then I would love my mum and dad as individuals, not as a joint offering. It turns out this was a wise choice and made home life more tolerable. My mum was OK, so was my dad. It was just that together they were a volatile cocktail that should have never been put in the same shaker. I am the dregs left in the bottom of the tumbler, the only sign that at some point they loved each other or at least had sufficient lust to procreate and make a new life. Otherwise, they are divorced, in every sense of the word.

Since my childhood, home has meant solitude, a peaceful solitude, not an angry solitude. Do you get that? Some people are alone and content, some people are by themselves and tortured. Well, I'm the former, not the latter. Mind you, I've met plenty of people who are angry and by themselves. They seem frustrated by the lack of return on their investment; that's what makes them angry fucks. They must think, *I am nice to people, so why isn't this effort reciprocated?* I feel like grabbing them, slapping them hard and telling them that all that effort is wasted energy, like trying to heat a building with your lighted farts. First, they need to be happy in themselves, happy in their own company, then everything else will be how it should.

My home is my palace. My space designed for me. My St Albans home is what some people might see as being 'tasteful'. It's certainly not flash in any great sense of the word. Yet the trained eye will notice that there is no crap here. The TV is Bang and Olufsen. The sofa is Conran. Everything is good quality. Not flash, just good quality. Every inch of it is me. It is like a monument to the person that is me. I have taste, I have overcome problems, I am successful. I am not the son of an Underground ticket collector, I am not a guy who scraped through university with a 2:2. I am better than that.

My home is about me and just me. Nobody helped me decide on a style, there was no female telling me what to buy, no girlfriend helping me to pick up bits and pieces. I made sure it was detached, in a bit of its own space with about a third of an acre around it, but it's walking distance to the centre of the city. I employ a gardener on the basis that I travel a lot. I pay him £300 a month and give him a budget of the same amount to work with. I suspect he fiddles this a bit, but I don't care. He knows that if he gets something wrong, I will tell him – sometimes in expletive-driven four-letter words, but I will tell him. He also knows that he is replaceable, so if he fucks up there are a dozen others who will take his place. That's me and people, you see. Everybody is replaceable. Even the kids that I move around can be replaced. People just let their emotions get the better of them. They whine about the past and don't focus on the future. I often wonder if people really think about the things they actually miss. I don't think they do. I think people prefer to wallow in the shit that is their own self-pity, rather than properly think why they pine after something. Self-pity is like a comfy armchair: we can sink into it and be comforted by its bollock-warming intensity. It doesn't change anything. The thing you've lost has gone. Get over it.

The girls I choose for the jobs have to have the same capacity. You'd be amazed how many are simply sycophants, thinking if they say yes to me, that's what makes them fit. You see, I want them to be able to do the right thing. To know the difference between a right decision and an emotional one. I'm not saying that all emotional decisions are wrong; people fall in love, get upset and so on. With emotional choices, sometimes they work out for the better, but often for the worse. Ask yourself, how many people do you know who have managed to maintain that *joie de vivre* that was there on their wedding day? Marriage is an emotional decision that usually works out for the worse, not the better. Which is why I've never got married, never got too close to anyone. People have this unnerving ability to disappoint us, to fail us. Just like my folks. Just like... no. I'm not ready to talk about that. Or am I?

It was during my postgrad. Leicester. Leicester has to be the most non- descript, arse-clenchingly dull city in England. It says a lot when it's most famous son is Gary Lineker. Yet Leicester was where I did my postgraduate research. Her name was Zie. At first, I thought she was German, but actually Zie was her way of shortening Lizzie. It was easy to think she was German. She was leggy with blonde, long, straight hair, perfect teeth and a sexy laugh. She wasn't bohemian and she wasn't particularly badly dressed, she just had a style of her own. A poise and a confidence that only she could occupy. I think the first time I saw her she confused me. She was drinking a coffee in the Junior Common Room, clearly flirting with one of the older female tutors, well-known for not being heterosexual. I had this underlying sense of anger: *How could such a pretty girl be a dyke?*

I sat at a table nearby and they were having a discussion about behaviourism.

'The thing is,' Zie was saying, 'is that Skinner never picked up on the ambiguity of behaviour.'

And the lecturer, whose name I can't recall, asked her what she meant.

'Well,' Zie said, 'take courting tonus. If I flick the back of my neck or touch my lips, or what have you, most behaviourists would take this to mean I was attracted to the person I'm talking to!'

The lecturer suddenly started mirroring Zie's behaviour which made the scene even more depressing for me.

'The thing is,' said Zie, folding her arms suddenly across

her chest. 'A change in behaviour means the ambiguity creeps in. If somebody's body language becomes closed, rejecting, does that mean that the person who is one minute seeming incredibly flirtatious is, in fact, not?'

At this, the tutor gets flustered, realises she's been played and makes her excuses that she has a tutorial booked back at her office.

She leaves and Zie just cold-shoulders her. She is left alone, but in a couple of minutes, she is giggling away to herself. She catches me looking and raises a hand.

'Sorry, sorry,' she says, stifling her giggles.

'It's OK,' I say and then she just corpses. Throws her head back and laughs out loud in sexy mirthful abandon. When she finally recovers her composure, she pats the seat next to her.

'Come and join me,' she says, laughing.

This was Zie. Confident, playful rather than wicked, but stunningly attractive, not simply pretty.

We talked for a long time that first afternoon. She was an open book, but one in which the words strewn across the pages were strangely ambiguous. She thrived on ambiguity. It was her touchstone. It wasn't that she couldn't be honest, it was just she couldn't commit to a single truth. In her mind, there were many truths.

She was originally from Cheltenham, her parents were GPs and she was an only, over-indulged child. All the time we talked, she kept the coffee, cakes and biscuits flowing. I was amazed. Zie was slim, pretty, but judging by the amount she had eaten, she could have been a Russian shot-putter.

So, by early evening, I was wondering where the conversation might be leading. Yet, abruptly, she suddenly announced she had to be somewhere else. No explanation. Nothing.

'See you around,' she said, leaving me feeling like a freight train had slammed into me at great speed. I was blown away and just wanted more of her.

That's enough for now. Still hurts to talk about it all. Beauty shouldn't be so painful.

Anna
6th May
Chiswick
19:30

He has been in touch. Told me I need to enact the 'dash to Gran' midweek next week.

I know not to ask questions. I will do as I am told. He will sort me out somewhere to stay. He will meet me at the airport. Told me to bring my passport which, of course, I would do anyway and he will sort everything else out.

This evening I hint to Cathy, through tears, that my gran has taken a turn for the worse. She is very concerned.

'What is it? What's wrong with her?'

This is easy.

I point to my chest. 'It is her heart. It has not been easy for her since Grandad died a few years ago and…' I make the tears flow.

She smiles at me, a wan, thin smile. She squeezes my hand.

'Come on,' she says. 'Things will be fine, promise.'

I think this is a stupid promise to make. Who is she to make a promise that she has no power to execute, no ability to determine? She is stupid. She will fuck her kids up with promises like this, turning them into heroin addicts because their mother is so delusional, pretending that the world can be made a better place by a squeezed hand, a weak smile. I worry for people like this.

I look up at her. I give her my best lost-puppy-dog look and then a sniffle. I try to pretend I am holding back the tears.

'It is so hard,' I say and take a long, deep breath. I wave my hands about a bit. 'I would love to see her, but there is Thomas and...' I let my voice trail off. I am, I think, quite good at this sort of thing. I don't know why, I was never into acting at school.

'If it helps,' says Cathy, 'I am sure we could spare you for a few days, if you need to go home.'

So then it is time for me to put on a singsong voice that says, 'Oh, no, I am sure it will be fine and little Thomas is so sweet.' I just remember to dab the edge of my eye with a tissue as I finish this sentence.

'Nonsense!' Cathy says. 'You need to see your gran! No debate.'

So we play around with the idea for a few minutes more. I think we come to a perfect compromise where we agree that if she 'takes a turn for the worse', I can fly back to Bratislava for a few days. I am all hugs and smiles and positive thinking. I think I am wondering if I am tempting fate; God knows what would happen if my gran actually gets ill! Then I realise that, for the moment, the worst that will happen is that gran will have a bad hangover and a headache from her addiction to plum brandy.

Cathy is behaving as if she should be recognised by the United Nations for her kind act of benevolence. Honestly! English women! I feel like saying, 'You have only agreed to give your au pair a few days off, don't let it go to your head!' She is though, like many English women, believing that her generosity somehow links her to the queen. So sad.

When I compare this flat to my place in St Albans, I have mixed feelings. I like the location here. I am a block away from the Regent's Canal, five minutes' walk from the Tube station and have everything at my fingertips. I am anonymous too because this is one of those 1920s mansion blocks: imposing, but the sort of place where neighbours rarely speak or only do so when they collect mail from their post boxes. Even then, half the people here are not British and have a limited command of English. To live here the only lingo you have to master is money.

The flat itself came furnished. Not quite to my taste. The sofa is big and leather, the bedroom furniture almost tatty, given the rent I am paying. There is a little balcony with a wrought-iron table and two matching chairs. You wouldn't really sit out there though, only at night. There is a spare room which I use as my office. A modern Apple Mac laptop sits on a desk; no screen, just a printer. That's it. If need be, I can be out of here in about twelve minutes. I've timed it. I have had several dry runs where I have practised getting everything packed away and out in the event that somebody comes sniffing. My secret is to only have enough clothes here for a couple of days. Nothing I would leave behind has any value to me. It can all be replaced. I don't have a car, so I travel lightly. There is a fire escape. So I can be out and down on the street with a holdall and a laptop bag, hailing a taxi, without going out through the main lobby. This is, to all intents and purposes, a space station, not the mother ship.

At night, despite the rumble of city noise in the background, the place is quiet. You sometimes hear people coming in late at night. Neighbours back from dinner, shift workers returning home. Yet the silence is reassuring. Nothing disturbs me here; everything is ordered, well-run.

The agent I rent it from is discreet too – this is my third tenancy with him, so he asks no questions. I think they assume I am a drug dealer, possibly even a pimp. I always take places on a twelve-month tenancy, I pay all the rent in advance, take places where gas and electricity are included and never renew. My payments are always honoured, my cheques never bounce; if what I do gives rise to a sense of unease, this is tempered by the fact that it really is easy money. I have thought about running two places at once as insurance. Yet it's not worth the hassle. I can't be traced, nothing is in my real name. Here I am 'Graham Smith'; all my mail comes in that name, all the bills come through him. I had a classmate at school by the same name. He was killed in a motorcycle accident just before his seventeenth birthday. Getting a passport in his name was easy enough. The rest of the paperwork flowed from that one document. Bank accounts, credit cards. As Graham, I am largely untraceable. Even as me, there is not much around to indicate who I am.

Tomorrow, Anna will meet me at Gatwick. She thinks we are going abroad which is fine. The important thing to establish at this stage is the need for her to get away quickly.

Anna
12th May
Apex Hotel
Edinburgh

So this is Scotland! I have been here two days and have seen

25

nobody in a kilt and no Loch Ness monster. A beautiful city though, it reminds me of Prague.

Cathy insisted on taking me to Victoria station. She said that it was the very least she could do in the circumstances. I thought it was OK. He would approve. If I had resisted too much, it might have made her suspicious. Was I really going home or for a few days away with a boyfriend? She even wanted to pay for a flight, but I managed to explain that my mum had already bought the ticket for me. Her kind offer wasn't necessary, but I laboured on the praise. I know she is expecting beatification from the Pope. She was gracious in her acknowledgement of my appreciation. I swear when I finish this job I am going to work in North Korea!

She has started asking about my family. I have made things up! My dad, I have told her, died when I was eight, just after the end of communism. He was a cellist with the Czech Symphony Orchestra. Dad would be pleased with this – not with being dead, but that he is not a car mechanic. He has always liked Dvorák and classical music. A nice promotion, no? My mum runs a bakery. This is nearly true: she supervises a bakery counter in a supermarket – again though, she will like the promotion. Cathy lapped all this up, even understanding how I got annoyed about the separation of my home country into two. I explained that I was always brought up to think of myself as Czechoslovakian, not Slovakian. This gave Cathy a chance to show how stupid she was. She asked, very seriously, 'Shouldn't there be three countries? What happened to Ko?' I pretended I thought she was joking. I hope she doesn't publish geography books.

He was waiting for me, exactly where and when he said. At the ticket barrier, Gatwick station, 10.36. The first shock was that we didn't get on a plane. We caught a train back to London. Then we travelled up to Scotland, First Class, and arrived at Edinburgh. He has allowed me to go sightseeing alone. We are sharing a room, but it is twin-bedded. There is no 'funny stuff', as he calls it, going on. On the train, he gave me a small case of clothes and a bag with a blonde wig. I had to pop to the toilets at King's Cross station to put the wig on. Long, blonde, straight hair. It sort of suits me, although I have never had long hair, always short. He also gave me a pair of glasses with no lenses, just plain glass. Add these and I look entirely different. I look like a doctor, I think! A clever, sexy doctor.

We have spent our days apart, but eaten together in the evening. The hotel restaurant looks onto the castle and to the city beyond. I tell him that Edinburgh is one of the prettiest places I have been, but he disagrees.

'I wouldn't call it pretty,' he says. 'Grand, imposing, aesthetically pleasing, but pretty is not the right word.' I think about this and agree – he is right. I like how you have a sense of water or how the main shopping street is only built on one side, so it is a bit like shopping in a park.

It is amazing how he and I never talk very much about anything that matters. When I think about this though, why do we need to? We are business associates, not friends. When I think about it this way, he is quite good company: he never pries, never pushes me, just makes sure I am playing by his rules. Occasionally we put on a show of intimacy when a waiter is near the table. When the wine waiter came over, as he was pouring the wine for tasting, he placed his palm on top of my hand and said, 'You look gorgeous tonight.' He turned to the wine waiter and said, 'I hope the wine tastes as good as she looks!' The guy blushed and I am left thinking, *You are like James Bond. Smooth, collected, very good at this. Always in control.* Because of this, it is easy for me to play my part; it is like playing opposite an actor who you know is the best. All our improvisation becomes easier, not strained.

When we raised our glasses to toast each other, he smiled. 'Here's to our future success,' he said. A toast that could be understood in a number of ways, but one for which I was happy to clink glasses with him.

When I have money in the bank and enough time has passed, I want to come back to Edinburgh, eat in this restaurant, enjoy the view and then take somebody back to my room and fuck their brains out. Tonight though, this is enough.

Kieran
Paris Open Tennis
16th May
17:00

Today has been difficult.

I have met with a client who wants me to take on another job. I have turned it down.

He got very agitated, but, as I explained to him, I don't need the work and, besides, it isn't what I do. People think I am some sort of gangster, there to do anybody else's dirty work at their beck and call. I am not. I am a specialist, not a generalist. I tried to explain to him that you wouldn't call a plumber if you wanted your house rewiring, so why call me for a job I am not qualified to do?

I don't accept every assignment. I was once asked to get identical twins for an Arabian sheikh. I explained to him that the risks were far too great. Firstly, because the chance of them eventually being detected would increase. Two little white boys with blonde hair and blue eyes would stand out like a sore thumb in Oman. The second reason was that if they were detected, there was a chance that the trail could lead back to me. He offered me sixty million euros, but I said that my freedom was worth much more than that and, with due respect, I wouldn't be accepting his assignment. We shook hands, and he understood. The best people to deal with are those who see you as a professional, not an amateur.

The guy today was an Indian surgeon. I eventually managed to placate him, persuade him that I was not the person he needed. It was a close-run thing though. I need to contact the client who referred him to me, tell him that my line of work is limited. I also need to explain that I will not be able, in the circumstances, to take any more referrals from him. The risks are too great.

Apparently, Bill Clinton once said the secret to success as a president is to concentrate on only the things a president can do. That's how I feel about my role. Nobody else is as good as me at my chosen role. Nobody is as meticulous, as organised and, most importantly, as successful. I understand that some people may confuse me with a common or garden criminal. I am not. I am above that – I provide a dedicated, boutique enterprise. I am not a hired gun, available for any old underworld criminality.

A frustrating, wasted day. Spoilt my enjoyment of Murray's win too.

Anna
Chiswick
21st May
7:30

Another day, another dime.

Thomas is running around on Acton Green. I am sat on a bench nearby. It is a very warm morning. His mum had to be in for an important meeting at 8am, so we left the house when she did. Thomas is happy, excited to be out so early. I am happy too. Sometimes that house is like a prison. A nice prison, tastefully furnished and with good coffee, but it is still a prison.

We are at a playground. There are a few kids already here, some with mums, some with au pairs. I know to keep away from them. I keep away from the mums because they are irritating, think they are lesser royals. They live in Chiswick, but you would think that they just happen to have left Buckingham Palace for a few hours. The other au pairs are just too nosey. They will ask questions that I may forget the answer to and in turn they may meet Cathy and… well, it is better to keep things simple. I exchange smiles and 'Good mornings' – that is enough.

Thomas is a happy little man. He is rarely any trouble. Comes to me when I call him – well, most of the time. Sometimes, I have to look him in the eye to get his attention, usually when he is engrossed in things. He likes to hug me too. Big hugs, like a small bear trying to impress me. Most of the time he is happy sitting nearby or singing away to himself in a tuneless way. I don't want children, not yet, anyway, but if and when I have them, a child like Thomas would be rather nice, I think.

He looks like his mum, but seems nearer to his dad in nature. He is quiet, slightly sensitive, but happy. When I have spoken to his dad, he is polite, gentle, aware of himself and keen not to over-impose. A good sort of doctor, I suppose. Thomas is very lucky; I often think he wants for nothing. His parents don't argue, his home is lovely, he lives in a wealthy city, in a wealthy part of the world. He will never want for anything, will he?

He has told me that, no matter what, things will be OK. Thomas's life will only get better, not worse. I wonder about this. I know that there is trauma ahead, but he is young enough to get over it, maybe even forget here, Chiswick, ditzy mums, GP dads, Anna the Slovakian au pair. None of us will be remembered in ten years' time.

A Tube train passes above the playground, taking more people into London. Their jobs are simple, innocent even.

Sometimes, when I think really hard about it, I wish my work was just as innocent.

Kieran
Maida Vale
23rd May
08:30

My journey back from Paris was tedious. The train was busy, got delayed at Lille for thirty minutes, and then they ran out of wine in Premium Economy. I had to sit listening to idiots blabbing into their mobile phones for what seemed like an eternity.

With nothing to do, I started thinking about a return journey Zie and I had made from Paris about ten years earlier. We had decided to go for her birthday. It was about the mid-point in our relationship. We had outgrown the head-over-heels bit and had moved on to the part just before people start taking each other for granted. The weekend had been one drug- and alcohol-infused frenzy. She was doing everything: acid, coke, dope, wine, absinthe – the whole cocktail of debauched living. I could keep up with her drink for drink, but I have never been one for drugs. We hardly slept; we were either in a club dancing or in bed shagging.

The train was arriving back at Waterloo, we had spent the whole journey in the bar, and we staggered down the platform each carrying our own bag. We got through passport control without a problem. At customs though, a police spaniel got overexcited by Zie's bag. Went nuts. Barking, yelping, it was like it was doggy Christmas Day, New Year's Eve and twenty-first birthday rolled into one. The customs officer took her to one side, made her open the bag and inside was a stash of weed.

My memory of what happened next is clouded by the fuzz of alcohol left over from the journey from Paris and the general miasma from our weekend. I vaguely recall that Zie tried to suggest the bag was actually mine, a story that fell apart as soon as the bag was opened as it contained women's underwear, makeup and nothing in my size. Then she was taken away. I was asked to wait in a nearby office whilst she was questioned and body-searched. She was later released and cautioned. She claimed she would have been held on remand, but for the fact that she gave the customs officer a blow job. I didn't believe this for one minute, but part of me, a tiny part of me, worried that this might be true. The whole thing seemed to go on forever, but probably only lasted a couple of hours.

Zie was furious when she was finally released.

'Thanks for standing up for me!' she said as we made our way to the Northern Line.

I didn't know what to say.

'Zie, you had half the stock of weed for France with you. What exactly was I supposed to do?'

This made her even angrier.

'You could have fuckin' lied. You could have claimed the stuff must have been planted on me or that the bag wasn't mine or any other shit instead of the pathetic, passive role you took!'

She marched off into the Tube station.

Then she stopped dead, realising I was the only one with money.

She turned back.

'Come on, let's go to Camden or Hoxton, I need my shit.'

I didn't want to do this. I'd had enough and, at the time, had no idea of the geography of London. Camden could as well have been Canberra and Hoxton, Havana.

So we had a stand-up row in the ticket hall at Waterloo Tube station. She ranted, she raved, she slapped me and, in the end, feeling humiliated, I gave her her train ticket back to Leicester and told her I was heading home.

She stood and stared at me. She was silent, a look of disgust playing on her face.

In the end, I got bored, shrugged my shoulders and headed off into the subterranean world of the Tube system.

'You'll not find better than me!' she yelled.

Maybe not, I thought. Yet I knew that all that would follow would be worse, not better.

That journey back from Paris was a salutary lesson though. It taught me that caution should be my default position, even when nothing criminal is happening. It would have been too easy to get caught, too easy for the police to suddenly investigate where the stolen giro cash had come from. It also taught me that Zie was the wrong person to hang out with. She was funny, she was passionate and wild, but she was also dangerous. Not just to me, but to herself. She was a dangerous, out-of-control risk, and there was no place in my life for that sort of thing.

Anna
Chiswick
21st May
22:30

Tonight has been strange. I watched TV with Cathy in the lounge. We ended up watching a programme called *Crimewatch*. It is interesting because it has reconstructions of crimes and the public are supposed to help in solving them.

Cathy seems to think it is comedy. When a reconstructed photograph of the person who is wanted appears on the screen, she shouts out the name of famous people who it could be. 'Cheryl Cole!' 'David Cameron!' 'Michelle Obama!' The first time it is funny, but after this it becomes silly.

So I ask her, 'Do you not like this programme?'

She just laughs.

'It's propaganda. Designed to have people quaking in fear that their lives and homes are in danger,' she explains.

She talks away, saying that she has never been a victim of crime; that most people have very little to fear, particularly in London; that fear of crime is worse than criminality itself as it makes us distrustful of everyone.

I listen to what she says, but think she is rather stupid. No, I think she is very stupid. She lives her life in a charmed bubble, wants for nothing. Drives a big car, has a nice home, lives in a wealthy part of London. I find myself becoming angry with her that she is so indifferent to the pain some of these people experience.

'What about the hit-and-run attack on the teenage schoolgirl?' I ask. The programme had included a story about a fifteen-year-old girl in South London who had been in a coma for three months, having been hit by a stolen car on her way back from school.

'Yes,' Cathy acknowledges. 'It's very sad, but I can't help wondering why her mum didn't meet her. Why was she allowed to make her way back like that alone?'

So I remind her that she is arguing against herself. A few minutes earlier she told me that fear of crime was the biggest problem. Now she is saying that it is the parents' fault because they didn't fear crime enough.

She waves her hand, dismissing me. Eventually, she changes the subject. It is nearly bedtime.

'I'm making tea, would you like some before bed?'

I want to say yes so I can tip it over her empty English head!

Instead, I say, 'No, thank you,' and make my excuses to retire to my room.

Now I can't get to sleep. I am angry about her indifference and lack of concern. I realise that, in many ways, she is the perfect victim. Maybe having a crime committed against her will cure her of her stupid ways and stop her from being so aloof. She deserves what will happen to her.

Kieran
12th September
Lisbon
09:45

I am back in my hotel room. Breakfast was excellent and I feel ready to face the day. I have to pick up a hire car later this morning and then I will drive down to Vilamoura. Anna is due in Albufeira in three weeks. There are some final preparations that need to be gone through.

As far as I can gather, they are renting an apartment in a holiday complex that is mostly the haunt of Brits. She has been told that they would like her to travel with them. So this looks like our best chance.

We considered a number of options for the collection. London was a possibility, but Anna would be implicated too closely there. Also, the Met are much sharper than the Portuguese police. For them, a difficult crime is sorting out an unpaid parking ticket. What we have planned will be way beyond their competencies, giving us at least an eighteen-month head start. In that time, we can option various false sightings in Spain, Tunisia and Morocco. Enough to cause confusion whilst we spirit the 'package' away.

I am already planning the next two jobs. The first is for a Jordanian couple. They are unable to have children and want a middle-class Muslim kid for their own. The second is easier. Another Russian job for a fawning mother who always wanted a daughter but is yet to have one. Time is running out for her, so they have asked for my help. So far this has been a good year for me. My income is up thirty-five percent and future order books are full. Everything has a price; I am just lucky that this year my profit will be up again. Twenty million euros. Not bad. I'll pay tax on that too, not like some drug dealer, finding ways to swindle the public through laundering it away.

Anna, for her part, has been excellent. I have tried to persuade her to stay on for another job. She won't have it though. Still, I reward good work, so her final pay check will be closer to one and a half million. I reckon this makes her one of the highest paid au pairs around.

I can understand why she wants out too. I have thought about quitting. I reckon I need 750K euros a year to keep me happy for life. I have no pension, but have been putting money aside. So, at the minute, I've enough for twelve years. In a year's time, I'll have fifteen years in the bank and, after that, I reckon I'm two years away from stopping. I'll pull the plug, delete all my e-mail accounts and split my year between Sydney and Dubrovnik. Two fantastic cities: sunshine, quality living, good food and friendly people. Never see another grey, rainy winter's day again.

Before that, I've got to keep on top of my luck. Actually, luck has nothing to do with it. I just have to be sharp, focused. Luck is for losers.

Anna
Chiswick
12th September
22:30

Not long now. I am just wishing the next few weeks away. He says it will be a maximum of six weeks and then I can do what I want. It is both an excitement and a worry. Exciting because soon I will have enough money to do whatever I want. Worrying because we may get caught.

As time has gone on, I have understood a little more about what it is we are doing. Thomas will go to a good family, much wealthier than his own. He will have a 'very nice life'. I think he has this now, but British humour often works on making understatements. It is sometimes hard for me to know when people are being serious here. Cathy will sometimes say something is 'quite nice' when it is actually stunning. The queen, according to Cathy, is 'well off', but I think she is horribly rich, the richest woman in the world. I wonder how much money somebody would need before the British would call somebody 'rich'.

Cathy is the same when she talks about Thomas. Sometimes, he seems far away, but Cathy just calls this 'being in a little dream world'. So she will ruffle his hair and wait for his playful smile or giggle. I wonder if there is something else. I haven't mentioned it to him. He has never asked me to comment on this sort of thing. Anyway, it is not my place. Cathy, she is his mother, you would expect her to notice these things, wouldn't you? She hasn't and it makes me wonder if she is really a good mother.

Cathy seems more concerned about plans for our holidays. We are going to the Algarve; we have a big apartment that looks on to a pool and they have other friends at the place we are heading for. We have also had a conversation about me going with them – it was very English.

'Would it be too tedious for you to come to the Algarve with us?' she asked. I thought, *This is such an English question.* The words 'too tedious' are ridiculous to me. Something is either tedious or it isn't. You never hear people say, 'Oh, this is not tedious enough,' so how can something be 'too tedious'? Still, I gave her my best OMG look and said I would be really excited to go to the shitty and pretentious holiday resort with her other self-absorbed and self-obsessed friends, that it would not be tedious, that it would be lovely. I have learnt, you see, that 'lovely' is another word that these English people overuse. The perfect adjective for anything pleasant. Dinner is never delicious, it is lovely. The weather is never fantastic, it is lovely. So using lovely in this context earned me a hug and a wrinkled-nose smile of approval.

The woman is weird, a total creep, not lovely in any way.

Kieran
Brentford
14th September
17:45

I always get nervous before final project inception. I shouldn't, because I have done it so often, but it's no bad thing. If I wasn't nervous, I wouldn't be paying attention to the details and if I wasn't paying attention to the details, things would go wrong.

At times like this, I seek out activities and people that calm me. In particular, my Uncle Tony and Brentford seem to have the combined effect of putting me in a better place. Tony is a former railwayman. He and my dad used to wind each other up endlessly. Tony always argued that the Tube was nothing more than a boring kid's toy, whereas Pops always said that trains were for the toffs. There was never any malice, but there was good-natured banter between the pair of them. I miss it and I don't miss many things. Going to the Bees with them both represented a great afternoon out – in the beginning, I never went for the game, I went for the company.

After Dad died, I didn't go for quite a while, not all the way through university anyway, not until after I'd started with this little number. When I did come back, Tony was always pleased to see me, even though he never understood why I bothered.

'You get to watch all the big teams and yet you still come down 'ere?' he'd always say with a chuckle. He'd run through the list.

'You get to see Bayern, Barca, Juve, even Sparta bloody Prague, yet you still give up your time to see Bees versus Tranmere!' He'd chuckle at this kind of thing.

I'm waiting for him now, whilst he has gone off to buy me a cup of tea. The thought never occurs to him that I should buy it, despite that fact that he is now retired and lives on a pension. That's Tony though, generous, fair and a devoted Bees fan.

When people first meet him, they think he's odd. He's balding and a bit rotund and you wouldn't call him a great conversationalist. Yet, and this is what annoys me about those who dismiss him, if people got to know Tony they'd realise he's sweet; there's nothing nasty about him and he would walk through walls to help those he cares about.

He comes back, carrying a couple of teas.

'You still in St. Alban's then?' he asks.

'Yeah,' I say, 'still up there.'

'Spurs country, isn't it?' he says, pulling a face.

'A few Orient fans though,' I say, trying to placate him.

'We're there in a couple of weeks, you gonna come?'

I nod negatively.

'I can't,' I explain. 'I'll be in Portugal.'

'Blimey!' he says. 'You don't half get around, don'tcha?'

He laughs to himself. 'Still,' he says, 'given the choice, I suppose Lisbon or Porto or places like that are much nicer than here.'

I nod, but then add, 'Yeah, but the tea's nowhere near as decent.'

And he laughs.

We carry on chatting; the second half is under way and, before I know it, the final whistle is sounding. We've thumped Tranmere 3–2. A good game, two good teams.

I'm leaving the ground.

'You got time for a pint?' he says, encouragingly. The trouble is, I haven't. I've got to get across to Chiswick to go through a few last-minute things with Anna. So we end up parting outside The Griffin.

I give him a big bear hug which is awkward 'cause Tony is not one for physical contact, but he's calmed me and I am back in a good place. Focused, ready to move forward.

'Righto,' he says. 'I'll have one for you then, alright?'

I smile. Give him a nod. Walk off towards the Great West Road. He's a good bloke, Tony, a diamond amongst the shittiness of the surrounding world, always bringing calm to me with his decency and general good-naturedness. I think if he knew what I did for a living, he'd be disgusted. Sometimes I'm disgusted, but at least it's an honest disgust.

Time to move forward. There's work to do.

Anna
Chiswick
14th September
21:30

The only thing I will miss about here is Chiswick itself. It is nice. The people are friendly (for London), the shops are good and there are some great places to eat. It is changing though. Even in the short time I have been here, there appear to be more estate agents than anything else, but English people seem to love to talk about how valuable their property is, so they must be serving a need.

I met him in a pub, not one that I have been to before, on Bollo Lane. It had a great atmosphere and he bought me dinner. I think it might be what you call a gastro-pub, but we just blended in, another couple having an early dinner.

He explained that everything had been arranged. The day before the 'lift', as he called it, I would get a text message from Slovakia saying that my gran was at death's door. I would have to head home to be at her bedside and would promise to return by the weekend, if I could. He was working on the idea that if they were only there for a week, they should suggest that we meet back in London.

He pushed a package across the table.

'Passports,' he said quietly, 'and your routes back to the Algarve and then on to me at the rendezvous point.'

There were also some car keys.

'The car will be parked about half a mile from the apartment. It has Spanish plates. A full tank of petrol – that should get you most of the way to Bilbao. You need to complete the journey as quickly as possible, not stop overnight. At Bilbao, there will be another car with more instructions. You will need to get across the border to Biarritz and there is a villa you can stay in there. Once you get to Biarritz, the money will be transferred into your account.'

This makes me happy.

'You can also go back to your natural colouring when you get back to Slovakia, but you might consider wearing this for the short period when you are collecting Thomas.'

He passes me a bag and in it there is a wig, same colouring as my hair now.

'What if things go wrong?' I ask.

'They don't,' he replied firmly. 'I've never had a job go wrong yet. There may be slight delays, but it's all down to skill, you will have finished your work for me as soon as I let you leave Biarritz.'

I am a bit bothered by the last thing he said.

'You mean, I can't leave until you allow me to?'

He smiles reassuringly.

'Just a precaution,' he says. 'We just need to be sure that everything is OK. I doubt that you'll be there any more than a couple of days. Anyway, it's not a bad place in September, most of the surfers have gone and the casino is a good place to while away an evening.'

I am a bit happier with this.

'I hope you have given me nice cars to drive!' I say.

'We'll see,' he says.

'Anything but a Skoda!' I say, laughing.

On the walk back home, up the avenue, I wonder which cars I will drive. Maybe a BMW, that would be nice, or maybe something like a Volvo. I know it will not be noticeable because he has stressed that everything we do must not draw attention to ourselves.

Once I am in the room, I open the package he has given me. There are three passports, all valid for three years. The first one is a British passport and my name is Jill Betts. Hmm, I am not sure about that name, I don't think it suits me. The second passport is French and my name is Anne-Laure Le Merre. That is a much better name, quite exotic-sounding to me. However, I am worried that I don't speak French, so don't know how I would carry this off. The final one is a Danish passport and my name is

Mette Greversen. So I have three identities to use. If I add my own passport, that is four potential identities and I can probably go anywhere in the world as any of these people. This is exciting!

From the instructions, I have been told to use the Danish passport for my re-entry to Portugal via Faro.

There is also another sheet. It has biographies for all three identities.

Apparently, as Jill Betts, I am the daughter of a former English Army Captain who divorced my Polish mother when I was fourteen – that is why I have the GB Passport. As Anne-Laure, my story is that my father taught economics at the University of Toulouse. My mother died during childbirth, she was Slovakian and I am now working as a PA in Bath. And, as Mette Greversen, I am an unemployed gym instructor. Nothing more is said about her. I wonder about these three lives. All of them are quite appealing. I am comfortable with the identities. Mette is probably the one who is easiest, simply because she is the one with the minimum information.

I am going to dream tonight of being all these people, of escaping to a new life, anywhere as anybody. Mette is ideal, if only I liked the gym!

Kieran
St Albans
15th September
16:00

I hate this day. Every year it comes around and every year I fucking hate it.

Four days after 9/11 and you're probably wondering what is there to hate? Surely, all the bad things that can happen were in

43

Manhattan on that fateful September day when the towers came down. Yet my life is not dictated by global events, nor, I suspect, is yours. Sure, I give a nod in the direction of these things, but our lives are underpinned by these things, not defined by them. Other events define our lives and one defining moment in my life happened on this day, in the nondescript shit hole of a city called Leicester in the East Midlands.

A policeman was waiting on the doorstep when I got home. Like a magician, he had my wallet in his hand, a wallet which I had thought was in my pocket. Magicians usually look pleased, a clever smile playing across their face. But the plod looked pained, as if his power to make my possessions appear out of thin air was a skill he had stumbled upon in an embarrassing accident. His look was the pained look of a man who had farted in the middle of a dinner party.

I hadn't seen her since the end of term. In truth, Zie and I were no longer an item – after the scene at Waterloo we never quite recovered whatever it was that we never actually had. All you need to know is that we were no longer together.

I had been in a pub, not far from my old halls. I'd arrived back early, looking forward to doing my Ph.D. So I was reading the Sunday papers, early evening, leafing between the serious stuff in the *Sunday Times* and the tabloid junk in the *News of the World* and *The People*. I was happily lost in myself, getting a bit pissed, but relaxed. Out of the corner of my eye, I notice a skinny, waif-like girl waving to me. I should have realised she was drowning not waving, but, hey, that all comes later. It was Zie, or at least a version of Zie that was thinner, as if she had been compressed via e-mail into a much smaller file. Everything about her was reduced. Her face, her hips, her tits and her hair; it looked like she had given away chunks of herself for medical research.

She wandered across the floor of the pub and I noticed her limbs were really thin and I wasn't entirely convinced that she would survive the journey from A to B. Somehow or other she made it, leant across and kissed me on the cheek and sat down opposite me. It was like something from the Michael Jackson video with the zombies in the graveyard. I was, to all intents and purposes, looking at the skeleton of Zie, not the person who she had been.

'Hello, you!' she said. Slightly too loud, slightly too affectionate. Something was clearly not right.

'You look great!' she continued.

'Hi, Zie,' I said. 'You look... well,' and I pulled a face.

'Oh, don't worry,' she said. 'I'm fine. Just been getting off my head on some heavy shit and, you know, chemicals mess you up a bit sometimes. Do you want to get me a drink?'

'Not really,' I said, trying to be honest.

'Why not?' she asked and almost shouted the words at me.

I just decided to tell her the truth.

'Because it looks to me as if alcohol is the last thing you need. I'll buy you a pork pie or a pizza or something to eat, but I'm not buying you a drink.'

'Well, fuck off then!' she said and stood up, scraping her chair back loudly.

She stumbled back across the pub floor to where she had previously been, giving me a single-finger salute once she had sat down.

I returned to my papers. Yet I could see, each time I looked up she was sat glaring at me, not drink, alone, like a wronged dog kicked out in the yard.

After about twenty minutes, she seemed to spot somebody else she knew, a woman, and the next thing I knew, the pair of them had a bottle of wine, drinking away.

I returned to my paper, but twenty minutes later she was stood back at the table, a leering mess.

'We need more wine,' she told me.

I looked at her. I was getting angrier and angrier, but managed to stay calm and cool.

'The bar's over there,' I told her, gesticulating in the direction of the optics and the beer pumps.

'We've got no money,' she said and I could see all this was requiring a great effort. She was swaying, not incoherent, but the sort of person who, if you met at random, you'd know to steer clear of.

'Me neither,' I said.

She tried to sit next to me, throwing her arms around my waist beneath the jacket I was wearing. I pushed her away, gently.

'Zie, please stop that!' I insisted.

At this, she just lost it. She started swearing, threw an ashtray at me – which missed, then she called her friend over who tried to calm her down and then was thrown out by the landlord.

After she had been pushed into the street, he came over to me.

'Were you fucking with her?' He was menacing.

'No way,' I said, 'just some loser I knew in my undergrad days.'

He calmed down slightly.

'This place is a peaceful pub. I hate morons like her, fucking useless!'

I nodded.

'I know, mate. Can I buy you a pint?' I was trying to be conciliatory.

'Nah,' he said. 'I'll get you one for your troubles. Pint of Everards?'

I nodded and thanked him.

I didn't think much more about it. Just read more of the paper and finished my drink.

I left the pub about 7.30. The street outside was busy and I noticed a police car and an ambulance. Thought nothing of it. It was a warm evening in Oadby. Incidents happened all the time. There was no reason to think that this one involved me in any way.

I picked up fish and chips from Luigi's on the way back to my flat. Ate them out of the paper, enjoying being in the fading light of an autumn evening. I'd just finished eating when I turned into the street I lived. Outside the flat there was the police officer, the conjuror, standing with my wallet in his hand.

As I approached, he asked: 'Excuse me, sir, do you know a Lizzie Sleigtholm, also uses the name of 'Zie'?'

I nodded positively.

'Ah,' he said, 'and is this your wallet?'

I agreed that it was my wallet.

'I'm afraid it was found on her at the scene of the accident.'

'Accident?' I repeated, stupidly.

'Yes, unfortunately the young lady... Well, can I come inside?' he asked, deciding not to continue the conversation on the doorstep.

I was aware that I smelt of beer and batter and that I was a little unkempt in my appearance, but I wanted to hear the rest of the story. What accident?

Once I had shut the hallway door, he removed his hat.

'Yes,' he said. 'I am afraid she hasn't survived the accident.'

I was confused.

'What do you mean?' I asked, although I actually understood. I just wanted the words confirming.

'She's dead, I'm afraid. Killed by a bus that she stepped in front of.'

He held my wallet out.

'Can you just confirm that this is, in fact, your wallet?'

'Yes,' I said.

'So how come she had it?' he asked.

'I've no idea. She probably stole it.'

I explained about our encounter in the pub, about how she wanted me to ply her with alcohol and that the afternoon hadn't ended well.

'But you knew her?' the officer asked, tilting his head to one side as he did so, inquisitorial.

'She was a sort of girlfriend,' I explained. 'A term or two ago.'

He had a look that suggested he was satisfied with this. I was a student, wasn't I? Most plods probably thought we swapped partners every half hour.

'For the record,' he said, 'can I take your name? There may be an inquest and you may be called as a witness.'

We went through the motions. I gave him my details and he left.

I felt, well, what did I feel? I think, no, I know, I was saddened. I probably cried for a little while. Then practicalities set in. I checked my wallet. It was about £20 lighter than I last recalled, but my credit cards and bank stuff all seemed OK. Yet I realised that I was only irritated with the inconvenience of it all, not with any sense of affection for her.

At the inquest, the coroner actually absolved me of any blame, suggested that I was one of the few people that had shown any common sense by not buying her alcohol. She was over two kilos beneath a healthy weight and alcohol simply raced through her veins, getting her intoxicated very quickly. So, he stressed, I should not be held in any way responsible for what happened subsequently.

I don't hate the day for Zie's death. I hate the day because it confirmed for me that I have a heart of stone, that I am an unfeeling bastard who only really cares about himself. No love, no compassion, just self-centred, self-absorbed.

So, you see, 15th September is that date for me when I became a harsh bastard. It set down the path for everything else that followed.

Anna
Chiswick
16th September
20:00

Pack, pack, pack. Why does she have to take so much on holiday? We are not going for another week, but she has already done her early packing. What is that for? I go on holiday I pack one bag the night before. She seems to think she needs clothes for every possible occasion and, of course, there are no shops on the Algarve. So the idea that she might buy something, rather than fill a suitcase with her expensive clothes, is not one which floats around in her stupid, empty head!

In the middle of this, I take a walk. Down to the High Road. I need air and I need a break from the bags, the kid's clothes and the endless combinations of outfits. I am walking down The Avenue, enjoying the late warmth of summer when a woman starts talking to me.

'It's a beautiful day,' she says to me.

I nod. 'Yes, it is quite gorgeous,' I say.

'Ah,' she responds. 'Where are you from?'

So I explain that I am from Slovakia.

She nods. 'Oh, yes,' she says, with a long pause. 'You people from the east, you are the root of all evil, or at least our papers tell us so.'

I am worried, more than a tiny bit. I have come across older women like this before. She is sixty and I am worried that she is a nasty sixty.

'Let me tell you,' she says, 'people here forget!'

What was coming?

'My grandfather, he was Irish. When he first came here, the Irish were hated, they were scum. They were barred from renting rooms, couldn't get served in pubs, seen as being the lowest of the low.'

She looked at me and I still wasn't sure.

'Then,' she continued, 'things got better. The Windrush arrived so there were people from the Caribbean to hate. No blacks, No Irish. We were united by the fact that the locals hated us.' I could feel myself relaxing.

'By the mid-seventies, the Hindus and Muslims were here. So there was somebody new to hate. In fact, but for the mad people in the IRA – not that they were wrong – us people of Irish ancestry were not really the problem. It was the hardworking Muslim shopkeepers and Hindu doctors that became the targets of bile and nastiness.'

I was beginning to like this woman.

'Finally,' she said, 'you lot, the Eastern Europeans, arrived, with your fancy ideas of working hard and earning a decent day's pay. Anathema to the lazy locals who hated the fact that you were showing them up to be the feckless wasters they surely are.' She laughed at this.

Then she turned serious.

'But listen to me, lovey. These people. They're a bit warped. After you, there'll be somebody else new. It will be another bit of the world, Colombians or bloody Ethiopians for all I know. Then you'll be British. You'll be expected to complain about the newcomers whilst singing "God Save the fucking Queen" and kissing the arse of Prince William. In the meantime, the real things that made the country great, the NHS, state education, tolerance, well, they'll all be overlooked. They'll also miss the fact that the place wasn't ruined by my grandad or by you, it was ruined by the greedy vermin they call Tories who just have their fat noses in the trough and expect the rest of us to wipe their arses.'

She paused for breath.

'They'll paint anybody who opposes them as caricatures, as pale imitations of some bygone Mickey Mouse type. You see, they do that because the people who control this wonderful and godawful place are scared shitless that they may have to change.'

She's smiling now, but then stops, just as we reach Turnham Green Terrace.

'This is a mad country, full of people who are 20p short of a pound. Yet, and this is the big thing, once they have been through their hate, they will give you their love and they will proclaim you as British. So hang in there, sweetie, it's all transitional.'

With that she nodded, smiled at me, and wandered off into the distance. So a tiny part of me, maybe less than thirty percent, wanted to be here forever. To stay as Anne-Laure Le Merre or somebody else, knowing that eventually this little island would take me to its heart and love me like one of its own. There is nowhere in the world like this. It makes me sad to think that I may eventually have to leave.

Kieran
17th September

They leave today. A flight in about an hour's time from Heathrow to Faro. Then they move to their resort in Praia da Alvor. So they should be settled by about lunchtime.

You would think I'd be nervous, but I'm not. Everything has been looked into, carefully planned. All the elements are self-contained. The only person who knows how they fit together is me. Cars have been sorted, accommodation has been rented, people briefed and payments made where necessary.

Tomorrow morning, I catch a Eurostar to Lille. They have a Europa League game and I am, ostensibly, taking a client to the match. I'll then take the train the following morning down to Nice. Catch a match involving Monaco, before heading over to Biarritz. I have no meetings in Biarritz. I have hired a woman for forty-eight hours; we are a couple taking a break. She knows that she is to make a fuss of me. There is no sex involved. We share a room, nothing more nothing less. The act only has to take place outside of the room. Even then, we are not Angelina and Brad, much lower key. I have deliberately chosen somebody who although attractive is not eye-catching.

You might be reading this thinking, *Lucky bastard!* You're wrong. It's not luck, it's skill. A combination of focused attention and precise planning. At any point, I know exactly where I need to be, exactly what I need to do and exactly what the risks are. You? You're busting your balls in a dead-end job, going home to screaming kids and badly cooked meals; you think a glamorous night out is going for a pub meal. Well, bollocks to all that. I say you haven't used your talents properly, you haven't worked out what your key strengths are. Forgive me for saying it, but you're a loser. I'm a winner. I'm corrupt too, but my corruption pays.

What does your failure deliver other than self-loathing and self-contempt?

I know I'm being unfair. I know that you probably hate what I do, but I also know you hate what you do, day in day out, even more. Whilst you will drag your sorry arse into another meeting or stand teaching a class full of disinterested teenagers stuff they don't want to know, my not-so-unhappy bottom will be taking a few days off with a few more million in the bank. Like I say, loser.

Anna
Praia da Alvor
18th September
20:30

I hate her! What a horrible woman!

We arrive at the airport and she says to me, 'Please could you sit with Thomas, they will not let him in the First Class lounge.' So, stupidly, I agree. We sit there and I do my best to keep him amused. We play a game where I ask him to find people who look like animals. We start with a horse and then move on. It is a rude, but fun game.

After about forty minutes, she and her husband come back. They stink of wine and are a bit drunk. We get on the plane. I go to turn into the First Class section and she says, 'No, you and Thomas are back there, it's wasted on him.'

I am furious. It is only separated by a stupid curtain anyway! All through the flight, she keeps waving through the curtain to us. This makes little Thomas and me cross. He keeps crying, wanting to go to Mummy, and other passengers keep getting annoyed with us because the silly boy is wailing. An hour into the flight, she wanders down into the economy cabin. She picks him up, gives him a cuddle, but then goes back to her seat. The stupid woman! This just makes him madder still. He's crying like he has lost all his teeth! I eventually manage to make him calm, but by then he and I both have headaches and everybody in economy wants us to die.

At the airport, we then have to wait forever because she doesn't like the colour of the hire car. Thomas is tired, I have a headache, her husband is embarrassed, but she ignores all of this until they find her a blue (not yellow) car that she is happy with.

Then, at the villa, which is in a holiday complex, the second we arrive their stupid friends are all over them. I am ignored, like I am the maid, whilst Thomas is fussed over, she is air-kissed and he gropes most of the women.

'Anna,' she says, 'take the bags in.' Not a please, not a 'would you?' No, an order. I think the English term is 'knowing my place'. I am the 'hired help', here to do everything and anything. So, like a fool, I drag all the bags into a hallway. There is a room plan which shows their room, Thomas's room and a room marked 'Child minder' which is mine. There is also a spare room. All the rooms, except mine, have their own bathroom. I have to use the main bathroom, despite the fact that there is another room which has its own facilities.

Before dinner, I ask her about my room and if it would be possible to have the room with the private bathroom. She has been drinking all day, but her response is still unpleasant.

'Anna, you are lucky to be here. The room you are in is more than adequate!'

We eat by the pool. Pizza which is not very tasty. I am then told to put Thomas to bed and that I will not be needed until morning. The message is clear. *Do not come back out here and join us!*

Well, to be honest, I am exhausted. A long flight, a tense day and a realisation that I truly hate her. Anybody else has got to be better for Thomas than her. My room is small, but it won't be for long. Soon I will be rid of her. I can't wait.

Kieran
18th September
Maida Vale
21:30

She has sent a text. It says, *I hate her.* This is worrying. I don't want her getting emotional. She has to stay calm.

I have decided against replying. Anna needs to realise that the objective is to complete the job, not to like the person we are dealing with. I am not so sure now that I would want her for future projects. Getting emotive is too risky. Luckily, things are structured so that little can go wrong.

Worrying though.

Anna
20th September
Hotel Eva
Faro
23:30

Things happened so quickly.

This morning he sent me a text. It said: *Today: 19:00.*

This was the cue and a few minutes later another text came through on my phone in Slovak. *Grandmother close to death – come home! Mum.* For a moment I panicked, thinking it might be true, but then realised what was happening.

I went across to my dressing table. I put a bit of talc in each eye and immediately the tear ducts swell and my eyes look red. It is a good trick that I learnt at school. So I then go into the kitchen and she is sat there. I wail.

'Anna,' she says, sounding concerned. 'What on earth is the matter?'

So I blub my way through an explanation, making sure to add relevant deep-breath gasps between sentences.

'My grandmother! She is dying! They want me to go home!' Then I wail a bit and notice that Thomas has thrown himself around my leg. He is trying to comfort me, I think, which is very sweet, but I think he will one day realise that grabbing the whole person is a much better way to comfort people than latching onto random limbs.

She allows me to blub away and it is quite hard work keeping the hysterics going, but I do my best. When she speaks, she is quite firm. She puts a hand on each shoulder and looks me in the eye.

'You must take a flight to Prague,' she says, very firmly.

I do my best not to laugh or to even call her an ignorant cow for not knowing that Bratislava is the capital of Slovakia. The thought occurs that this would be like a Slovakian saying to a cockney, 'You must take a flight to Cardiff!'

I blub a bit more, but she adds a negative twist.

'You can take unpaid leave and meet up with us back in London.'

This woman has no generosity of spirit! Her first thought is pay. Wow! I stay in grateful peasant mode though.

'Thank you! Thank you!' I say.

She then adds, 'Do you need to borrow the money for the flight?'

I have been told that British people are kind and generous. Of course, London is also the centre of the world's financial institutions. I half expect her to mutter quietly about interest rates and the like, same as on those adverts you hear on the radio.

'No, no,' I say softly. 'I have the money for a flight. Is it OK if I go and check online?'

She nods and hugs me. I am surprised that she hasn't given me a bill for her time as a counsellor – perhaps she will give that to me back in London?

'OK,' she says. 'We will pay for a taxi to the airport.'

At this, I am shocked. Genuine generosity, unbelievable.

'Thank you, thank you,' I say. 'You are very, very kind.'

Then she does that annoying wrinkling of the nose thing, hugs me again and tells me to go and get sorted.

Whilst I'm pretending to sort flights out, Thomas comes into my room.

'Can we play in the pool?' he asks, his voice sad because he knows the answer.

I cuddle him. He is sweet, not yet infected by the mean-spiritedness of his mother.

'I promise I will see you soon. OK?' This is, perhaps, the first truthful thing I've said for about an hour.

He nods, but his bottom lip trembles away.

The next few hours are spent pretending to sort flights out. I get a taxi to the airport at about six.

I was told that the plan was for me to fly to Bratislava and come back to Portugal as Anne-Laure Le Merre. After I checked in though, I got a new text message: *Don't join flight. Re-enter as Anne-Laure immediately.*

Fortunately, I had the wig and some dark glasses in my rucksack that I was carrying. I slipped into a rather smelly toilet and made all the changes in a cubicle. It only took me a few minutes to find passport control. As it was a French passport, I was waved through the EU channel.

Then a strange thing I wasn't expecting – a Portuguese man approached me.

'I think you dropped your phone,' he said, handing me a gold-plated mobile. As he put it in my hand, my old mobile vibrated.

Destroy this now. Use phone you have just been given, the text message read.

I looked up and the man who gave me the phone had disappeared. I wondered if he was nearby, organising everything from close quarters. Yet looking around all I could see were tourists and the odd suited businessperson. He wasn't there.

I popped into another toilet, this one not so smelly, went in to another cubicle, dropped the phone on the floor and then stamped on it. I removed the SIM card, bent it, then scraped the mess up and dropped it into the toilet pan.

As I left the loo, I received another message. It told me to head here. Check in as AL and follow the instructions in the safe. There was a code for the safe door: 2009. I thought, *That wouldn't take a genius to work out,* but I was still quite impressed about all the planning.

Now I have a glass of wine, there is a suitcase full of Ann-Laure clothes and car keys for something that will be parked in the short stay car park on Level 4.

Will I sleep tonight? I don't know. All this clever planning is making me very confident that everything will work. Tomorrow something new starts, tomorrow I have the opportunity to begin my new life. I will not be a frumpy au pair working for a ridiculous family. I will control my future and, hopefully, my past will not control me.

PART TWO

Lisa Lagnoo
Praia da Alvor
24th September
09:30

So here's the deal. I actually don't want to be here. Normally, at this time of the year, I'd be covering the party conference season. Stupidly, in my appraisal session this year, I said I wanted to branch out. So, in the spirit of my desire, which only came about because I couldn't think of anything else to say, I am not shagging a Labour MP or giving a BJ to some up-and-coming Tory wonderkid, I am in a one-eyed hole in the Algarve, covering a crime story. OK, so it's a big story, I just can't believe that people come to places like this for a holiday. That has to be a crime in itself, doesn't it?

What I have so far is that a nice couple from Chiswick have had their only son nicked whilst they were having dinner by the pool. One of my tabloid brethren, a bit of a pisshead if you ask me, has come up with the headline: BABY THOMAS STOLEN WHILE MUM AND DAD GOT DRUNK. Well, there isn't much evidence for that. It has about the same validity as ADMIRAL NELSON HAS TWO ARMS, but the shit that sells his paper has nothing to do with the truth. What he sells is a mirror that he can hold up for his readers to look at and, through the haze, they can make out their own faces. 'We've done that kind of thing,' his readers might think and that spurs them on to read more about how these sad arses got caught out.

I wish I could say it beats having my tits groped by some Home Counties Tory or my arse grabbed by a trade union

61

baron, but, in reality, both are much more enjoyable than the tedium of the Algarve. The police here are useless too. This was confirmed to me by a colleague from Lisbon who explained that Portugal was to policing what England was to sobriety. He told me this in a bar yesterday lunchtime and I just pulled a face which hopefully conveyed disdain, but I'm worried he mistook this as a come-on. He's like a young version of Kenneth Clarke and I am 100% certain that he will not be getting inside my knickers. I will either have to be bored or desperate or desperately bored. It means though that I suspect this story is going to move very, very slowly.

There is a suggestion from the more mischievous hacks that they, the parents, might have done it. To be honest, even if there wasn't a hint, it's worth hinting at. Our readers like tragedy, but they also like betrayal and complexity. So if we lead them along a particular route of enquiry, not by suggestion you understand, it will keep their little piggy noses interested in what may not be a particularly riveting story. Truth, anyway, rarely sells newspapers. Speculation sells newspapers, be it about politicians, the weather, footballers or foreign affairs. My ideal headline would be: MAN UNITED MIGHT BACK TORIES IN COLD WINTER. That more or less has everything. The winter is not going to be cold, but everybody assumes we will have a cold winter. There's always some idiot who works on the basis that 'there's no smoke without fire', without realising that we are just blowing smoke up our readers' arses. Plus, at the same time, every other hack will wonder how we broke the story, claiming that they had heard the rumours too, but dismissed them as being baseless. The joy of journalism is that when you make shit up, half a dozen other people claim the shit was theirs in the first place.

There is some shit on these two though. For example,

there's an au pair in the background who has disappeared to Slovakia. I've got somebody back in London trying to track her down – does she have a back story? Family rows? Randy doctor groping her? Got to be something in that.

There's something about the mother too – I don't know what – that just doesn't stack up. She seems a bit too together. Shouldn't she be falling apart a bit more? Their only child! Stolen. At times, she gives the impression that she's lost an Oyster card, not her only child. Is she being sedated? That would also help with the story. DISTRAUGHT MOTHER BECOMES ZOMBIE AFTER CHILD IS TAKEN. The trouble is that most of our female readers aren't much more than zombies themselves. Make breakfast; take kids to school; housework; watch *Loose Women*; supermarket; collect kids from school; dinner; sex; sleep. That's an exciting day too!

Meanwhile, I am killing time, waiting for things to happen in Praia da Alvor. I think usually a big news story would be a pensioner getting locked out of their apartment or maybe somebody shoplifting in a local supermarket. God knows, I understand why people do it here; anything to escape the creeping monotony, the sense that time has stopped, that it is forever 1986 and that everything has been frozen amongst the Sangria, king prawns and suntan lotion.

Lisa Lagnoo
Praia da Alvor
25th September
14:30

Excitement! Well, no, not really. The police have called a news conference for tomorrow to talk about 'developments in their investigation'. This could mean something or it could mean nothing; as usual they're not giving anything to us hacks that really matters.

I spent the day sat across the bar opposite the Billy Warner or Mark Butlin complex they were staying in. I was hoping to see if anybody coming out would take a beer or a coffee here. The trouble is it is one of those all-inclusive places. So the dumb-arses staying there are unlikely to come across the road and spend €4 for beer when they can guzzle as much as they want across the way.

Still, the wine was quaffable. So much so that I zipped through a good couple of bottles before my thoughts were interrupted by a call from the news desk.

'Lisa!' the news editor barked. 'What's the story?'

I hate questions like that, but Danny Drummond is notorious for talking like he's running a Radio 5 phone-in.

'Hi, Danny,' I say, doing my best not to sound like I am sozzled. 'I think the story is "Portuguese police clueless in hunt for missing boy".'

Danny likes this. It fits with our general editorial *raison d'être*. Foreigners stupid, Brits super-intelligent. Most of our readers make UKIP seem like pinkos, so it plays well with those who buy our paper.

'Great!' says Danny. Happy that I am getting an angle on a lean burn story. 'So what are they saying?' Danny barks down the line.

'That's just it, Danny. They're not! They won't answer questions. Won't give us any news on how the investigation is progressing.'

This is a lie, but I am a convincing liar. I have years of experience of it.

'OK, so can you raise that question at the news conference in the morning?'

Fuck me, I missed that, but I'm not flustered.

'No problem,' I say.

'I'm sending you some stuff we've picked up from their families and friends,' Danny explains. 'The usual stuff, nothing earth-shattering. Can you knock it into seven hundred and fifty words for tomorrow's edition? Get it to me for seven, so we can run it online.'

'No problem,' I say. 'You'll have it by six!'

'Excellent! Great stuff, Lisa – let's give this story some traction, yeah?'

'Will do, Danny,' I say.

We hang up. Two minutes later, I am checking my e-mail where there is a bundle of stuff collected by the research team. Totally uninteresting, but the trick is to mix the quotes from real people against the story.

I draft a headline for the sub-editor to play with.

PORTUGUESE POLICE – SLEEPING THROUGH THE MYSTERY

I then match a couple of quotes from neighbours and the like with a generally unfounded article about how our paper believes that the local plod are lazy, fat and feckless. When I have finished, I edit it down a bit, move a few facts for effect – and there you have it.

I go back to my room for a sleep, but at about 7.15, Danny calls again.

'Lisa! Great stuff. The boss wants to run it on the front page. We're also going to do a leading article. Usual shit, you know. What's the point of being in Europe if the useless wankers can't solve crimes? You happy with that?'

Blimey! Front page, a leader comment and the boss is happy. Tomorrow, I'll have three bottles of wine!

Fuck! This is getting serious.

So I turn up for the press conference and the local Chief of Police lets fire.

'It is not helpful that certain elements of the media are choosing to tell lies about our investigation. People like Ms. Lagnoo must know better than to expect to be given minute-by-minute information. Salacious gossip is not an alternative to accurate, balanced and fair reporting.'

All eyes were on me.

He continued, 'Britain has always been known for balance and fairness. The British are our oldest ally and we wish this to remain the case. Yet Ms. Lagnoo does nothing to support this case by peddling lies and quarter truths. We expect more.'

Bloody hell! Luckily, other colleagues come to my defence. Up pops a guy from *The Mirror*.

'You're hiding your lack of progress by attacking Lisa Lagnoo. Wouldn't it be wiser to concentrate your energy on finding out what has happened to little Thomas? Isn't that what you're paid to do?'

There is a small ripple of applause at this point, a sense as well that colleagues are closing ranks. The Chief of Police snaps back, 'You fail to appreciate the challenges and the efforts we are making. There is nothing else to say!'

With that he gets up and leaves the small podium.

I am suddenly surrounded by TV cameras and microphones. In several different languages, I am asked the same question.

'Lisa Lagnoo, how would you like to respond to the attack by the Chief of Police?'

I am good at my job and I hold a long-term ambition to break into broadcasting. I make the tone of my voice a little deeper, put on my best hurt look.

'You know,' I begin, 'it's a bit upsetting for me, but it must be devastating for Thomas's parents. We are talking about the search for a little boy who has gone missing. Instead, the local police want to turn this into a political story. His parents must be feeling sick to their very souls and, frankly, I share those feelings. Instead of using me as a scapegoat, they need to get on with the job and find Thomas!'

More questions are thrown at me, but I decide to quit whilst I have the emotional upper hand. As soon as I step outside, my phone rings. It's my editor.

'Bloody amazing, Lisa! We'll nail them for this!'

'You saw it?' I ask.

'Saw it! It was live on Sky, BBC News 24, CNN, the works. Fucking well done!'

He hangs up. I'm still being pursued, but restrict myself to polite 'No comments'. I'm careful not to become the story, but I know, at least for the next twelve hours, I am the story.

There are days when I hate this job, but not this morning. This morning feels like I have the best job in the universe.

Lisa Lagnoo
Praia da Alvor
26th September
11:30

One of the researchers has got back to me from the London desk. They have been trying to track down Anna, the au pair. They have checked with all the airlines flying out of Faro and they have no record of her travelling with them. Now, it could be nothing. I suspect the guy doing the research is a bit excitable anyway, intern doing work experience before going off to journalism college, but I wonder if it points to something else. His boss, Clara, has been doing some sniffing around about the husband. She says that the one thing that keeps cropping up is that he has a 'way with the ladies'. I am wondering if this means he's been shitting on his own doorstep and fucking the au pair? Doesn't tell us anything, but it gives us the basis for a new angle. LITTLE TOMMY'S DAD IS BONK MAD! works as a headline in my opinion, but now may not be the right time to use it.

The police didn't hold a press conference today. I am not surprised. They have been condemned for playing the politics of this by every English paper. There was a particularly well-written leading article in the *Express* that indicated they were playing the man, or in my case woman, and not the ball. There's even a possibility that I might be invited on *Newsnight* this evening. That would really help raise my profile.

Happy days!

Lisa Lagnoo
Praia da Alvor
26th September
22:50

That was exhilarating! *Newsnight* isn't quite what it was in Paxo's day, but Kirsty Wark is still good.

There was me, a spokesman for the Portuguese police and one of our nondescript government ministers.

Wark came to me first of all, probing away at why I thought

68

the local police weren't doing a good job, what else I thought they should be doing. I was able to reference how in the past, with Southam for example, police maintained clear and open lines of communication with the public; that the public were often the best detectives out there and that communication was the key. At one point, I said something like, 'We don't have half the facts to go on, we don't even have quarter-facts, in fact all we know for certain is that a little boy is missing in suspicious circumstances. We need more.'

In a PR disaster, the Portuguese spokesperson was fat and lacking in charisma. He explained that this was a police investigation, not salacious entertainment for the media. This allowed me to jump in.

'What a ridiculous statement. All research indicates that the first thirty-six hours in any investigation are crucial.' I had no idea if this was true, but I was convincing in the way I said it. 'We don't want this crime to remain unsolved, we want you and your colleagues to find little Thomas. Why do you keep suggesting that we are somehow reporting this case as if it were an extended soap opera?'

He flustered about with that, then Kirsty turned to the minister present, who offered platitudes about co-operation being important, sharing resources from Scotland Yard if necessary and giving the general impression that most of what I was saying was where he was coming from. And then it was over.

I'd been doing the piece down the line in a little studio in Faro. So at the end of the interview, I just got a 'Thanks, Lisa, great stuff' from the director in London and then got whisked back in a car to my hotel at Praia da Alvor. My phone was going mad: texts from colleagues, calls from the boss and so on. A few of the texts suggested that I should do more telly, more broadcasting. By the time I got back to my hotel, I really was as high as a kite.

In my room, I checked coverage online. Sure enough, the quality media had picked up my quote on the first thirty-six hours, so that pure speculation on my part had now become a 'fact' of the story. I wish the public knew how lazy we journalists are, that often what we say is baseless and made up. Hell though, it beats doing a real job for a living.

Lisa Lagnoo
Praia da Alvor
28th September
14:30

Yesterday was quiet. No developments. I filed a short story claiming that even the locals were getting frustrated by the lack of progress. There was no evidence for this, but, in the absence of hard facts, making stuff up was the next best thing. Of course, you have to be careful. For example, a line in my report said: 'One local I spoke to claimed that the police in Praia da Alvor were only ever interested in minor tourist crimes and that for them a lost passport was a big issue.'

In fact, that had been said by a local waitress who commented that normally Praia was crime-free, nothing happened. The police here had very little to do other than deal with drunken tourists who had lost their passports.

Call it journalistic embellishment. My line is more readable and keeps the attention at home.

Yesterday afternoon, we had a team conference call. People were delighted that we had managed to set the tone for the media coverage and were seen as having started a campaign for little Thomas. There was a worry that other titles might get a better angle. So we got the team looking at how we might spin the story or find new lines. One thing I wanted the team to check was what had happened to the au pair, Anna. We knew that she had not been seen since before Thomas was taken, so where was she, what could we find out about her? We also wanted more angles on the doctor. Could we find out more about his sexual activities? Was he really the devoted husband or a man whose reputation was strongest in the bedroom? This wouldn't tell us much about the crime, but it would keep the public interest going (I find it odd that no editor explained at the Leveson Enquiry that any story that the public were interested in was in the public interest). Finally, we wanted to look for local suspects. Had somebody taken Thomas who he'd already met whilst on holiday? Somebody working in the resort? Another guest?

The last angle was probably going to be the most productive. By this morning, I had received a number of e-mails about some of the guests. One of them, a Mr Kellison, was suspended from a teaching job recently. Another guest, Derek McHugh, turns out to have been a small-time gangster from Lewisham. He'd done time, but only for low-level offences.

I was pondering all of these possibilities at lunchtime, playing with a tuna fish salad and enjoying a local rosé wine. My thoughts were interrupted by a woman looming over my table. At first, I didn't recognise her. She was dressed in a white T-shirt and jeans and her hair was worn loose, down to her shoulders. Then I realised it was the waitress from a few days ago. Off duty, she looked younger and prettier than when she was working.

'People say you are a reporter,' she said. Her English was good, not particularly accented, but slow.

'That's right,' I said and gestured for her to take a seat at my table.

She sat down.

'Can I get you a drink?' I asked. One of my rules of journalism is that if a punter approaches you, be nice. In a situation like this, it usually means they have something to share.

She smiled. 'Rosé too,' she said, rolling the r at the start of the word in a way that an English person would find difficult.

A few moments later, she had her glass next to her and started to talk.

'Thomas,' she said. 'I think the police are looking in the wrong place.'

'Go on,' I said, smiling to encourage her to say more. 'This sounds interesting.'

'There is a man,' she said. 'He is German, he has been here all summer.'

This was good. Our readers hate foreigners, but hold Germans in particular contempt – for them, the Second World War is a ceasefire, not over.

She then proceeded to explain that the German had arrived in May. He was in his fifties and when he first came he had a very pretty, very young woman with him. She was maybe sixteen or seventeen, possibly even younger.

'Some of us were concerned. We thought this girl was too young to be with this man. There was no doubt that they were together and also that their relationship was intimate.'

'Maybe it was his daughter?' I suggested.

'No,' she said. 'People had said they had seen them together intimately. There was even a rumour that a maid had discovered them sharing the same bed. I do not think it was his daughter, no.'

She paused.

'There was another thing,' she continued. 'He also seemed very interested in children, particularly little boys. We began to wonder did he have an obsession?'

I was trying not to get too excited. During the course of the conversation, she explained where he lived, but she wasn't sure of his name. 'Fumpf, I think,' she offered.

I was keen to make the conversation end now, so I just picked up my phone and said 'Hi', pretending there was a call coming in. I grunted and made false conversation for two minutes, then hung up.

'I have to go,' I said. 'Work beckons.'

I called the waiter over, knocked back my wine and thanked her.

'You are?'

'Janna Jorges, but most people call me JJ.'

As soon as she was far enough away, I called one of the research team.

'Do a search on Fumpf, a German guy. I want anything you can find on him, possibly to do with sex with underage girls.'

Then I waited.

An hour later, I had six pages of cuttings about a Dirk Fumpf, an Austrian, convicted in Hamburg of sex with underage prostitutes. This was good. We would run the headline: IS THIS THE SEX FIEND THAT COULD HAVE TAKEN THOMAS? More importantly, we would point out that we had uncovered his existence without too much digging. Why hadn't our feckless Portuguese colleagues done the same?

Bloody bingo!

Lisa Lagnoo
Praia da Alvor
29th September
10:00

We are the lead on most of the breakfast TV programmes. Our story, naming Fumpf, is being viewed as a classic scoop. I did the *Today* programme at 7am and my interview has led the BBC radio bulletins all morning. I also did Breakfast TV and Sky. On Sky my interviewer asked, 'Are you saying that Herr Fumpf is a suspect?'

We'd been advised by our lawyers to be very careful on this one.

'No,' I responded firmly. 'What we are saying is that he's a person who should be on the police radar given his history. The fact that our colleagues in the Portuguese police service have missed this suggests to me that they don't have sufficient focus or experience to make progress with the case. Every day that goes by reduces the chances of Thomas being found. The situation, frankly, is intolerable. If I was faced with the same catalogue of errors in my work, I would seriously be considering my future.'

'So you are saying the senior police officer should resign?'

'That's for them to decide. We want Thomas found. Nothing more. I am sure that the British public would have more confidence that he would be if the investigating officers were shown to be more than incompetent.'

As I was doing the interview down the line, the Home Secretary was next up. He too called for 'wholesale change' in the way that the case was being conducted. Then, in that dead-air bit at the end of the interview, he came down the line in my headphones.

'Lisa,' he said, 'this is off the record, but I just want to say I am extremely grateful for the work you and your colleagues are doing here. Keep it up.'

Once out of the studio, I immediately phoned the boss.

'Look,' I said, 'the Home Secretary is creaming in his trousers about what we're doing. He told me down the line at the end of the interview.' We then discussed how we could get this on the record. I suggested that he spoke to someone in the newsroom at Sky. We should let Sky run it as an exclusive, using any recording they were bound to have. The boss agreed.

So I have just finished watching a Sky exclusive where they have tape of the Home Secretary praising me. The headline caption is: LISA LAGNOO PRAISED BY HOME SECRETARY. They have now moved on to a profile of me which is making me cream in my knickers. Better still, they have cut to Fumpf's apartment where the local police have just arrived to arrest him.

I got fucked more at party conferences, no doubt about that, but this is comparable to the best orgasm I have ever had and there's no sweaty backbencher or failed union leader drooling over my tits!

Anna
5th October
Biarritz
9:30

The doctors are examining him again. I don't know what the problem is. We have been here a week and we have not been allowed to go. It is concerning. He is concerned, Thomas is agitated, but he is being kept drugged a little and I just want to get on with my life.

I sometimes think that when everything is going well it means things are about to go wrong. Everything went too well.

Taking Thomas was actually quite easy. I knew the routine. He would be put to bed at 7.30, his mother and father would eat at the bar by the poolside, near to the apartment. They would leave the window on the patio ajar. I had been told to make sure I opened that a bit more as this would help police to think that somebody had come in that way. He had given me a skeleton key to the apartment.

In the hotel, I changed into my new image. I put a permed blonde wig on, glasses, heels. I thought I looked like a Russian prostitute. The idea was that I would be so noticeable that I would be unremarkable. Just a good-time girl in a sleepy back water, maybe allowing herself to recover from too much sex.

I timed my arrival for about 8.00. The car was not a special one, a SEAT Leon, powerful but nondescript. I parked it a few metres away from the entrance to the apartment complex. Then, a few minutes later, having glanced to the pool and seen both of them there, I made my way in.

Little Thomas was sleeping. I gently woke him and he immediately looked excited. I made a 'hush' sign with my fingers and said that we were going to play a game. He recognised me, which I thought was amazing, but kids are good like that, I think. I mimed that he had to be quiet. He understood. I wrapped him in a big beach towel, covered his head and stepped out into the reception. My heart was thumping in my chest, but there was nobody there and nobody saw me. I bundled him into the back of the car, made him hide in the seat well in the back and drove off into the night.

After about twenty minutes, I told him he could come out. He was in his bed shirt and already a bit sleepy. I passed him some orange juice which he drank greedily. He didn't know, but the juice had a powerful sedative. He was soon sleeping, very soundly. Once I had been driving for an hour, I pulled over into a motorway service area. There was another car there which I already had the keys for. This was a more powerful Porsche Cayenne. Much more to my liking. I carried Thomas to the new car, strapped him into a child seat in the back and dropped the old car keys into a grid. Seemed a shame to waste such a nice car, but those were my instructions.

I drove for about another twenty minutes and then, when

the road was quiet, pulled the blonde wig off. Nobody would have seen me through the Porsche's darkened windows. Yet it felt good not to look like a Russian prostitute anymore.

We drove through the night, into Spain and towards Madrid. At about 8am, I pulled into a motel. A room had been booked for us there. I was offered help with my bags, but explained that I didn't need any. I parked the car near the entrance to the room, took Thomas in and then ordered room service to bring breakfast.

He had been sleeping soundly, the effects of the sedative. I waited until after the food had been delivered before I woke him. He rubbed his little eyes with the back of his hand, a sleepy gesture, but he seemed unperturbed as he tucked into his breakfast, eating like someone who had not had a meal in a long while. It was only after breakfast he started to get a bit upset, asking for his mummy and looking tearful. I made him another drink and slipped him some more tablets and within fifteen minutes he was sleeping again. I showered, dumped the plates on the landing outside and hung up the 'Do Not Disturb' sign. I climbed into the bed next to Thomas and fell into a deep sleep, not waking until four in the afternoon.

As I got out of bed, Thomas also woke. He seemed calmer.

'I'm hungry,' he declared. So I promised him more food if he behaved well while I bathed and washed his hair. I also dyed his hair a different colour, dark brown, and said I would do the same to mine. He giggled when he saw me with the same colour hair and seemed to buy into the game.

After burgers and Coke in our room, I got us ready for the final stage of the journey. We were driving overnight to Biarritz. I decided to keep him awake for the first few hours and didn't give him any sedative. We had now swapped the Cayenne for a VW 4X4. Boring, like English tea, warm and dependable, but not thrilling. Thomas seemed to like it though and didn't actually need any sedative. He fell asleep an hour into the journey, leaving me to contemplate the future.

I would soon have money in the bank and the chance to start a new life. What do I want? One million euros is a good amount of money. I will still need to work, but I can choose where and how I work. I am thinking of moving to Greece or Turkey. The winters are short. I hate the cold. Maybe I will buy a bar? Or a café? Bars are a bit risky, too many fights. A café, on the other hand, would be nice. I could put money aside to get me through the bad times and then live off the earnings from my place. Maybe I could call it Café Thomas? The only reason I will have the money is because of the little boy who lies slumbering on the back seat. It would be a nice way to say thank you.

I kept playing around with these ideas as I drove. Then, about an hour out of Biarritz, I was aware that Thomas was moving in the back. Perhaps he was finally waking up. It was 6am as we crossed the border into France. I glanced over my shoulder into the back seat and then saw that Thomas wasn't just stirring, he was convulsing. His whole body was shaking and his arms and legs were flapping around.

I pulled over into a rest area, jumped out of the front of the car and opened the rear door. He was awake, but not awake. He had a bruise on his forehead and his arm, but seemed dazed. He had also messed his trousers.

'Thomas! What is the matter?'

He clearly was somewhere else. Gazing into space, a bit confused, shaking slightly. I cuddled him, stroked his hair, tried to calm him. He eventually seemed to come to.

'Trousers smell!' he said.

'It's all right,' I said gently. 'I have some spare ones. Shall we get you cleaned up?'

He nodded. I fished into a bag in the boot, pulled out some clean clothes, wrapped him in a big beach towel and took him into a rest room. There was a disabled loo – we went in there and I cleaned him up. Within a few minutes, he was in fresh clothes, but still out of it, still a bit quiet.

'Are you hungry?' I asked.

He shook his head.

'Mummy?' he said and began whimpering.

I hugged him.

'It's OK, we are nearly at the end of the journey.'

He tried to smile, but it wasn't a convincing one.

I loaded him back into the car and then set off on the final stage of the journey.

An hour later, we were pulling up in front of a rather grand-looking chateau. It had big security gates at the front with only one route in or out. There was a long, tree-lined avenue that ran up from the road to the main house. It looked like the sort of place a Bond villain would live in.

He emerged from the front door as we arrived. He had no expression on his face, but just pointed to a garage block, indicating I should park there.

Once inside, he approached me.

'Hello, Anna, is everything OK?'

'No,' I said.

He led me into a big kitchen in the main house. Thomas was gathered up by a young French woman, Elena, who spoke very good English and explained how they were going to get him breakfast and orange juice. Thomas seemed happy with the proposition, but glanced at me.

I nodded. 'It's OK, Thomas, go and enjoy breakfast.' I smiled at him. He ran across and hugged my legs, but then held out his hand to the new French girl. It amused me and I realised that, to some degree, all kids are tarts, happy to give their affection away for chocolate croissants and orange juice.

I then explained to him what had happened, the episode in the car, the contortions, how he messed himself.

He was calm, but had a concerned look on his face.

'OK, I will get some medical people in, do some tests. You're probably both tired. Get some sleep. You have a villa to yourself in the grounds. I will get one of the team to take you there. We might be here for a week or so. You'll find a full wardrobe of clothes and everything else that you will need in the villa. You can sleep until late afternoon. A doctor will be here by then.'

A few minutes later, I was in my new surroundings. A member of the team, a very handsome man called Jorges, showed me around, pointing out all the essential features. From the outside the villa looked sixteenth-century, but the interior was incredibly hi-tech. Flat-screen TVs, room-to-room music systems, air conditioning and even a small sauna. In the garden, there was a pool, about thirty metres long, together with a Jacuzzi and plunge pool. Whoever owned this place had taste and money.

I am soon asleep, underneath white cotton sheets in darkness. I am relieved not to have sole responsibility for Thomas now and sleep so much better because of this.

Kieran
5th October
Biarritz
14:00

You can plan for virtually everything – bad weather, financial hardship, failed love, ill health. You make contingencies, set things into place. It smoothes things over, but doesn't quite remove the sense that a situation, despite all the planning and backups, has left you somewhat fucked.

I have just finished a conversation with Dr Fish. Fish is reliable; I have known him for about fifteen years. He retired quite recently, but is on my retained list of people who I have working with me. I have entertained him here in Biarritz on many occasions. He is erudite, charming company, a Brentford fan, a wine buff and a man of utmost discretion. For me, his discretion is bought for £100K per annum, plus his daily rates. He has often said he will do the work for free, but that is not how I operate. If things ever were to go wrong, I want to be clear that I always paid my dues and paid well.

Yet this is not good news. He is pretty certain that the kid has epilepsy. Now, whilst my contract with the purchasers has a 'sold as seen' clause, there is also a clause that says the buyer has the right not to take the goods if they are not 100% delighted. In these circumstances, they still pay all my costs and I am left with 60% of the original fee and a child to dispose of. Epilepsy is not a 'fashionable' disability either. You don't believe they exist? Well, let me assure you they do. There is a certain honour in having a child with particular disabilities. Deaf kids are always seen as quite cute, even kids with Downs Syndrome have a certain status value, but epilepsy, well, that's well down the list of designer label disabilities, like autism, not something that parents hanker after.

I will discuss how this all came about with Anna. There is no evidence, but she may have given him a little too much sedative. Dr Fish doesn't think this is likely to have induced the epilepsy, but if I can pass it off as a temporary thing, we might still be able to seal the deal. The Russian couple are flying in tomorrow to meet Thomas. The one advantage I have is that emotionally they will have bought into the concept. They will be planning a life with Thomas and it may be that their heart will rule their head.

I know, though, that this is a long shot. Business is business and people don't want faulty goods.

Fish has agreed to meet the Russians too tomorrow. He will put on his best gloss. Yet even his upbeat optimism won't be enough. They have their own medical people. They will probably advise against proceeding. As I said, I am somewhat fucked.

Anna
Biarritz
5th October
17:00

What was he trying to do? I am so angry! Everything bristles – from the ends of my hairs to the tips of my toes.

We sat down. He said he wanted to talk about the situation with Thomas. That doctors had confirmed that Thomas has epilepsy. They had also suggested that it might have been a side-effect of the sedatives, so they spent the next hour grilling me on exactly how much I had given him. Precise amounts, exact times and so on. Then he went over it again. Three times. From the start, working back and then a combination of both.

At one point, he asked, 'How come Thomas did not demonstrate any signs of this before he came to us?'

I tried to keep calm, but I am not a nurse or a doctor.

'How am I meant to know? I am not qualified to see the signs – are you?'

He tried to calm me, but I wasn't accepting that.

'You can't blame me for this! I have done everything you have asked me to do and done it well. I spent months living with that shitty family, gaining their trust so that you, you, could complete your deal! You never told me I was meant to be a medical expert. You tell me, when did you ask that of me? To be a medical person? You never!'

I slammed my hand flat onto the table top at that point. He just smiled.

'You're quite entertaining when you're riled,' he said.

I asked him what this word meant, 'riled'; I had not heard it before.

'Provoked,' he said. 'Worked up.'

'You are blaming me!' I said.

He then adopted a patronising English tone. He was saying I was not to blame. That my work was commendable. I told him he could stick his English commendable up his rear end. Then I had enough. I got up, stormed off to the villa, changed into a bathing costume and swam a furious sixty lengths of the pool until I could hardly breathe.

I am now trying to calm down. I have not made little Thomas sick. I have cared for him, looked after him. I would never make him sick.

Kieran
6th October
Biarritz
17:00

One reason why I enjoy doing business with Russians is that they are pragmatic. They get things in a way that others don't and they see business as business. They will argue with you, bang the table, shout and swear, but then insist on sharing a glass of vodka to cement the friendship.

My Russian clients arrived by helicopter mid-morning. We were all assembled on the lawn to welcome them, including little

Thomas, who got very excited as the chopper came in to land. This excited the Russians too. Seeing a three-and-a half-year-old leaping up and down is a good way of cementing a deal.

We all had coffee together in the gardens under a canvas canopy and overlooking the *Jardin à la Française*, modelled on the gardens at the Palace of Versailles. Thomas moved around the group quite naturally and was friendly towards the Russians. Of course, he didn't know that they were his prospective new parents. Whilst the husband was older than the boy's natural father, his wife was younger than Thomas's mother. A pretty, leggy Russian blonde princess who spoke perfect, non-accented English. The only way you could tell she was Russian was by the clothes she wore and the amount of bling. If you listened carefully, you would also notice an absence of idioms and slang. She could, however, easily pass herself off for an icy, Cheltenham College-educated Sloane.

We retired into the drawing room alone and were joined by Dr Fish. Fish had a way of talking that was ideal for the situation we were in. It was always precise and slow and not littered with *um*s and *erm*s. We soon came to the medical report and I handed over to Fish.

'Well now,' he began, confident, assured. 'Young Thomas is a very healthy, very active little boy. He's everything you would expect for a child of his age. Very bright, inquisitive, reasonably well-behaved too. He is a very pleasant and very likeable little boy.'

At this point, Fish paused, made sure that there was an air of positivity, making eye contact and smiling at the Russian couple before continuing.

'So,' he said, 'a very likeable and balanced child. There is, however, one problem. We want to share this with you because we have a policy of openness and honesty.'

At this point, the wife placed her hand on her husband's, seeking assurance. He patted her arm.

Fish continued: 'On his journey, little Thomas had some sort of seizure. We believe that all the symptoms indicate it was an epileptic seizure, but we cannot be certain. As you probably know, epilepsy can be controlled and can be managed. Having said this, I am no expert and, on a purely objective basis, I would recommend that you have this problem checked out by an independent expert. I have a colleague in Lausanne, a Professor Parlour, who is renowned in this field. If need be, we can bring him and his team here to give you an in-depth assessment. Now, before I continue, you may have some questions that you wish to ask?'

Fish held both his palms upwards and out, encouraging the Russians to speak.

They both glanced at each other.

'If we could,' the wife asked, 'would it be possible to discuss this point on our own for a few minutes?'

Fish, ever the servant, deferred to me, with a look in my direction.

'Of course,' I said. 'We will leave a copy of Dr Fish's report, in Russian and English, for you to look through. Shall we give you fifteen minutes?'

They nodded agreement. I am sure they were impressed by the attention to detail, but I am also sure that they valued our honesty.

We left the room.

I put my arm around Fish's shoulder once we were outside.

'Well done,' I said. 'Your usual high standard of professionalism.'

I went and checked e-mails and sent Elena, my chief of staff here, who speaks fluent Russian, in with some more coffee. She was told to try to find out their mood.

She reported back.

'The wife is up for the challenge, but the husband is worried about what people will think. I get the impression though that he will do anything to keep her happy.'

This was useful. It gave me an angle to push in our discussions.

A few minutes later, we were back in the room.

'We think we would like you to bring in your expert,' the wife said. 'We trust your integrity, you have been open and honest with us and, in the circumstances, some people would not have done this. If it is possible, I would like to stay. My husband has business in London anyway, but if I could stay on that would be helpful.'

Her husband interrupted, 'I could have your specialist, Mr Lounge, flown here by private jet if need be.'

Fish smiled to himself.

'Parlour,' he said, correcting the husband.

I interrupted. I was not keen to have a third party involved in transportation. 'We have booked Professor Parlour and his team to be here by lunchtime tomorrow. They have a large amount of equipment to bring, so travelling by air may not be the best option. Your offer is nonetheless greatly appreciated.'

The husband nodded at this.

I continued: 'I will arrange for accommodation for your wife in the main chateau. You are welcome to stay as long as you like. However, can I suggest we aim to conclude this all by the end of the week, one way or the other?'

Again, there were general nods of consent. The wife then raised a question.

'If we don't take Thomas, what will happen to him?'

I didn't need to answer this and simply replied, 'Appropriate arrangements will be made.'

That was my business, not theirs.

This was all a few hours ago. Fish has now gone to play golf, the wife, whose name it transpires is Sofia, is settled into a suite in the house and has been taken shopping by Elena. We are due to have dinner with Thomas and Anna later.

At this stage, this is the best I can hope for. The deal may still go ahead.

Anna
6th October
Biarritz
23.15

I am drunk. Worse, I think I am in love. Oh, my God!

We had dinner. It was a very French meal. Lots of courses, lots and lots of wine. Thomas was with us for the first couple of hours. Then Elena took him to bed. He came to me, said, 'Goodnight, Anna!' loudly and brightly, then planted a sloppy kiss on my cheek. He melted my heart.

Sofia spoke: 'He is so gorgeous. Such a pity about his problems.'

I gave her a look because Thomas was still at the table. So I spoke to Thomas: 'Oh, we know what your problems are, Thomas! Not enough ice cream and not enough tickles,' and tried to tickle him there and then. Thomas squealed with delight. He ran across the room to Elena and waved goodnight to us all.

After he left, I turned to Sofia.

'I think it might be a good policy not to mention Thomas's problems whilst he is in the room. It could upset him.'

She gave me a very hard stare.

87

'Are you buying him?' she asked coldly.

'No,' I responded. 'I just know that Thomas can be a little sensitive, you should be aware of that.'

He interrupted: 'Anna has got to know Thomas very well. She knows him better than all of us.'

'An au pair?' she asked dismissively, laughing as she asked the question.

I responded in Russian.

'I'm not an au pair. I speak Russian, French and English. Nor do I need a sugar daddy to support me. I am like you. A criminal, stealing children. Don't pretend otherwise and don't you dare look down your nose at me!'

He was at a disadvantage here as Elena had gone. Sofia looked taken aback by my fierce response and my perfect Russian.

She responded in English. 'I am sorry; I didn't mean to underestimate you. My mistake.'

He was still looking unsure, but seemed satisfied that no harm had been done.

'Anna has been a very reliable and very valuable member of my team. I would, without doubt, work with her again.'

I liked that; he was singing my song, telling people I was good. Yet I didn't like the idea of having to do this again.

'Oh,' I said jokingly, 'I don't think you can afford to hire me again!'

He raised an eyebrow at this. Dr Fish, sensing the tension, interrupted and changed the conversation to the history of the chateau.

I continued to think about the idea though, doing another job. I liked the fact that I was good at something. I liked the money too. Doing this twice would make me secure for the rest of my life. I could have two cafés in Greece!

I drank more and just listened to the conversation. I watched this Sofia woman and imagined the relationship she would have with Thomas. I wondered if she would always make him feel bad about his 'problem'? Would they keep his name or would they change it? 'This is Igor, our son. He has a problem, but we love him anyway.' It seems to me that you should love your children unconditionally. There is nothing bad about Thomas. He is sweet, gentle, loving and trusting. He is missing his mum I think, but he is being brave. That is good.

The more I drank and the more I thought about it, I realised that this woman was not good for dear Thomas. That she would not love him, but own him like a pet dog or an expensive sports car. Perhaps when she got bored with him, she would have him put to sleep, like a dog that was no longer needed. This was not what I wanted for my Thomas.

I stood up – it was 10.30. I pushed my chair back from the table.

'I am,' I said, and it was a great effort to get the words out, 'going to bed.'

I stumbled out of the door back to the villa. As I walked through the grounds, in the chill of the autumn air, I felt an inner warmth. It was an inner warmth for little Thomas. It was then that I realised I was in love with him. It made me giggle, smile and, worst of all, feel very sad. Who gives away their love? What kind of stupid idiot am I?

Kieran
8th October
13:00
Biarritz

We are all due to meet for a final debrief from Professor Parlour at two. I am not keen on him. Unlike Dr Fish, he is somewhat loud and arrogant and boasts that he is the best expert in his field in Europe. Fish assures me that Parlour is discreet. I am still uncertain about him.

Sofia has been getting to know Thomas a bit more. Thomas is very relaxed with her, but his affection is directed towards Anna. It was a risk keeping Anna on, but I need her here until the deal is complete or until we have to deliver the alternative. She probably doesn't realise, but she has already been paid in full. So there is no reason why she has to stay. I meant what I said at dinner the other evening though – I will be sorry to see her leave. She has been good and good people like her are hard to find. I have two more jobs lined up after this one. One is Edinburgh-based; the other is Stateside. I think she would be good for the US job, but I sense that she is not that interested. She has time though; it won't start for another twelve months. She needs to lay low for a year, keep out of trouble and check in with me before we set things in motion. America is easier than here in some ways and harder in others. Easier because the federal system means once you have crossed state lines, you gain more time. Harder because my networks are less developed out there and because the Mexican drug cartels are muscling in on every show in town. Not that Europe is much better: Romanians are exerting a disproportionate influence on most dishonest jobs.

Still, that is all for the future. For now, we need to seal the deal with our Russian clients. Life will be much simpler if they can be persuaded that Thomas is a low-risk purchase.

Anna
8th October
17:30
Biarritz

They have gone!

The meeting with Professor Parlour seemed to go on forever. It would have been over quicker if he had spent less time looking at my tits, something he seemed to do when he was not talking. He is quite a good-looking man, but nothing makes a handsome man uglier than roving eyes.

He had detailed charts and presentations. Not just about Thomas, but also about the incidence of epilepsy in general. How one out of forty people in the EU are affected by it; famous people like the pop star Prince and writers such as Laurie Lee and Fyodor Dostoyevsky. It was interesting and also serious. Professor Parlour was trying to explain that epilepsy was not a tragic affliction, but a simple feature of life which affected many people, but which could be overcome.

He then went on to talk about Thomas, in particular. How he appeared to have epilepsy in a very mild form and how childhood epilepsy often cleared up around about the onset of puberty. He stressed that he could not guarantee that Thomas would ever be seizure-free, but his prognosis was that seizures were unlikely to be *grand mal* and more likely to be either night-time seizures or *petit mal* or absence seizures. In Professor Parlour's experience, absence seizures could be managed with a combination of medicine and lifestyle management. He stressed that lifestyle management might mean not getting over-tired or avoiding certain trigger foods, such as alcohol or particular flavourings.

Parlour saved his trump card to the end.

'We have come a long way since the medieval period. Then people with epilepsy were burnt at the stake because the assumption was that they were somehow possessed by demons. Now people who have epilepsy are present in all jobs and at all levels of society. Indeed, in my own experience, epilepsy has not prevented me from becoming the foremost expert in this field in Europe, possibly the world. Thomas has huge potential – you need to help him fulfil it.'

He sat down and I wanted to applaud him. It was a 'Wow!' moment, a point when you felt that you had learned something new and important. Dr Fish also chipped in that he had always found Professor Parlour's judgement to be sound.

The Russians asked for time alone to reflect. A half-hour, they said, with no interruptions.

They were given that, exactly as requested. Now they have gone. They have gone without Thomas. I am so happy!

Kieran
8th October
Biarritz
22:00

I have sent Fish away. I wonder if Parlour overegged the pudding by revealing details of his own epilepsy? I am not sure if the Russians appreciated that.

So we now have a problem. A child to dispose of, with a plan B that isn't particularly nice, but protects all of our business interests. The worst part is plan B involves dealing with the underbelly of the market, dominated by nasty Romanian henchmen.

I have briefed Anna. She seems reasonably OK with the prospect of working longer and I explained that there would be a small amount of additional pay, maybe not much more than €50K, but she seemed fine with this.

'What will happen now?' she asked.

I explained that the plan was still being developed, that we had to maximise our return on the deal, but hopefully we would cut our losses. I don't think she gets the detail of what's in prospect. If she did, she would be far more upset.

Nothing for days and then there are developments.

Fumpf was released last week – no charges have been brought against him but he is officially helping the police with their enquiries. Then nothing, the news dried up. We have run a few features in the paper about unsolved kid snatches in the past, crazy Austrian criminals (Hitler always sells papers) and stories about Thomas's life in Chiswick, but to be honest, nothing that moves the story on.

Then, about half an hour ago, something appears on the wire from Reuters: 'Spanish police announce breakthrough in Thomas search.' It detailed the fact that soiled clothing has been found in a motorway rest area near Santander. Tests suggest that the DNA on the clothes match the DNA of Thomas. No more details are available.

We are rushing around in a frenzy, awaiting a news conference from the Portuguese police. In the absence of hard information, journalists do what we know best – we interview each other.

So far, I have done snippets for BBC Breakfast TV and Sky. I am also scheduled to appear on the *World at One* at lunchtime.

The general line of questioning from other media outlets has been to seek facts. How far is Santander from here? How long would it take to get there? I don't really know the answer to this, but reckon it would take a good day's drive. It allows me to go back to my previous theme.

'It seems clear to me that the police have let Thomas slip through their fingers by not closing roads and border crossings at the outset.' This is good television and makes the story much more appealing to the UK audience. Whilst the focus is on a little boy going missing, the subtext remains how those awful foreign policemen are just incompetent and how the stupid EU, with no border controls, allows criminals to run amok.

At the press conference, we get more details. The clothes were new, sold by C&A across Europe. They were soiled. The DNA on the clothes is an exact match.

I am the first to ask a question.

'How confident are you that Thomas is still alive?' I ask. This gives the room a buzz as the fifty or sixty journalists grunt for an answer.

'At this stage, we have simply found clothes,' the Portuguese detective responds. This doesn't satisfy me or anybody else.

I decide to try a different tack.

'Earlier in the enquiry, you detained an Austrian man, Herr Fumpf. Does he have a connection with the Santander area?'

This question is brushed aside.

'It is far too early to say or to make links with specific individuals.'

This doesn't impress anyone either. A guy from *The Mirror* points out that a criminal investigation should be focused on specific individuals who may have committed the crime. There is a murmur of approval in support of this point. Whilst the questions continue, I text my local photographer: *Keep Fumpf apartment under scrutiny, photos of any comings or goings.*

I push for a further question – finally, I get my chance.

'Have the parents been advised of the latest developments?' I ask.

'We are meeting with them later this morning.'

'So are you telling us that you have given a media briefing ahead of talking to Thomas's parents? If so, that's unbelievable!'

The room is now in uproar and all that happens is that the police spokesman keeps on repeating the line about meeting with the parents later on.

I decide to leave.

A Sky reporter grabs me on the way out.

'A quick comment for the camera, Lisa?'

I agree and give a short rant piece to him.

'Quite unbelievable. Here we have the world's media being given more information than the parents. I don't know about your viewers at home, but I find that entirely insensitive.'

Of course, if the opposite had happened I would have said, 'There is huge media interest in this story and we are willing to help in any way. Not sharing important information means that we are not able to support the police investigations.' It is classic lose-lose journalism. Whilst your average *Guardian* reader will see through it, most people are more simplistic. They want goodies and baddies and, for our readership, all foreigners are baddies.

I phone the team in London. I want to explore as much as we can find out about Fumpf. Does he have business interest or property near Santander? Where is he? The team agree to do a conference call at noon. Then I get a call from the boss. Could I write a two-hundred-word leader column for tomorrow's edition? I agree to get him a first draft by later in the morning.

So the battle is on again. Fumpf is my target.

Lisa Lagnoo
Praia da Alvor
3rd October
11:00

I am reviewing the leader column I have written:

Our readers will rightly be appalled by the developments in the little Thomas case. Portuguese police seem to have acted entirely without judgement in briefing the world's media before speaking to the boy's parents. One thing we do well in Britain is make sure that families are kept in the loop during such investigations. The authorities in the Algarve have failed miserably.

More importantly, the case raises major questions about open borders in the EU. We have always worried that criminals, not just illegal immigrants, will exploit the porous walls between nations. We think this is another reason why so many of our readers are exasperated by the whole European project. If you are a Brussels Bureaucrat or a criminal, the Common Market is a blessing. For the rest of us, it is a headache that makes life worse, not better.

Yep, doubtless some of the posh words will get whittled down, but that should do it.

I e-mail it to the editor, safe in the knowledge that this is bang on the money.

I have just had an e-mail back. The only word changed is 'porous' to 'leaky'. I'm pleased with that – a good half-hour's output.

Lisa Lagnoo
Praia da Alvor
3rd October
14:30

The conference call was excellent. Lots of really positive developments – the team are working hard. They discovered that

Fumpf has no connections with Santander. Yet there is better news. He has connections with Bilbao which is equidistant from the motorway service area to Santander. Apparently, he taught German there when he was in his twenties. This link will form the basis for our front-page story tomorrow.

Our proprietor has also thrown his weight behind a 'Find Thomas' campaign. The parents have agreed to this as they are convinced that he is not dead. Personally, I am not convinced, but they want to hold out hope. I would probably do the same. Anyway, there is an England game at Wembley tomorrow. Thomas liked football and we have booked pitch-side advertising hoardings with 'Find Thomas' hoardings beneath our masthead. This won't do anything to find Thomas, but gives us a good profile.

The local plod are continuing to be useless. They cannot confirm or deny if Fumpf has been taken in for questioning. His apartment had no activity, he hasn't been seen or heard of for about forty-eight hours. We think he is back inside for questioning, but can't get any answers. There is a follow-up press conference tomorrow morning. We will learn more then.

I have been invited on to *Newsnight* again this evening, another down-the-line interview. The focus will be on the European dimension – they know about our proposed leader column. They have some nutter from UKIP on, a Labour MEP, who is part of the Social Affairs European Parliament inter-group, and me. Should be interesting.

I have decided to take the afternoon off. I am treating myself to a massage and a haircut, so that I am relaxed for the *Newsnight* appearance.

The editor is all over me like a rash at the moment. Not only is he claiming I am doing a great job, but he's also touting this as being evidence that the paper is committed to personal development. I think he's listened to his own spin for too long, but if he wants to sing his own praises I'm not going to stop him.

So all of this is great. Totally enjoying being here, the raised profile and everything. Seriously brilliant.

Lisa Lagnoo
Praia Da Alvor
4th October
11:30

Oh, Christ! This is bad!

The morning started well. A group of us from the other titles had breakfast together before the news conference scheduled for 10.00. I was being teased about my constant media appearances. *Newsnight*, Sky. A couple of the wags suggested that, on a normal news day, I would be lucky to get a soundbite on Three Counties Radio's lunchtime news slot and that my next step had to be either *Big Brother* or *I'm a Celebrity*. To be honest, I'd love to do either, but waved their suggestions away as being distasteful.

We arrived at the venue for the news conference together, only to be told that there had been a development and that there would be a thirty-minute delay.

This sent us all scurrying and speculating. Rumours were rife. Somebody had established that a body had been found. Was it Thomas? It would fit with the delay. Maybe the parents were being asked to identify it?

I got on the phone to the team in London. They reported that the Chief of Police for the Basque region had been on the phone to our proprietor first thing this morning. He was none too pleased with our front page about Fumpf for reasons that would become apparent. This was followed up with a call to our editor from the Interior Minister for Portugal, pretty much along the same lines.

At 10.45, a senior media officer and the regional Chief of Police appeared on stage. The Chief spoke: 'Ladies and gentlemen, we have an important announcement. At 08.30 today, a body was found on a beach in Lagos.'

There was an audible gasp in the room, one of those moments when the only thing that could be heard was the speaker's voice and the sound of the photographer's electric drives. Was this Thomas?

'The body is that of a forty-seven-year-old Austrian national, Dirk Fumpf. The wrists had been slashed and nearby there was a suicide note.'

I felt a frisson of excitement. Had we got him?

'The suicide note was written in German, but here is a translation of the important section.'

The senior press officer then started reading: 'Until recently, I have loved living in Praia Da Alvor. I have been recovering from cancer. Whilst this destroyed my marriage, it gave me the opportunity to rest during my recuperation. For the first few weeks, my daughter, Greta, was here, but she has now had to return to her studies in Vienna. The past forty-eight hours have seen me accused of the kidnapping of the English boy, Thomas. Worse still, sections of the English media have made my life intolerable. I have been accused of...'

I had stopped listening. I was aware that all eyes were on me. My phone vibrated with a text message from my editor: *GET OUT NOW!*

As I rose to leave the room, I was pursued by the same hacks I had been joking with at breakfast. I ran as fast as I could back to my hotel. I used the stairs rather than the lift which was a mistake as it meant a couple of photographers got to my floor before me. Those pictures would be valuable and syndicated almost immediately.

I barricaded myself in the room, turned on Sky to catch the end of the press conference. It was the Chief of Police speaking: 'The free press have an important role to play in protecting society against excess and exposing corruption. Yet they also have to be responsible. Lisa Lagnoo and her colleagues have some serious questions to answer. Their amateur approach to their investigation has seen an innocent bystander take his own life. Sadly, we cannot bring a criminal prosecution, but we can ask that other members of the fourth estate reflect on these events and temper their future coverage accordingly.'

Lisa Lagnoo
Faro Airport
19:00
4th October

Packing was depressing.

Every five minutes, my room phone would ring or there would be somebody hammering on the door asking to speak to me.

The editor spoke to me. Gave me the line they were going to take. His argument was that we were not to blame for the Fumpf incident. If the police had been more forthcoming with information about the investigation, this kind of misunderstanding could have been avoided. He had cleared the line at the highest level in the paper. He also stressed that everybody was very impressed and proud of the work my team and I had undertaken. The Fumpf factor was 'regrettable', but our coverage of the story had seen our circulation increase by 15%. In addition, advertising revenue had also increased.

Despite this, there now appeared to be a fashionable witch hunt against us. The FA cancelled the pitch-side advertising campaign for this evening, citing 'reputational risk'. They had given the space to *The Sun*, which our editor thought was entirely appropriate given that they 'have about as many tits in their average edition as work at the FA'. This, at least, made me laugh.

I asked what he could do about the constant hounding. He called back a few minutes later. The police were being vindictive. The hotel had already asked for assistance, but they cited 'other priorities', including the ongoing investigation into a recent suicide, meaning they had no available resources to deploy. The paper were trying to organise private security for when I left.

At about 5.30, the corridor outside was cleared. Security had arrived. By six, I was being taken down to a waiting car for the short drive to the airport. We were pursued by a media pack and then confronted by TV crews from Portugal and Austria as I checked in. I maintained a steady silence.

I am now in a VIP lounge, alone, away from other travellers.

My flight leaves in twenty minutes. *Newsnight* and Sky News were both keen to have me on this evening. Needless to say, I won't be doing it.

Next year in my appraisal, I'll keep my mouth shut.

PART THREE

Anna
Area Servizio Bidirezionale 'Novara'
11th October
08:45

I am tired, Thomas is confused and I am feeling sick.

I never expected this to happen. I am sipping a strong black coffee whilst Thomas dozes in the back seat. I will have to get rid of this car later this morning. That may be a challenge. I am wondering about catching a train, but I am not sure where to. I could drive, but again I don't know where to go. Home could be a possibility, but home is the obvious place they will look for me.

Outside, it is raining heavily. Driving on the autostrada has been difficult. Like driving at sea, lots of spray from big lorries heading for Trieste and beyond. I've also had to keep one eye on my mirror as I need to be sure I am not being followed.

I have three enemies to avoid. Police, Romanians and him. They all want me for the same reason. I have stolen a child and they need to have him back. I will probably get the best treatment from the police. I do not want to hand myself in. It would mean going to prison. I would get a big sentence – twelve to fifteen years, I think. I do not want to lose my freedom.

The Romanians will probably be the worst people to be caught by. They will either kill me or hold me captive, probably selling me into some sort of prostitution ring. Thomas will also suffer a worse fate. I do not want that.

If he catches me, I think I will be made to pay a penalty, but again Thomas will not be safe. I only want this little boy to stay with me and, of course, to be safe.

Kieran
Padua
09:00
11th October

I don't often get angry, but I am fucking angry now. What was the stupid bitch thinking of?

We met near Venice airport. It was the Romanian's choice, a hypermarket car park. I wonder if the Romanians base their plans on watching episodes of *Breaking Bad*? It seemed too conspicuous to me.

I was travelling alone in my Mercedes Anna and Thomas were following in the Cayenne. We had stopped overnight in Nice. We left late in the evening yesterday. Anna seemed very upset. She had assumed I had found new parents for Thomas.

'Don't the parents want to meet Dr Fish?' she asked over dinner.

'No,' I replied, trying to close the conversation.

'But they need to know about the epilepsy and how to manage it, no?'

I changed the subject, but Anna is not stupid. She was hired for her intelligence, so I suppose she is simply demonstrating one of her strongest facets.

'Why are you asking me about the wine?' She is getting angry. 'Thomas! Tell me what is happening with him!'

Fortunately, we are in a private dining room at La Reserve, Nice. I have used it before with clients and my €100 tip to the waiter buys discretion.

'Anna, you don't need to know,' I tell her, firmly.

This made her even more upset.

'You have used me and now you have something not so nice planned for Thomas!'

106

This was outrageous.

'Can I remind you that so far you have been paid €60K, plus €1m and all your expenses? Is that being used?'

'It isn't being used, but you know what you are doing is not right!'

'I run a business, not a religious order. Business and money have no morality.'

She was cross, but also able to regain some composure.

'I feel sick. I do not want to eat any more stupid food,' she said and pushed her plate away.

I wasn't too bothered. It seemed to me a good idea that we leave sooner rather than later.

I called for the bill, paid and arranged to meet Anna back in the hotel car park. She would put Thomas into the Cayenne. I would sort check-out.

I met Anna next to my car. She asked me one question.

'The people we are meeting. Answer this question, honestly please. What is their nationality?'

With hindsight, I should have lied, but I decided on honesty.

'Romanian,' I said.

Anna gasped. I saw tears well up in her eyes, but then she seemed to regain her self-control.

'OK,' she said. 'In your business, there is no morality. I understand. Everything is a commodity to be traded, yes?'

I nodded agreement. It seemed she was learning the rules.

We drove through the night, across the border into Italy, past San Remo, across towards Turin and then to the hypermarket where we were meeting them.

It was about 6.30 in the morning when we pulled off the autostrada near Venice. The roads were quiet. Anna was maybe five hundred metres behind me. I pulled into the car park. However, instead of heading over to the area where the

Romanians were waiting, she headed straight for the store. I assumed she needed a toilet break.

I pulled up adjacent to the Romanians. They were horrible shits. Ugly, unsophisticated Neanderthals.

'You have the boy?' the leader, all bling and gold teeth, asked.

'He is with my colleague; she will be here in a moment. You have the money?'

He nodded.

'One million euros,' he said.

'We agreed three!'

He put his hands up, then started laughing.

'Don't be so uptight! It is a joke!'

These people were clowns, dangerous jokers.

He passed me a holdall.

'You want to count it?' he probed.

I opened the holdall, flicked through a few of the bundles of notes, making sure they were real.

'I don't need to count it,' I explained, 'If it's not all there, you will have made a very serious mistake. Your boss knows this.'

The guy nodded.

Then we saw Anna climb back into the Cayenne. There was a one-way system in the hypermarket which she obeyed. It meant she initially had to head away from us, back towards the road.

The Romanians were amused.

'Who follows one-way systems?' They roared with laughter. 'Your colleague is a pussy!'

A moment later, they weren't laughing. They were outraged.

Instead of turning towards us, Anna turned back towards the autostrada.

The leader ordered one set of apes to follow her. But they

were slow. By the time they had got into the car, Anna was three minutes ahead, probably five.

The leader grabbed at the holdall.

Fuck it, I thought. I threw the holdall five metres behind me. He wasn't happy, started reaching for his gun, but in the nanosecond between the reach and connecting with his weapon, I landed my boot in his groin. He sank to the floor. Taking advantage, I then smacked him in the face with my foot, the sort of kick you occasionally see defenders make in lower divisions with the ball sailing clean out of the ground.

I picked up the bag. Threw it into the Merc. Balou, the head chimp, was motionless on the floor. I didn't care if I had killed him. I probably hadn't. Now all I cared about was getting Thomas back. Anna had taken my stock and if she was caught with it, all hell would break loose.

I'm now in the centre of Padua. I am initiating a backup plan that means getting myself back to England. I will travel by rail. There is a train in twenty minutes that will get me to Paris in time for dinner. I should be in St Albans this time tomorrow. I'll then be better placed to put together a recovery plan.

I am fucked!

Anna
Valma
12:45
11th October

I have taken a chance, but my head start has given me an advantage. I am trying not to be predictable.

Looking at the map, I realise that I am not that far from Zurich. This morning, I was about ten hours away; now I am

109

about five. I have decided I need money and the only money I have is in Guernsey. So, here is my thinking: if I go to Zurich I will be able to transfer money into a bank account there. I will open the account in Jill Betts' name. I will leave a small amount in the Guernsey account but put most of the balance (now more than €1.5m!) into the Jill Betts account. I will then transfer €500K into an account under the name of Mette Greversen. I am not sure of the precise mechanics, but each account will need a checking facility. I think €100K for each account should be sufficient.

As for after that, I am not sure. I can't keep driving forever. So in the first instance, I think we need to settle somewhere, maybe until Christmas. I am thinking Dubrovnik. It is a good choice because it is still in the EU; I will not have to deal with border controls to get there. After that, I don't know. A clearer plan will emerge.

I am worried about Thomas. He is getting bored and agitated by all this travel. It is exhausting keeping him entertained and driving. I have told him that we are playing a game of hide and seek, so he has to stay in the car so that we can win. He has said a couple of times that he is bored. I have got round this by giving him cuddles and tickles. Now 'Anna, I am bored' has become an invitation for tickling. He says it with a giggle.

We are both eating baguettes. Thomas is only slightly taller than the huge cheese and tomato thing he is munching at. Occasionally, he smiles at me; he seems comfortable. He has stopped asking about his mum and dad. Kids are adaptable.

We will soon be back on the road. l have bought a CD with children's songs. We will sing them for the next few hours. At least for the moment, his fate is in better hands with me than with the Romanians. I am happy about that; it doesn't make me a saint, but it makes me better than the Romanians.

Kieran
Hotel Marcel
Paris
22:00
11th October

She is leaving the room now. Elegant, discreet, beautiful.

I started paying for sex many years ago. In this job, you can't sustain a relationship. Either people want to know too much or they get weirded out by the secretive nature of my work. One-night stands are no use either. There is always the chance you will bed a bunny boiler – unhinged, dangerous and the last thing I would need.

I needed it for the relief. Today has not exactly been stress-free. All through the journey north, I kept on getting text messages from the Romanian boss, demanding I return the money or face the consequences. He also wanted compensation for the damages to his ape. I am not too worried. He won't find me and the one million was €75K short. I've dumped that SIM card for now, so he won't track me beyond Paris.

Anna is a bigger problem. Firstly, she has shaken my faith in my own selection process. I thought she was dependable, reliable and trustworthy. Her disappearing with Thomas gives me a problem. If she is caught with him, it could lead things back to me. All the obvious places she has to lead a better life would be out of bounds. Sooner or later, the police will come looking for her; the investigations will show her as a missing, but vital, link. It is better I locate her before the police. It will avoid complications and enable us to come to an arrangement.

Of course, I have given her minimal information. She doesn't actually know my name or where I live. The money that has entered her account has passed through four or five other accounts before arriving there. It could be traced, but it would be difficult, particularly as all the initial originating accounts are closed.

She does, however, know where the Biarritz place is. Whether or not she knows it is mine is questionable, but that could be the only solid lead that links me to all of this.

It is a headache – I now have to do my best to stop it becoming a migraine.

Anna
Jenatsch Apartments
Zurich
12th October
16:00

That was, in truth, relatively easy. It makes me think that being rich must be a good thing. Nobody asks too many questions when you have money.

The bank in Zurich was very accommodating. They even allowed Thomas into their staff crèche for a few hours whilst we sorted out the business. So now all the money is where it should be and tomorrow morning we have to buy a new car. I will leave this one in Zurich – at the airport, I think.

I have given myself a budget of seventy-five thousand for a car. I have asked Thomas what new car I should buy and he said 'a red one'. This made me laugh. I hope he doesn't become a boring man who only wants to discuss engine size and reliability.

I have started to wonder what is happening with the investigation. I bought myself an iPad. I have Internet access here and looked online today. The last big event appears to be the death of an Austrian guy, a suspect, hounded by the English media. I am a little worried that the clothes they discovered could link to me, but I don't think Anna the au pair is yet a suspect, so I am not too concerned.

Thomas is settling into the routine. I will have to buy him some more clothes soon. He is having his afternoon nap. I will check online where the best place is to buy clothes for a little boy in Zurich. Tomorrow morning, I am due back at the bank to collect all the paraphernalia for my new accounts, cards and cheque books. We need to get away from Zurich. It is very expensive. We need to head to a place where our money will last longer. There is an English word I am thinking of that describes what I am; I think it is the right word. Not just for me, but for Thomas. We are fugitives. It is a strange thing to be. I hope I am good at it.

Kieran
St Albans
13th October
13:00

Back home. It feels good to be back. I have a number of things to sort out.

The Russians have paid all the relevant amounts into my accounts. With the Romanian cash, I am about twenty percent down on the deal. Not a great place to be, but you take the rough with the smooth. I need to line up a couple more deals to compensate me for my losses. I also need to consider an alternative strategy to the way I recruited Anna. I can't afford to make the same mistake again.

The next job in Edinburgh is for the Jordanian couple. They want a little boy and I have identified a guy who is a Finance Director in Scottish government. He had pictures of his kids all over Facebook. I wonder if people realise how the information they post is being used by people like me? My clients live in Dubai. I am due to meet them next week. I know that doing another job will take my mind off the shortcomings of this one. I'll also get to see an exhibition tennis match whilst I'm away. At least it's not golf!

Finally, there is all the other shit to deal with whilst I'm home. Bills to pay, cars to service, laundry to sort out. Oh, and one million to pay into the bank. I'll need to sort a trip to Guernsey out before I head to Dubai.

Life – one thing after another.

Anna
St. Gallen
13th October
17:30

This car is great. Thomas loves it, I love it. A big BMW X5. It is red. Thomas is delighted. It only cost €60K and, because it was used as a demonstration car, it has everything you need. Satnav, great sound system, air con, the works. I will have to buy some music. I know all the kids' songs we bought a few days ago. I think the sound system should be put through its paces by something more demanding than 'The Wheels on the Bus'.

Zurich is behind us. We are heading for Dubrovnik. I am now travelling as Mette. I keep on trying to perfect a Danish accent. Maybe I am going too far and also I don't think it is that different to my own. I will do my best though.

I am not taking the shortest route. I want to avoid going back through Italy. So our route is through to Munich, then down to Salzburg and into Slovenia. Tonight, we will stay in Munich, then Zagreb and finally go on to Dubrovnik.

I think I am happy. Thomas seems very happy; he is excited by the Alpine scenery. In a few days we can settle, find an apartment in Dubrovnik until Christmas. I don't know what will happen after that. We will take life as it comes.

Kieran
St Albans
14th October
22:30

This work makes you paranoid. I know that. Yet sometimes things happen that seem more than coincidence.

St Albans isn't famed for its cosmopolitan character. I like it because it is so bland. Nothing to get excited about. Life is quiet here, although Friday night can be a bit 'Wild West', according to locals. I think they have a slightly warped perception of the frontier days. Two spotty kids swearing at each other outside McDonald's would not have caused too much concern for Wyatt Earp, nor would fisticuffs in a local kebab shop.

The past two days though, I have noticed two cars with Romanian number plates. One car with Romanian plates would be unusual. Two represents a plague.

It could be nothing. It could be paranoia. Or it could be something more.

Anna
The Westin Hotel
Zagreb
15th October
22:00

We are very tired. Too tired to eat; we both just need sleep.

We have just arrived in the hotel room. It is big. Normally, Thomas is excited by new hotels, but tonight he is too sleepy. I bathe him, but he is also a bit bad-tempered and won't wash himself. It's OK though, I understand.

Once he is asleep under the sheets, I have a shower. I pour myself a G&T from the minibar. I need sleep.

Tomorrow is the final stage of my journey.

Kieran
Departure Lounge
Guernsey Airport
17th October
15:45

My flight to Stansted goes in thirty minutes. I hate budget airlines. They are full of budget people, people who have twenty percent off their intelligence, looks or common sense. A few of the passengers look Romanian. I know they aren't, but they are dressed like Romanians in their dowdy clothes and ten-year out-of-date fashions.

When I left home this morning, I saw no Romanian plates. It was early though – 6am. I had a car collect me and drive me to Stansted. I have business in London tonight, so will catch the train to Liverpool Street. Dinner is booked at seven at Skylon on the South Bank. I am meeting a bent copper I know – well, a retired detective – for tips about how you go about tracking somebody down discreetly. Then, the day after tomorrow, in the afternoon, I fly off to Dubai.

I'm as jumpy as hell. It's not good – people remember nervous people more than they remember quiet people. I need to calm down, blend in. Not being noticed is my trademark.

Anna
Villa Josef Broz
Dubrovnik
17th October
17:00

Ah, this is very nice. This is nicer than a hotel and a place we can stay for a few months.

I toured the downtown accommodation agencies when we arrived. They didn't have much, but we gradually managed to find two that were suitable. One was just inside the city walls, but it was too risky as too many people would pass it. This is north of the old city, near to the funicular. It has three big bedrooms, a nice luxury finish, a covered pool and Jacuzzi and a bit of a garden. In a few weeks it will be too cold for Thomas to play in the garden, but the pool is heated, so I will be able to teach him to swim.

Thomas is excited by the pool. From the moment we arrived, he wanted to play in it. So we both went in naked the first time. He thought my naked body was a funny thing, kept on pointing at my boobs and giggling. Afterwards we went to a local hypermarket to buy things, including clothes for Thomas. I need more too. I have been washing underwear each night in a hotel room and travelling with the same three or four outfits. Jeans are fine, but I need more tops and some warmer winter clothes.

117

I am also thinking about the practicalities of life with Thomas. How do I get time for myself? It is very easy if you have documentation for a child; they can join a crèche or start education. I have no documents of this kind for Thomas. I need to get some, otherwise we will spend more of our budget on corrupt solutions.

I am wary of criminal contact here. It is Eastern Europe. The Romanians will have an influence. I know that there are Serbian gangs active here too and my best choice might be to look for them. I am not a criminal. I have started to do some online research and think that three documents will cost me about sixty thousand euros. When we have them, we will be able to travel outside of Europe. At the moment, our movements are restricted to the EU. I still have ninety thousand in Mette's account. I will need to transfer the sixty out of savings, but that should be OK. I am beginning to realise that the life of a fugitive isn't cheap. We have to be careful with money. This may be difficult.

It is possible that after Christmas, with the right documents, we will head south again. I am thinking about Turkey. Turkey is cheap. I may even find a business to buy there. I need to start earning money. I have Thomas's future to think about.

Kieran
18th October
St Albans
01:15

The first thing I noticed when I got back was that the garage door was open. I always leave it locked. Something was up.

It didn't help that retired DCI Andrew Robertson drank like a fish. Even pacing myself had left me a bit light-headed. Far too late in the proceedings, I remembered he had resigned due to his alcohol problems, not because he was bent.

I made my way to the front door which again was ajar. I turned the hall lights on and there were no obvious signs of an intrusion. The lounge had not been disturbed, the kitchen was fine.

I opened the door to my study. That was where the damage was. They had tried to force open a filing cabinet to no avail. They had also taken a laptop. It was my decoy laptop, one that had no important data on it and no e-mails.

I quickly did a recce of the rest of the house. If it was kids, DVD players, CDs and the like would have gone. Nothing of that kind had been taken.

I climbed the stairs to the bedroom. My drawers had been opened, but the safe, containing all my fake documents, had not been disturbed. Not many people would think to look for a safe in an en suite bathroom.

Then I noticed something on the bed. An envelope.

There was nothing in the envelope, just writing on the front.

'Give us our money back.'

The Romanians.

Anna
20th October
Villa Josef Broz
17:00

Some things I am good at, some things I am not.

I am good at cooking, tickling Thomas, keeping the villa tidy and making quick decisions.

I am not so good at bathing Thomas, keeping the car tidy and being patient.

That last one is a problem, I think. It means that I will take risks. I liked working for him because all the decisions were made by somebody else. I just had to do what I was told when I was told.

Now I have to make my own decisions. I have made enquiries. I started by trying to find out which of the bars around Dubrovnik were run by Serbians. There are about seven, but four are run by the same people. To me, that was a big clue. Same people means that they are organised.

Yesterday, I decided to visit. I went in and asked if the owner was around. The girl behind the counter asked, 'Who are you to know?'

I responded by asking her, 'Who are you not to tell me?'

She laughed at this response.

'OK,' she said. 'Who shall I say is the big shot that wants to see him?'

'Not a big shot,' I say, smiling. I hold out my hand. 'I am Mette from Denmark.'

She shakes my hand. Then she disappears for a few minutes, goes to the back of the bar. She returns with a big, broad man, about six feet tall.

He speaks to me. 'I am Stephan,' he says. 'I have no vacancies.'

'Oh,' I tell him, 'I don't want a job. I have a business proposition for you. May we talk somewhere private?'

We go into his office – it is dark and dingy. There are a pile of pornographic DVDs in one corner. There is also a lot of paperwork and a metal box, overflowing with Euro notes. I wonder if he wanks over the DVDs or the money?

'What is your business proposition?' he asks, gesturing that I should take a seat.

Here goes, I think.

'I have been told you, or maybe your associates, can help arrange passports.'

'Passports!' he says. 'We are not government!'

I laugh. I decide to keep pushing.

'I know you are not government. You see though, I also know that you are a particular type of businessman and that you have many associates.'

'Who tells you this?' he asks, tilting his head to one side. 'Were they drunk?'

'You think I am the sort of woman who hangs out with drunks?' I ask him. Before he can answer, I continue, 'I have my sources and I came to Dubrovnik especially for this purpose.'

'Passports are not cheap,' he says.

'Oh, OK, I will leave then,' I pause. 'First, you think I hang out with drunks and then you suggest I am stupid. I know what the passports cost. I need three – for a child.'

He blows out his cheeks. Yet I know we have crossed the threshold.

He makes some calls. Then, after ten minutes, he writes down an address.

'You have a car?'

I nod.

'OK.' He passes me the piece of paper. 'You need to go to this address, a garage, for 2.30 tomorrow. They will discuss what is possible. Ask for Katrina.'

'Thank you,' I say. I shake his hand. 'Nice doing business with you.'

He doesn't smile, but sort of grins.

Tomorrow I have an appointment that will, I hope, make Thomas's life with me a bit easier.

Kieran
Terminal 4
Heathrow

121

20th October
17:30

I have been stuck here for two hours. Delays due to French air traffic controllers being on strike. This is seriously unhelpful. I needed to get Dubai sorted out without any hitches. I am baffled and nervous.

My first question is how the hell did they track me down? If they can find me, then the police can find me. So my whole cover could be blown. I wonder if they got lucky, but all they knew was that I was British. Nothing else. So have they been randomly breaking into homes all over the UK, dropping the same note on to a bed? I fucking think not!

Then I am wondering how to handle it. I could quickly dispose of St Albans; it's only a dormitory for me anyway. Before I left today, I had the twelve data sticks with all my essential data couriered to a safe place. So there is nothing left there that is particularly valuable.

The house is worth £600,000 but I would be happy to let it go for £500,000. I mean, I can even afford to let it rot if need be. The house though is not the issue – it's the fact that they tracked me down that is eating away at me. If they find me once, they can find me again. I was mad to call them apes. Madder still to take their money.

My difficulty is that I could give the money back. The value is neither here nor there. If I give it back though, they have power over me. If I don't, they will continue their hunt. Neither option is pretty.

As a fallback, I have alerted the team in Biarritz that I may be coming for an extended winter stay. I have to regain control of the situation – once I have done that I will know what my best option is. The question remains, how?

Anna
Villa Josef Broz
21st October
17:30

It was a place with no real features. I arrived, as told, at 14.30. I asked for Katrina.

She was a heavy-set woman. No, that's not accurate, she was a fat woman who obviously was very keen on cakes. She chain-smoked as well.

We stood at the back of the workshop and she discussed my requirements.

I had brought my three fake passports and three photos of Thomas.

'I need him to be British, French and Danish.'

She looked at my documents.

'You want him as your son on each one?'

'Yes, he sometimes travels with his father, so I want him to have his own documents.'

She looked again at my passports. She took a few drags on her cigarette, then looked at me.

'The British and French documents are twenty thousand each. The Danish document is twelve and a half thousand. For all three, we will call it fifty-two. We can do it for forty-five if you do some work for us in return.'

I shook my head, disagreeing.

'No.' I was very firm. 'Fifty-two is a good price. When can you have it done by?'

She took a long drag on her cigarette.

'Two days,' she said.

'So I will make it fifty-five if you have the documents for this time tomorrow?'

She takes another couple of drags on her cigarette. Then she offers me her hand.

'Deal,' she says. 'Come back tomorrow with the cash. The documents will be ready.'

I drove back here. The conversation took no more than six minutes. Thomas had been waiting in the back of the car all the time, sleeping.

Tomorrow, he will be properly mine. Tomorrow, we can start to really plan his future.

Kieran
British Airways Executive Lounge
Dubai International Airport
22nd October
17:00

Have I made a mistake?

I reckon if I continue as if they have got the wrong man, life will be fine. So here's what I have decided. I will move another single male into the property. I will pay them to live there if I have to, but the important point is that the person continues to live there. I will spend the winter in Biarritz and operate out of there. There are no technical restrictions on me doing this – I am free to come and go.

I have placed an advert on Gumtree: 'House available, St Albans, close to all local transport, all mod cons. You must be a single male, 5'10 with a BMI of less than twenty-five, professional, British.'

I don't mention much more, but know that I will get a good response.

I am flying direct from here to Paris. I will catch a train straight down to Bordeaux and Dr Fish has agreed to drive me on to Biarritz. He is going to be a house guest for a few days and is bringing his golf clubs. I really loathe golf, but it will be good to have him around for company. He always helps me to clarify my thinking. With any luck, we will be at the chateau by midnight.

My flight is being called; I just have time to check the initial responses to the St Albans ad. So far there are twenty-four. There will probably be double that by the time I arrive in Biarritz. I need to work out who I can get to show the property. That can wait though. No point in rushing into a plan.

Anna
Villa Josef Broz
23rd October
14:00

Now Thomas Greversen has a doctor, a nursery place and a dentist.

It feels good to have him settled. I have spent two days drumming into him his new name. I have told him if people ask who he is he is to say, 'I am Thomas. My mummy is Danish.' We practised for several hours. He seems OK with it, although at first he said that I was not his mummy and that I was not Danish. I explained that it was part of the hide and seek game.

'Are we still playing that?' he asked.

'Absolutely!' I said.

He giggled. I think he will be OK.

I have realised that today is actually my birthday! Amazing! I had nearly forgotten. I don't need to buy myself anything. It is also a month since I took Thomas. Only a month – goodness!

Later, I will take Thomas for a special ice cream to celebrate.

Otherwise, today is just another day. I am older but I am not sad by it because I am much happier too.

Kieran
Biarritz
24th October
19:00

At breakfast today, Dr Fish asked me something.

'Kieran,' he said, 'I know that you're busy, that you have a demanding, how shall I say, business to run. Yet, I'm wondering when was the last time you had some time off, didn't think about work or do anything to do with work? Just relax?'

I thought to myself and I couldn't really remember. I don't do holidays and my work is everything. In the end, I answered, 'Not for a while,' and smiled at him.

'Right. Well, I am as you know a doctor—'

'Retired,' I said, interrupting him.

'Yes, yes,' he said, acknowledging my point. 'You'll recall though that I didn't give back my qualifications when I retired and I still have the same diagnostic ability?'

This is typical Fish: amusingly assured, but deliberately light in tone.

I nodded in agreement.

'Well' he said, 'my professional opinion is that you need a day off. So, anticipating that we were going to have this conversation, I have booked a table at Aux Allzes for lunch. I happen to know that they have a very fine seafood menu and some excellent wine. In fact, I'm willing to sacrifice an afternoon of golf to keep you company there so that I can monitor you not working and also ensure that you take in sufficient quantities of what us medics call "life's finer things".'

I smiled again.

'The table is booked for 1.30. I have taken the liberty of asking Elena to drive us down in my car. She will collect us at 18.00 from a venue to be determined as I rather fancy you and I extending lunch by finding a bar with Sky Sports, so we can see how the Bees are doing this afternoon. Does that sound to your liking?'

And it did. We spent an excellent afternoon together, a man's afternoon. We ate oysters, steaks, drank several bottles of very good wine, talked about nothing in particular but everything in general, and then made our way to a local bar where we drank some more and watched the football results come in. Brentford's score was one of the last through, but they had beaten Brighton 2–0, a satisfying result.

Elena collected us at 18.00. I thought I noticed as we drove back to the chateau, a car parked about a kilometre away. The car had Romanian plates.

'Elena,' I said, 'drive past the chateau!'

Elena knows that when I give an instruction it is exactly that. It is not a request – it is an instruction to be obeyed.

Fish wasn't sure what the fuss was about, but he himself was also a little worse for the wear.

'What's the…'

I put my finger to my mouth, hushing him.

'Elena, can you look in your mirror? The white Opel we have passed – is it still parked there?'

'It is,' she said.

'Pass me your phone,' I say.

She passes it to me and I dial the house.

Jorges, our security man, answers the phone.

'Jorges,' I tell him. 'Put the house into lock down. We will be back in ten minutes, but we will use the southeast entrance to the grounds. Lock the gates at the front and ensure that the CCTV cameras are recording.'

I turned to Dr Fish.

'It was a great afternoon. Sadly work has intruded, as it always does.'

I'm sitting in the security control room. The monitors are showing nothing untoward and this is very much a precaution. We will stay locked down for the next forty-eight hours. This means no incoming calls, e-mails or anything that can be traced. I had built the procedure in anticipation of a police raid, but it works just as well for any level of risk, including Romanian apes. Now we have to wait.

Anna
Villa Josef Broz
25th October
08:15

There is a doctor here.

In the night, I was woken by banging. I thought somebody was trying to get in, maybe trying to break in to Thomas's room. So I ran in and he is on the floor, near the window, arms flapping about. It is, I realise, another seizure.

After a few moments he is calm but his clothes are soiled again. He regains his focus and starts to cry. I cuddle him. He settles.

I take him to the bathroom. We are both sleepy, but I wash his bottom, get him changed. Eventually, he is back in bed. I kiss him, he smiles weakly.

I go back to bed, then about an hour ago, the same thing. This time I phone the doctor.

She is young, has a nice manner with Thomas and speaks good English. She examines him, takes his temperature and then turns to me.

'So this hasn't happened before?'

If I lie, there will be no need to look at his family history.

'No,' I say.

She sighs.

'Well, childhood epilepsy. It is a mystery and at his age I wouldn't use drugs to control it.'

She strokes Thomas's head. He is still looking a bit dazed. Yet I can also see that he is becoming brighter; life is returning to the back of his eyes.

'You be a good boy for Mummy.'

And Thomas looks mischievous and just shouts, 'Ssh, hide and seek!'

I give him a look that indicates he has been naughty.

'Stop being silly, Thomas!' I turn to the doctor. 'He sometimes says the strangest things!'

She laughs.

'He is a little boy, he will one day be a little man and we all know men say the strangest things. I think he's just practising.'

She leaves, gives me a mobile contact number if I need her again and says she will send a bill to me.

I am worried for little Thomas. I am also worried for me though. Can I cope with this? A stupid question. I have to cope with this.

Kieran
26th October
Biarritz
21:00

Fish has gone. Nothing happened.

For two days, we didn't venture out. There is always sufficient food in storage for us to be able to last out for twelve days. Two days wasn't much of a test.

The lock down area is under the garage. The entrance is concealed at the end of the mechanic's pit and can only be reached if a hydraulic lift is raised. The lift can only be operated from within the lock down area. So once we are in, we are safe. It is spartan compared to the rest of the chateau. There are nine rooms. They are furnished in the style of a budget hotel chain; not too spartan, but not too luxurious either. Fortunately, there were only seven required this time. Dr Fish kindly offered to share with Elena. She politely declined.

We had two veritable feasts. Good wine, good food, good conversation. It was as if there was a revolution in the streets above and we the Politburo had taken to our bunker. Anybody watching the chateau would have seen the gates shut. A complex timing device gave the impression that the place was occupied. Lights in different rooms came on and off when they should. Curtains opened, shutters were turned back. It would take closer scrutiny to reveal any more, but closer scrutiny would be caught by the CCTV cameras.

Then, after two days, a run-through of all the monitors and a review of the recordings, we emerged.

Before he left, the doctor said to me: 'Do you need to share this problem? Do you need to talk?' He placed his hand on my shoulder as he did this.

The last thing I want to do is drag the good doctor into this mess. He really needs to know as little as possible. If he knows too much, he could be targeted. So keeping him ignorant is beneficial to his own safety.

In the end, it was just a Romanian car. The team at the chateau thought it was an exercise. That suits me. Hopefully, it will only ever be an exercise. Nonetheless, I have talked to Jorges. I want some heavier protection. Whilst I have always been one to avoid the heavy end of things, I have suggested we locate a few semi-automatics. A precaution. Nothing more. Jorges is investigating this possibility.

He explained to me: 'If you want guns, that's fine. You have to understand though, it is not like in Hollywood. You will need to learn how to use them, how to load and reload, how to shoot. OK?'

I agreed. This is a serious business. I will find a local gun club and learn how to shoot.

I think things are getting very dangerous. I am exposed. I don't like any of this and need space to think through my options. I may need to escape to somewhere more remote. Where?

Anna
Villa Josef Broz
27th October
22:00

He has been better today. More focused, more like the normal Thomas.

I keep wondering when he will start forgetting his mum? When will he realise that we are not going back to them? I need to tell him. I need to explain it, but I need to do so in a way that doesn't hurt him, doesn't make him feel rejected or stolen. He is, of course, stolen. He just doesn't need to know that.

I think, in the end, we tell lies to children all the time. Father Christmas is a lie; the Easter bunny is a lie; so is the Tooth Fairy. One more lie will not damage Thomas too much.

Kieran
Ramsey Arms
Fettercairn
28th October
17:30

Uncle Tony and my dad used to bring me here when I was a teenager. Good Scottish walking country. A small hotel with great food and great whiskey, not far from Montrose.

It isn't the most remote place, but it is quiet – at this time of the year, very quiet. The clocks go back tomorrow, so it will also be quite dark. This fits with how I'm feeling.

I took the train up from London, hired a car in Edinburgh. I have managed to get a short walk in already, just around the village and surrounding hills, but it blew the cobwebs away.

Having a pre-dinner whiskey in the bar, the local malt. They do a great cullen skink here which is worth the hassle of the journey and the piss-taking from the local jocks. Mind, typical of small Scottish villages, many of the locals prefer not to eat here. They argue that the Ramsey Arms has got ideas above its station. Not everything about Scotland is communitarian; this is one of many examples of a community simply showing prejudice against enterprise. Suits me. I have a seat by a roaring fire, a menu to work through and a couple of decisions to make about who I should offer St Albans to.

Tomorrow, I am going to do a fifteen-mile walk to Montrose and back. By the end of it, I hope to have made the right choice.

For now, I'll settle for the cullen skink with a decent bottle of Merlot.

Anna
Hotel Kopeci
29th October
10:00

Istanbul! Yes, Istanbul!

I wanted to take a chance, test out the documents. A risk? Well, of course, but we would have to have taken that risk sooner or later.

We flew. Thomas was very excited. Only a short flight, but he sat with his nose pressed against the window all the way. Then we had a day sightseeing. The Grand Bazaar, the Blue Mosque, Topkapı Palace. All wonderful.

We fly back today and I know that we have made a breakthrough. We are now able to travel where we want and when we want. This is good. We can plan for a different future.

Kieran
Ramsay Arms
Fettercairn
30th October
10:30

Finished two Skype interviews.

The first guy didn't seem suitable. Asked too many questions about what I did, wanted to know what the catch was with him living there rent-free. Seemed dodgy. An accountant – what did I expect?

Second guy much more suitable. Very similar to me in build and not far off in looks. He was sanguine when I mentioned that the place was rent-free and said, 'I'll do my best to keep it maintained to a high standard.' This was the kind of response I was looking for. He also asked practical questions. Would he need to transfer the utilities into his name? Would he be able to have people to stay (not long-term, he assured me)? How was he to contact me in the event of an emergency? Was there a contract? I explained that I would continue to pay for all of the services, that there was no contract, but he could have the place until the beginning of June.

We agreed to meet in London later in the week. I will make a quick visit to St Albans on my way south. I have decided to drive back, rather than take the train. This will mean I can call in at the house and drop the hire car off in London. I have documents to collect, mostly data sticks, and the guy who is taking the place would like to use the garage. I suggested that he might want to use my car, but he explained that his Jaguar Sport is his pride and joy and having it garaged was an essential. That's the trouble with petrol heads, they get all their priorities out of kilter. I need to see Tony too. I want him to act as a contact if anything goes wrong with the house.

Unfortunately, the past few days haven't resolved anything in my head. I think I need to live in the gap. It's only in movies or novels that people gain an epiphany. In real life, we stumble on, banging into crises, groping our way through the darkness. For most of us, it seems to work most of the time. Whatever plan I have could be subject to change. Still, I did some great walks and had some amazing food. Sometimes, we have to be patient in life, rather than torture ourselves. That, in itself, can be torturous.

Anna
Villa Josef Broz
1st November
09:30

Two more seizures last night. One at two, one at four. I have left him sleeping this morning.

I thought the Russians cruel and heartless. Now I am wondering if they didn't make the right decision. This is hard work and so unpredictable. So far though his seizures have been at night, not when he is awake. I have spoken to the doctor and she has said that nocturnal epilepsy is less to worry about than if Thomas was having daytime seizures. I think she is right, but it is still hard work. Poor Thomas.

Kieran
Churchill Hotel
London
1st November
20:00

So it's war!

I never wanted this, they did. I never intended to hit back, but now they leave me with no choice.

I was moving the car. I had decided to park it at Tony's as this would kill two birds with one stone. I would also be able to hand him a spare set of keys to St Albans. The kid is due to move in the day after tomorrow, complete with Jaguar Sport.

I am driving around the M25 to West London. The weather is wet so I am keeping my distance from the vehicles in front. Of course, this doesn't stop people driving up my arse, but that's the M25 for you, populated by sales reps and arseholes, often one and the same person. My car, a big Audi A6, can handle the conditions fine. Yet, just after we pass the M1 junction, something starts to feel wrong. The braking is getting spongy. I wonder if there is air in the brake pipe or something similar, but to tell you the truth, I know nothing about cars.

I slow down a little, drop to the legal speed limit and increase the distance between me and the car in front. Then up ahead, suddenly, there are lots of brake lights coming on. I hit the pedals again and not much happens – the car slows, but it's not slowing fast enough. Fortunately, the middle lane is clear, so I throw the car across the carriageway and slam it into third. It skids about on the wet surface. There is more traffic ahead. There is nothing for it – there is a van on the inside lane which I manage to clip as I head for the hard shoulder. I just catch its front bumper. There is a bang, but no crunch, so I reckon I haven't done much damage. Then I manage to steer onto the hard shoulder, but there still isn't much happening with the brakes. I decide there is only one thing for it: pull up onto a grassy bank and hope that by engaging neutral and pulling on the hand brake, I'll be able to stop.

It's a bumpy five or six seconds and the windscreen cracks as I bounce along, but eventually I come to a halt.

About twenty minutes later, the police and RAC man are on the scene. The guy from the RAC carries out an examination of my car. He calls me from the safety of his breakdown truck out into the rain to show me something.

'You're a very lucky man,' he says. 'Look at this, the brake fluid pipe has been interfered with.'

Then the Old Bill come across and before I know it questions are being asked about who would do this. What do I do for a living and so on. None of this is helpful.

The RAC drive me and my briefcase to Ealing. I drop the keys off to Tony and give him a grand for his troubles.

'Why are you giving me all that money?' he asked. 'You don't need to do that.' It was non-negotiable. A grand for Tony would keep him in Brentford tickets for the rest of the season – well worth the investment. Anyway, he wasn't one to argue. He accepted it, but was bewildered by my generosity. In his mind, people did things for mates without reward.

I left Tony and headed into London. I had arranged to meet a lawyer friend who was going to have my data sticks put into secure storage. The day-to-day information I needed was online, behind a series of well-secured firewalls. This stuff was more mundane. And I decided not to go back to St Albans. I booked a room at the Churchill. London seemed the sensible option for tonight.

Of course, the garage doors had been opened after the Romanians broke in. I had been stupid and not checked the car in the intervening period, having no need to use it in the subsequent twelve days. This being the first time meant that their little surprise had been delayed.

Breaking into a home is one thing, putting my life at risk is an entirely different and much more serious proposition. Not to mention getting the police involved in the fringes of my life.

It is time for action.

My first action? Call the Romanian chief chimpanzee.

Anna
Villa Josef Broz
1st November
21:15

Thomas is sleeping.

137

I am thinking that it is becoming too cold here. We need to go somewhere warmer. I am not sure where. My research online shows that a British passport is the easiest for us to travel on, particularly if we are going to countries Britain owned in the past.

I look at a list of former British colonies. Australia? New Zealand? It is starting to be summer there now, but I think they are places where it costs money to live. Sri Lanka, Malaysia or India would be much cheaper.

I don't know about Sri Lanka. I think it might be dangerous. Malaysia seems too far away, but India – well, I know about India. I have always wished to go to Goa. The weather apparently is great from November through to February. Looking online, I have found a villa with a big pool for less than €300 per month. This is nothing!

I am thinking I will sleep on it, but I am also thinking I have already made up my mind.

Kieran
Churchill Hotel
London
1st November
21:30

It's like a combination of chess and Russian roulette.

I phoned him. There was no point delaying. I had bought a cheap pay-as you-go mobile earlier this evening.

I dialled the number I had used to make the initial contact.

'It's time for you to stop playing games,' I said calmly.

'Games?' Ape responded. 'Why do you use that word?

138

You owe us money and you have cheated us. This is not a game!'

'I want you to stop. I don't want you breaking into my nephew's house, do you understand?'

'Oh,' he answered. 'It is your nephew's house is it? We have never seen your nephew there.'

'He has been working away,' I say.

'Really? Where? In the South of France perhaps?' He added a laugh at the end of this.

'I am happy to return your money,' I said, wanting to steer the subject away from any hint that they knew more than they thought they did.

'You will need to pay interest,' he said.

'What do you propose?' I asked.

'If you pay the money back in a week the interest will only mean that you need to pay us one point seven five million.'

'One and a half million,' I said.

'Well,' he replied, 'I could consider that, but I couldn't guarantee that my team would be happy. They are still angry with the physical assault you committed. The additional charge would, how can I say, ensure that all future claims are considered settled. Do you understand?'

'What assurances do I have?' I asked, but I knew the answer to my question.

'You have none,' he said. 'If you don't pay the money though, well things will just get worse. You see, you made a mistake. A little mistake in kicking my man in the face, but a big, big, big mistake in trying to cheat me out of money.'

'I agree,' I said. 'It was an error of judgement. I apologise.'

'No, no, no,' he replied. 'An error of judgement is when you spill milk as you put it into your English tea. There is a small stain left on the white tablecloth, but it will wash out. This was a colossal mistake; the stain may never wash out and it is blood not tea…' The line goes quiet. Then he continues, 'But of course, we will do our best to put this behind us.'

It is a sort of assurance.

'So how do I get the money to you?' I ask.

'You bring it to me, in Bucharest.'

'I am not coming to Bucharest,' I tell him.

'Well, you give me an alternative then,' he says.

I think for a moment.

'Dubrovnik,' I say. 'Hotel Bellevue, five days' time.'

He goes quiet.

'You still there?' I ask.

'Four days,' he says.

'OK,' I respond. 'Just you, nobody else.'

'We can have dinner,' he says with a laugh.

'I think,' I say, 'that I may have a stomach bug coming on. Dinner is not going to be possible.'

He laughs.

'Your choice,' he says.

The call ends.

I still don't trust him. Yet I suspect this has become a question of honour. I have asked him to come alone, but I doubt that he will. So I will bring Jorges and Elena for backup.

I will sleep more soundly tonight, but there is no doubt that this has been an expensive mistake. A big, big, big mistake.

Anna
Villa Josef Broz
2nd November
11:00

Why are people difficult?

I have spoken to the stupid man who we have rented the villa from. I explained that I may be leaving earlier than planned, something has come up. He has said that if I leave early there is an additional charge to pay. I asked him why when we have paid up until Christmas and he said 'administrative costs'. I was not happy with this and called him an idiot. He told me not to be rude, it was just the way the system works.

He made me mad. So I asked, 'What would the charge be if we left our things in the villa until Christmas and then had them put into storage?'

'Only the cost of removal and the cost of storage,' he said.

'Which is what?' I asked him.

'I think about two hundred euros,' he told me.

Now, here is the crazy thing, the administrative cost for terminating my agreement would have been €500. So it is cheaper for me to use a removal company and keep the villa in my name than it is for him to rent it out again. The bigger stupid thing is that I forgot. I forgot I have plenty of money. I must stop trying to live like a girl with no money.

I have decided that in three days we are going to India. To Goa! I have found us a big villa with a huge pool and a beach nearby. It costs nothing – for six months about four thousand euros. We are travelling as British so I will now be Jill Betts with her son, Thomas Betts. I think Tommy Betts is a nice name, no?

So we leave in three days. I have to sort out storage for the BMW – I have called the local dealer and he is happy to look after the car for up to six months. He offered to buy it off me, but I want to keep it. He said he will garage it and keep it 'mothballed', whatever that means. Sooner or later we will come back to Europe and car is the quickest way to travel.

Which means we are ready. I think we will stay in Goa until March or April, I can't decide.

Kieran
2nd November
Guernsey
12:00

I have a suitcase with one and a half million next to me.

I have a flight to Paris and then a train from there to Marseille. Another long day today, but business is business.

I am a long way behind in planning my two new jobs. At the back of my mind, I am wondering if I should back out. Take a year off or something. At the minute, it feels like an uphill struggle to keep things moving forward. There is plenty of money in the bank, easily enough to keep me solvent for two or three years. Maybe I could write a book in that period? I have plenty of stories to tell. The trouble is that if I step out of the game, it will be hard to step back in. Clients go cold and even the agencies I source my actual sports tickets through will stop being as accommodating. The signs are there now. I was trying to get tickets for a Calcutta Cup game in February, but my usual source seemed particularly nonplussed about the possibility. Whether or not my Russian client would understand rugby is beyond me, but that's not the point.

It is irritating. When I have an idea, it eats away at me. That's how I got into this work in the first place. A *Sunday Times* article about rich, childless couples trying to adopt. I thought, *I could deliver a service here*, and the rest as they say, is histrionics. Yet just because you're good at something and it pays well, doesn't necessarily mean it's worth the aggro does it?

Regardless of any considerations for the future, I need to sort this shit out with the Romanians. I am not looking forward to the trip to Dubrovnik. I have some insurance in place. Elena and Jorges are meeting me in Marseille. They are going on ahead of me, posing as a couple away on a romantic break. I am sure the Romanian Ape will have somebody in the background. It has been tempting to organise a hit on him. Yet there is already too much mess here without creating more crap. An assassination would just mean more trouble and a merry-go-round of retribution.

The motorway is always efficient; more accidents happen on country lanes and sometimes the sensible route is the best route, even if it is not the one that gives the greatest personal satisfaction.

Anna
Villa Josef Broz
3rd November
22:00

I have learnt my first Indian phrase: *Namaste*. It means something like, 'I am honoured.'

Hindi looks a very tough language to learn, but apparently Hinglish is widely spoken. This is a very quick version of English spoken with an Indian accent. I hope that I will be able to follow it.

Tonight, I will dream of elephants, Indian princes and golden beaches. We are nearly there.

Kieran
4th November
Split
12:30

The last family holiday, before my parents divorced, was taken here. It was just after the fall of the Berlin Wall. Europe was liberalising quickly, there seemed no end of possibilities. Now it is no longer as different as it was back then.

I am having lunch in a café in the main square. In some respects, I could be anywhere, the shops and retail outlets feel pretty much like anywhere else. I think this place still feels a bit behind the times, but now it feels three or four years off the pace – when I first came it felt decades behind everywhere else. The food has got better too. In the past, it was hot dogs and burgers. Now there is a bit more local stuff, but where I am eating serves excellent tapas. Progress can be measured in the absence of hot dogs and the preponderance of posh eateries.

Elena and Jorges are at the Bellevue. Apparently, Elena has already developed a liking for the Tamaric wine. She has good taste. They have seen nothing untoward, nothing that worries them. There are a surprising number of Americans staying, another change over the years. In the past, no God-fearing American would have set foot in such a communist backwater, with the exception of Coca-Cola executives, flogging bottling plants to Tito.

Tomorrow evening, I hope to have the Romanian apes off my back.

Anna
Villa Josef Broz
4th November
22:00

Last night I had bad dreams. For the first time, I had dreams about Cathy. She was not happy and the dreams were vivid.

In the first dream, we were in a version of her house in Chiswick. The postman kept arriving with Christmas parcels

– the parcels contained babies' clothing, but, once unwrapped, there were dead babies inside the clothes. Cathy was distraught. She kept blaming me.

'I never used to get these parcels before you came here!' she kept screaming at me.

The next dream I had was that she was on a horse. We were by the swings that I used to take Thomas to. She was chasing children on her horse, catching them with a lasso. She would haul them up to her saddle and they would be struggling. She would look into their faces and say, 'Thomas?' When she realised they weren't Thomas, she would throw them away and their bodies bounced along the ground like rag dolls.

In the final dream, we were at her house, but there was snow on the ground. Thomas ran ahead and then police arrived. They grabbed Thomas, but had their guns trained on me. I woke up before I knew what happened.

I know that dreams are nonsensical, but they scare me. They leave me afraid. I try to tell myself that they are only dreams, but if I am honest, sometimes I know the reality of what I have done is worse.

Kieran
Hotel Bellevue
Dubrovnik
5th November
14:30

I had just arrived. I had left my phone charging overnight and had forgotten to turn it on until late morning. That was a mistake. Lots of message and texts, all from Elena.

The first text read: *Do we intercept? Please advise!*

The second message read: *Jorges confirms it is them.*

The final message read: *Followed them to the airport. They are checking in for a flight to Zagreb!*

I listened to the voicemail messages. Again, all from Elena.

The first message said: 'Hi, boss, please advise. I have just seen a little boy, waving at me from a taxi. I am pretty sure it is Thomas. Will follow, but what should I do?'

The second message said: 'They are at the airport. I am keeping my distance. Why haven't you responded to my earlier message? Jorges is with me and he too is convinced it is Thomas. Anna is with him.'

The third message just confirmed that they were at the airport boarding a flight for Zagreb.

I phoned immediately.

'OK,' I said. 'Don't approach them. This could be a trap set up by the Romanians. Come and meet me back at the hotel.'

I couldn't be sure, but it seemed highly likely that Anna had defected to the Romanian cause. Maybe they caught up with her on the motorway? Maybe they were going to use her as a decoy? Maybe it's her who has been feeding them information about Biarritz and St Albans. (Did I ever mention St Albans to her? Surely I wasn't that stupid!)

We are all in my hotel room now. Elena is going through what happened.

'I was walking back to the hotel about an hour and a half ago,' she explained. 'I looked up and noticed a taxi waiting at traffic lights across the road. There was a little boy in the back, waving at me. It took a few moments, but I realised it was Thomas. He was smiling, but also making a hushing sign. I don't know what that was about.'

She paused, took a mouthful of wine. 'I stopped a cab and asked him to follow the taxi that was maybe one hundred metres ahead;

at the same time I called Jorges. According to my driver, we were heading to the airport, so I asked Jorges to meet me there. They didn't have much luggage and were checking in for an internal flight to Zagreb. Jorges arrived and he confirmed it was them.'

I weighed up what I had been told. This felt unlikely to be a coincidence. Did the Romanian have a photo of me with Anna and Thomas? Was the idea to take the money off me, but then turn the tables? They would now have the boy and their money back.

Yet it didn't make sense. They wanted the boy for other purposes, not to entice me. So the second possibility was that she was here trying to do her own deal. Maybe that's why he wanted to meet in Dubrovnik. Maybe he had already arranged to meet her here.

No. It wasn't adding up.

'Jorges,' I said. 'We need to be on high alert this evening. I smell a rat. Arrange for a table as close to us as possible. You are both French, OK?'

I would see how the conversation with the Romanians developed – if need be I could confront them with what we knew. Jorges, I hoped, had packed a shooter.

Anna
Flight ZG411
Croatian Airspace
5th November
14:45

I can't be annoyed with Thomas, but what has he done?

We had just taken off from Zagreb when he asked me, 'Elena, from the big house – is she playing hide and seek?'

I wasn't really listening, so just said, 'Mmm.'

'What happens if she sees me?'

I still wasn't listening.

'No,' I said, not really paying attention. He was just a little boy, gibbering away.

Then he tugged my sleeve, forcefully. 'You're not listening!' He was getting agitated.

'I'm sorry,' I said to Thomas. 'Ask me again.'

He sighed, as if he were talking to somebody quite stupid.

'Elena, is she playing hide and seek?'

He had lost me.

'Who is Elena?' I admit, at this point I was amused.

'From the big house. When we first started playing hide and seek!'

I thought for a moment, then realised who he meant. I leaned in close to him.

'Thomas,' I said quietly. 'Have you seen Elena?'

He nodded.

'Where?'

'When I was in the taxi.'

'And did she see you?'

He nodded again, but was starting to look upset, as if he was realising he had done something wrong.

I gave him a cuddle and a smile.

'It's OK,' I said, 'she won't find us,' and he seemed settled by that.

Inside, I was feeling sick. How had Elena tracked us to Dubrovnik? Maybe we were leaving for India at the right time!

Kieran
Hotel Bellevue
Dubrovnik
5th November
23:00

He arrived on time and was shown to my table. Elena and Jorges were in place, a table away.

'This is not very private,' he said as he arrived, looking in the direction of Elena and Jorges at the table next to us.

'French,' I said.

'They may speak English,' he suggested.

'From what I have observed, only enough to order food and wine. Providing we talk about more than bisque and so on, we should be fine.'

He looked across. Seemed satisfied.

'Why do pretty French women choose such jerks? I would hate to be giving that arsehole a blow job.'

I think this comment was designed to get a response. Elena and Jorges just carried on chatting away in French. Professional as always.

We ordered food. He has the table manners of a badly trained pig, eating with his mouth open, shovelling food in without pause for breath. Maybe I wouldn't need to have him killed – at this rate he would choke on his own bad manners.

'So,' he asked, shovelling steak and red wine into his enormous mouth. 'You have the money you owe me.'

'Here? You know this restaurant is good, but it isn't *that* expensive.'

He laughed. It was a forced laugh, not natural, carrying all the sincerity of a local radio DJ.

'So when will I get the money? In a fortune cookie at the

end of the meal?' He smirked at me, delighted with his great joke.

'I have some questions for you.'

'Oh, like your *Who Wants to Be a Millionaire?* programme?' *Such high culture*, I thought, but ignored his comment.

'Anna. She is the girl who took Thomas, the boy I was going to trade with you – have you been in contact with her?'

He affects a blank look and nods his head vigorously from side to side.

'I don't know any Anna. What makes you think she would be in touch with me?'

'She was here today, in Dubrovnik. She had the boy with her.'

He looks at me blankly and then smiles.

'Maybe she is looking for you? To give the boy back!' He roars with laughter at this. I am not quite sure why.

'So you are absolutely, one hundred percent saying she has not been in touch with you and you've not seen her?'

'I am a businessman. Why do I need to lie to you?' He sneered at me when he said this in the way that businessmen who deal in drugs and child sex rings probably do. 'Curious though, don't you think? Even more curious that we will be eating our desserts shortly and I have still not had the money you owe me.' There was menace in his tone as he said this.

'You will get your money,' I said. I was firm – not speaking with menace, but still resolute.

'Are you playing me?' he said, narrowing his eyes.

'What purpose would that serve?' I said and smiled at him.

'Your fantasies about this girl being here with the boy, the allegations you have made. You don't want to make a big, big mistake, do you?'

At this point, he deliberately tipped his wine glass over. The tablecloth turned crimson and staff rushed over to clear up the mess.

'Look how terrible mistakes can be – the mess, nobody likes clearing up a bloody mess,' he told me.

Order was restored, eventually.

When the staff had gone, he asked, 'Why don't you want to go into business with me? I'm sure I could make your business lucrative.'

So I explained.

'The work I do is complicated. It requires careful and meticulous planning. My work is based upon precision, like a Swiss watchmaker. I think your approach is more industrial. So let me put it as clearly as I can. I don't work with unskilled shits like you.' And I smiled at him.

'That is rather an unpleasant comment. In fact, I would say it is more than unpleasant. Distasteful, disrespectful. I want my money. I do not want my dessert.' His face was expressionless as he said all this.

I rose from the table.

'Excuse me for a moment,' I said.

He nodded, but was looking away, almost as if the act of looking directly at me would cause him to be violently sick.

I went back to my room. I fished out the holdall with the money. I thought about taking a few bundles out, but thought better of it. It felt like I was dumping a girlfriend I should never have dated and for some reason an image of Zie came into my head.

Returning to the restaurant, there was a large blonde woman standing over the Ape.

'Why are you on my patch?' She was standing over him, waving her arms around. I waited in the doorway to the restaurant.

'Calm down,' he said patronisingly. 'I am passing through, on my own. I am not doing anything on your patch.'

She was fearsome. Kept dragging on a cigarette, housed in a long cigarette holder.

'You have thirty seconds to fuck off back to Bucharest.'

She took a long draw on her cigarette.

He laughed at her.

'A whole thirty seconds. It will take them longer to bring the bill.' He was chuckling to himself.

Then, with no warning, she pulled out a gun from her handbag.

Instinctively Jorges stood up – she turned the gun on him.

'Sit down,' she barked, training the firearm on him.

Jorges did as he was told.

'You need my permission to be here,' she said, turning to the Ape. You do not have my permission!' She fired the gun; the bullet entered his head and exited the rear, sending blood spattering everywhere. A waitress screamed as he flew back off his chair and landed on the floor, blood oozing from the wound at the back of his head.

She took a drag of the cigarette. Looking around the restaurant, which now only contained Elena, Jorges and some of the waiting staff, she shouted, 'When the police come, if you value your lives, you tell them it was a man that did this. A tall man with a beard who he had been having dinner with. You understand? Destroy any CCTV footage! You can take payment for any damage from this.' She threw a bundle of euro notes on the table. Jorges later told me he thought there was about ten thousand in the bundle she threw down.

She took another drag on her cigarette, put the gun back into her handbag and then calmly walked out of the restaurant.

We all stood motionless for a moment. Then, almost on cue, we all headed for the exits as quickly as we could. The three of us agreed to get away from here as soon as possible.

I am waiting for them now in the car park – they are just coming out of the lift. In the distance, I can hear the sound of a police siren. We should be long gone by the time they get here, along with the money.

PART FOUR

Anna
Mobor Beach
South Goa
2nd January
11:00

We have a routine now. In the morning, we get up, we have breakfast. Thomas has boiled eggs with toast soldiers. I have a glass of orange juice and some black coffee. If Thomas has had a bad night, I make him sleep for another couple of hours. If he is fine and free from seizures, then we have a swim in the pool. Thomas in his little water wings tries to keep up with me as I swim twenty lengths. He normally manages one length of the pool, swimming like a doggy. Then we go for a walk on the beach. We walk for an hour, picking up shells, paddling, saying hello to people. My hair is long and black now. I am Mrs Betts. I have cut Thomas's hair short and it is dyed black. He is so tanned that from a distance he looks Indian.

We get back from our walk and Neetha, our housekeeper, is usually there with Ravi, her little boy. Thomas and Ravi like to play in the garden with each other. Thomas enjoys playing hide and seek with Ravi. By lunchtime he is exhausted, so he has a little sleep. Then the four of us eat food together, usually something simple like samosas or bhajis. Apparently, this is seen as being very democratic – not many Europeans eat with their staff.

After lunch, Neetha prepares dinner. This is usually more elaborate, often vegetarian, and all I have to do is heat it through. In the afternoon, Thomas and I might play some more in the pool or go and have some kulfi in the village. I am trying to reduce the amount of ice cream he eats as I think this triggers his seizures. I am not sure.

We are both happy. This is a very easy way to live. There is a hotel nearby, a Holiday Inn. On Sunday, when Neetha doesn't work, we go there for food. I have a massage, Thomas plays in the crèche.

If I have a complaint, it is only that life can be a little boring, particularly after Thomas has gone to bed. I am reading lots though. Sometimes I take books from the hotel library to read at home. Every night by ten, I turn my light out. It is time to sleep. Each night I wonder, is this the end of another day in paradise or another day in prison?

DCI John Hardcastle
New Scotland Yard
London
2nd January
09:00

I have been asked to review claimed sightings of Thomas Moore since his disappearance in Praia da Alvor on 23rd September last year. These sightings are based upon calls to the 'Find Thomas' line set up on 24th September.

There have been 429 sightings and I have listed the countries in which members of the public claim to have seen him:

Portugal - 48
Spain - 52
USA - 44
France - 36
England - 29

Italy - 17
Poland - 15
Croatia - 12
Switzerland - 5
India - 9
Bahamas - 4
Greece - 6

There is no common link between the sightings. Many seem either mistaken or just made up. For example, six of the sightings in India are in Delhi. Two are in Goa. They occur at the same time. I can only assume that these are cases of mistaken identity.

Of the sightings in Portugal most were made around Praia da Alvor in the thirty-six hours immediately after his disappearance. About a quarter have been investigated. However, a number claim to have seen him walking on a beach alone, eating burgers in McDonalds and, on one occasion, driving a forklift truck. These sightings have been filed under 'misleading' and I suspect that many of them have been reported by people who have been drinking or who are unable to distinguish fantasy from reality.

For the purpose of this exercise, I have reviewed those sightings where they claim to have seen Thomas with a significant other, i.e. another adult. This makes more interesting reading.

Spain - 8
France - 6
Italy - 5
Croatia - 10
Switzerland - 4
India - 2

For the moment, I am proposing to exclude all other sightings and concentrate on them, if need be, at a later date. I will then investigate all three-year-olds known to be employed as forklift drivers in the Lagos region of Portugal. I suspect, however, that this line of enquiry will fail to shed any light.

Anna
5th January
Mobor Beach
21:00

The first thing I am certain of is that they didn't see us. I am one hundred and fifty percent certain of that. The second thing is, it was definitely them.

We were enjoying our morning walk on the beach. We had just walked past the Holiday Inn and I glanced towards the pool – you can see it from the beach. They were on a pair of loungers together. He had gained some weight. Sofia was the same as always – thin, long-limbed, elegant. It was impossible not to recognise them. I pulled my sun hat down a little more over my face and made Thomas wear his sunglasses. I didn't rush or change my pace – that would have drawn attention to us. Instead, I carried on walking in the same direction, chatting to Thomas, getting him to collect shells. The usual sort of thing.

By the time we had turned around and walked back, they were gone, probably to eat, sleep or steal a child.

I am not so bothered. Russians are increasingly common in this part of Goa. Neetha does not like them. She says they are rude, drink and smoke too much and treat the locals like dirt. To me, they sound typical rich Russians. They are people who believe that because they have become rich they are special; not lucky, but somehow gifted. They were the same people who were in the Politburo in the past and who had dachas and Black Sea villas when the communists were in power. Now they can flaunt their wealth in our faces, but they are still horrible, arrogant and nasty.

I will avoid the Holiday Inn for the next week or so. It will mean missing our Sunday treat there, but that is no bad thing. We will go somewhere else for a change. I am pretty sure that Sofia and her husband are not here looking for us. In all probability, they will be gone in a few days. Just Russians coming here to insult the locals, ignore the culture, drink cheap whiskey and ogle the pretty Indian girls.

DCI John Hardcastle
New Scotland Yard
6th January
12:30

I have reported to my superintendent, DCI Liva. She always gives me a hard time; I think she is a bit bloody painful. She works all the hours she can largely because her personal life is a mess. She is always lording it over colleagues about how hard she works. We call her Slobber because Liva sounds a bit like saliva.

I presented my report. She thinks it's good, but doesn't support all the conclusions.

Of the thirty-five more detailed investigations I carried out, only six claimed to have seen Thomas with a man. Twenty-nine claim to have seen him with a woman. The description of the woman varies a little, but the height and build are always the same. She is also approximately the same age too. Somewhere between twenty-eight and thirty-four. Slobber thinks that this probably applies to half the women who are mums anywhere in the world. I tried to explain that the likelihood is low given the commonality of descriptions.

It drives me mad, but she has asked me to look again at all the Spanish and Portuguese sightings. Is the same woman in any of those? If not, she thinks I might be on to something.

I hate the way that my work is dismissed like this. I think that my opinion really isn't valued much. Maybe if I behave like Slobber, spend all my time at my desk, pretend I'm a workaholic, people will take me more seriously. The trouble is, that is not how I am built, that is not how I roll.

When I was doing my training, my training manager, DCI Robertson, an old-school type, always said that being a good copper is often about going with your instinct and intuition. That's what I came into this job for. I don't get why we have to go through every file, every document when the answer is staring back at you. Trouble is that in this job you don't ask questions of your superiors, you do as you're told. I've seen people with far less talent than me get on simply because they do as they're told. So what if we don't find little Thomas for a few weeks more? At least we will have done it by the book, eh? Well, good luck to the book.

Anna
Mobor Beach
22:00
8th January

I have been doing something over the last few days that I have avoided. I have been looking at the media coverage of Thomas's disappearance online.

It is interesting. In the initial few days, there was lots of coverage. Headline news for days. Now it is only occasionally mentioned. The media only seem to have an interest in the short term – new stories come along, old stories are forgotten. I wonder if that means Thomas is forgotten.

There was, however, a recent feature in a Sunday paper. It was an interview with Cathy. She seemed quite philosophical and mentioned that 12th January will be Thomas's fourth birthday. I will do something to celebrate. In the interview, she was saying that she and her husband are convinced Thomas is still alive and that they will see him again. I wonder how she knows? Is there a spiritual tie between a mother and her baby?

One thing that is clear is that the papers and the police haven't a clue where Thomas is. No mention of Switzerland, Dubrovnik or India. The closest was a report of a shooting in Dubrovnik of a Romanian gang boss by a woman whose description seems very close to my passport lady. They mentioned that the Romanian was wanted in relation to a child sex ring and had a picture of Thomas alongside the article. I think the picture was just an illustration to grab readers' attention, not really a link as such.

So there is nothing happening that threatens our little life here. Just the boredom.

DCI John Hardcastle
New Scotland Yard
10th January
16:00

Everyone is off down the pub. It's Slobber's birthday. I don't fancy going and I'm still finishing off the trawl through the Spanish sightings.

Only two of the sightings have any credibility. One was by

163

a lorry driver. He claims he saw Thomas being carried from a Cayenne by a blonde-haired woman into a hotel room – it was about 6am. The second sighting was about twenty-four hours later. Same woman, different vehicle, and this has her taking a little boy into a toilet. He comes out changed and she drops the old clothes into a bin.

All the other Spanish and Portuguese sightings don't add up or contradict each other. For example, there is one that has Thomas in Vilamoura at 18.00, whilst another has him in Lisbon at 18.00. They can't both be right, which to me suggests both are wrong.

I am hoping to wangle a trip out to Spain so that I can interview the lorry driver. He lives near Barcelona. Weather should be nice. I bet though, having done all this hard work, Slobber gives the job to somebody else. She wouldn't have me going on a little jaunt like that, would she?

Anna
Mobor Beach
11th January
10:00

Last night was very bad! Thomas had four episodes. Each one seemed to be more disturbing than the last. I am worried about the increase in the frequency of his attacks.

Neetha contacted her doctor for us, Dr Saxena. He is with Thomas now.

He emerges from Thomas's room and joins me in the kitchen. He sits with me at the table and Neetha brings him tea.

'He is a very bright little boy – how old is he, did you say?'

'He will be four tomorrow,' I say.

'Ah, very good,' he says and makes a note on a pad he keeps by his side.

'And you say these attacks have been happening for the past three or four months.'

'That's right,' I agree. 'One doctor has said that because they are nocturnal they could have been going on for longer.'

The doctor nods and smiles.

'Yes,' he says, 'that may be true. We just do not know. Tell me, has anybody suggested he have a scan?'

'Not so far,' I tell him.

'I think a scan would be useful. Whilst not wanting to alarm you, it may help us be sure that the problem is purely neurological. There is a hospital a few hours away, The Chodankar Medical Foundation; it has good facilities. It would be my recommendation that you have a scan done, just to be on the safe side.'

He smiles reassuringly at the end of the sentence. I wonder, if there is nothing to be worried about, why does he need the reassuring smile?

'OK,' I said. 'How much will it cost?'

'Not too much,' he said. 'I know the senior consultant. I will get a good price. Would you like me to call him now?'

I nod.

He picks up his mobile phone. His tone changes – he is most brusque as he barks into it. He seems to be pushed from pillar to post, then he arrives at the number he needs.

'Vikram, *namaste*.' I hear my name mentioned, I hear him say 'Thomas Betts', then I can't follow much. It is all too quickly said.

He puts his hand over the phone.

'Can you go the day after tomorrow?'

I nod.

'I will make it in the afternoon – it will take two to three hours to get there from here.'

He completes our business.

'So,' he says, 'I will arrange for a driver to collect you and your son at 11am on the 13th. I suggest he only take fluid in the morning as it may be that we have to anaesthetise him for the scan. Little boys sometimes are a bit scared. Also, I will let you have my bill after all of this. It will not be huge. Is that alright?'

I nod. He seems kind. I want Thomas to be better and anything that can control his seizures will help. Poor little Thomas, I am feeling so sad for him.

DCI John Hardcastle
New Scotland Yard
12th January
11:00

Amazing! Slobber said yes.

I have cleared it with her and made the travel arrangements. I have also made contact with the Spanish police and they have booked me a translator and an interview room with the lorry driver for the end of the week. I'm also going to see the other person who spotted them when she dumped the clothes. I can't see them until after the weekend which means I will have to spend a weekend on expenses in Barcelona! As luck would have it, they're playing Real Sociedad in a league game on Sunday too. Well, it would be silly not to, wouldn't it?

So, that's me sorted for the next few days. Not sure if I will get any leads but you never know.

Anna
Mobor Beach
12th January
18:00

Neetha had baked and iced a huge cake. It was in the shape of a football and had the words, 'Happy Birthday Brave Little Thomas' on it. We had it with ice cream and lemonade on the veranda.

Thomas and Ravi played in the garden, running around dementedly. Thomas was very excited, but also seemed very happy. Whilst they were playing, Neetha and I chatted.

'You never mention your husband, Thomas's father,' Neetha said.

'We are divorced,' I replied, hoping that this would close the conversation down.

'Ah,' Neetha responded. 'Your romantic Western marriages. I have never understood why so many people from Europe frown on arranged marriages, but don't realise you have so many divorces. Your romantic notion is sort of flawed, no?'

I move the conversation off my own fictitious marriage on to hers.

'So was your marriage arranged?' I ask her.

'Oh, yes! Absolutely,' she replies, giggling.

'And do you love your husband?' I asked.

'What a silly question,' she says. 'Look at that little ball of energy running in the garden. If I didn't love my husband, would I have allowed Ravi to be brought into this world?'

I nodded, understanding the point.

'Real love,' said Neetha, 'grows with time. It does not diminish. Your Western romance appears very strong to start with and then fades away.'

She is looking at the boys playing all the time she says this.

'So,' I ask, 'can you find me an Indian husband?'

Neetha laughs out loud.

'Oh, Mrs Betts, you are far too grand for an Indian husband!'

We both laugh at this.

'You're probably right!' I smile back at her.

We sit quietly. Then Ravi falls over and starts crying. Neetha hurries across the garden and picks him up and she is back to being a mother and I am back to being her employer. Our moment of conversation, as equals, has passed.

After they have gone, I ask Thomas, 'Did you have a nice birthday?'

He is quiet for a moment.

'It was nice,' he says softly, 'but I really miss Mummy and Daddy and my friends at home.'

He looks down at the table, but I can see his bottom lip quivering.

I put him on my lap, cuddle him. He starts to cry.

'It's OK, Thomas, but don't cry on your birthday. Where I come from that is considered very bad luck.'

I rock him in my arms, kiss his little head. I am worried. Is Thomas the loneliest little boy on earth?

DCI John Hardcastle
Terminal 5
London Heathrow
14th January
09:15

So, here I am, a few days in Spain away from the office. I feel quite the international businessman. I could pass for it too, being plain-clothed.

I wonder if people recognise me as a copper? I mean, other coppers obviously do. We just know each other. It might be because, unlike Joe Public, we're not servile, we just see each other as colleagues. Joe Public, on the other hand, either hate us, are scared of us or are over-respectful. So the plods at the airport – well, they just knew. I think even the passport control people knew, although maybe they clock the bit on your passport where it says occupation. Cabin crew also seem to recognise it, but then again the ticket says DCI Hardcastle. Still, nice to have a bit of respect.

Looking forward to this. I don't often get perks with the job. A nice foreign trip and a chance to catch a football match, that'll do me. Looking around the departure lounge, I reckon half the people on this flight could be villains. Some of them look well dodgy which probably means they're bloody coppers!

Anna
Chodankar Medical Foundation
14th January
15:45

He is showing me the computer image again.

'You see,' he says, 'it is this mark here.'

I look: the screen has Thomas's head and a grey blob.

'I think,' he says 'it is a haemangioma, low grade, benign. I would, however, recommend surgery to remove it.'

I have a sharp intake of breath. I can feel myself starting to cry.

'Dear, dear madam,' he says. 'This is all fairly routine. If we can remove it, we will have removed the cause of your little boy's seizures.' He smiles at me.

Vikram Annul is a very handsome man. He must be in his late sixties, but he has a good physique. Broad-shouldered, tall, he is like an ageing Bollywood idol. His manner is a bit direct though.

He continues, 'Whilst we could do the operation here, I wouldn't recommend it. However, you should discuss that option with Dr Saxena.'

'Where would you recommend?'

He smiles.

'Mrs Betts, in London you have the best hospital for children in the world. It is the Rolls Royce of children's medicine and there is nowhere better!'

I look blankly at him.

'Great Ormond Street! You would be mad not to go there!'

I am stunned. We have to go back to London? This is not the news I want.

DCI Hardcastle
Guardia Urbana
Barcelona
15th January
11:00

I am in an interview room. I have a translator with me, a lovely woman called Nelly Sanchez, and a local detective, Luis Poula. We are interviewing the lorry driver who thinks he saw Thomas.

On the table are my files, which I have open. On the inside cover of the file are lists of the key players in the case with pictures of Thomas, his family and so on. We have been chatting for about twenty minutes.

'So,' I ask, 'what attracted your attention to the woman and the boy initially?'

He pauses. He looks at Nelly.

'It's embarrassing,' he says. Nelly translates this as he speaks.

'Don't worry,' says Nelly. 'I am not here to judge you. I am here to help collect evidence.'

He relaxes.

'Well, I thought, she has a great arse and great tits, considering she has had a baby.'

We all laugh.

'OK,' I say.

'Yeah,' he says. 'It just didn't fit. She didn't quite look mumsy enough. Too confident.'

This triggers a thought in my head.

I take the picture of the au pair from the folder.

'Was this the woman you saw?' I ask.

He looks at the picture.

'Well, if it isn't,' he says, 'it could be her sister. She was blonde, not a redhead, but they look very similar.'

I glance at Luis and Nelly. This is important.

'You're sure?'

'One hundred percent,' he says.

'OK,' I tell him. 'Thank you. This could be what we call a major breakthrough in the case.'

He smiles.

'Is there a reward?' he asks, laughing.

And Nelly replies, 'Yeah, I don't slap you and don't tell your wife you ogle other women!'

We all laugh at this.

Yet it's true. This could be a huge turning point in the investigation.

Anna
Mobor Beach
13:00
16th January

I am talking to Dr Saxena in the kitchen. He is explaining, in some detail, the consequences of a benign tumour.

'It will not kill Thomas, but it will affect his quality of life. You see, I am no expert, but I suspect as he gets older the night-time seizures will become daytime seizures. I think we would want to avoid that possibility, yes?'

I nod in agreement.

'Why have it done in England?' I ask.

'Well,' he explains, 'the key is the anaesthetist. With children, you have to be particularly careful to get the drugs right and I honestly think, without being unkind to my countrymen, that it would be better to have it done in London.' He smiles at the end of this sentence.

'But we could do it here?'

'Yes,' he replies, 'but tell me, why would you not want the operation in London? There it will be free on the NHS. Here you will pay and the quality of care will be lower. It doesn't really make any sense.' He seems to know I am not going to bother answering his question.

'Anyway,' he says, 'there is no hurry. You take your time to come to a decision. You are his mother, you will know best what is right for him.'

I nod agreement, but I know that this is not so. I am not his mother. If I go back to London, there is every chance he will be identified and taken away from me. I will probably be sent to prison until I am old and then I will be deported. I do not know what the right thing to do is. This is not how I imagined our future being.

Dr Saxena gets up to leave.

'You are both very strong. I know you will all be OK. Fate will look after you. I will say a *puja* for you both.'

Prayers? Do the gods side with the thief or the owner? I think we know the answer to that question.

DCI Hardcastle
Guardia Urbana
Barcelona
16th January
10:00

This is unbelievable.

I have been on the phone to colleagues in Portugal. Eventually, I found an English-speaking member of the team involved in the case. I asked what follow up had taken place regarding the au pair.

'None,' the colleague told me. 'She left before the boy was taken. She is not a significant player in the case.'

I explained that I had evidence that a lorry driver had positively identified her, with Thomas, two days after he had disappeared.

'Then he is mistaken,' he said.

'So, let me get this right. Somebody identifies a missing boy with a person close to the case and your response is that he is mistaken?! Do you have any better leads?'

'No, but she left the country.'

'Where's the evidence for this?' I am getting very irritated with this sloppiness. 'Do you have evidence from any airline that she actually left the country?'

'No, but she told the parents of the boy she was going to see her—'

I interrupt: 'Hang on! You mean you haven't actually checked out if her story is true?'

'Why would we need to do this?'

I really am getting annoyed now. 'Why would you not bother to do so?'

I slam the phone down in frustration.

All that it will take is a few phone calls to customs at the airport, the airline companies who she was supposed to be flying with and immigration at the other end.

Portuguese police, I don't think they could catch a flipping cold!

Anna
Mobor Beach
17th January
23:30

I am trying not to be emotional about this. The best way to approach this is to look at the facts.

Firstly, we have plenty of money. This means we have plenty of choices. Our position is not without hope, but it is complicated.

The second fact is that Thomas has a non-life-threatening brain tumour. It does not have to be removed now, but it needs to be removed eventually.

The third fact, and this is hard, is I am not his mother. I am Anna – to him I am a friend who he is playing a big game of hide and seek with. He loves me, he has love for me, but not in the way a child loves his own mother.

Fourth, a big one – I don't know what to do next; my

174

options are unclear. And fifth, I am not sure if the best thing for Thomas is for him to be a fugitive. This is only an opinion, but I am wondering, would he not be better at home in Chiswick?

I know I will reach the right conclusion eventually. I wonder how long it will take. I also wonder how long before our luck runs out?

DCI John Hardcastle
Nou Camp Stadium
Barcelona
18th January
20:30

Halftime in the football. Cracking seats, amazing atmosphere, but I can't focus on the game. All I can think about is the case. I've booked a call with Slobber tomorrow morning, first thing. I have discovered a bit more.

Not only did the au pair not get on the flight she was supposed to, but there is no record of her leaving Portugal – well, at least not by air. I actually worked most of yesterday and today. I was calling all the airlines operating out of Faro, checking if she had flown with them. The package ones were OK, but bugger me, British Airways? Could they be any more unhelpful? KLM were good; they even suggested some tips, like checking for late additions to the flight manifest, as these were often different to the core manifest. Yet it became clear that the woman did not fly out of the country.

So then I looked at where else she had been spotted with Thomas.

First sighting I get is in Zurich at a hypermarket on 12th October. A woman with a boy like Thomas is seen buying clothes. I wonder if they have CCTV? That's almost three weeks after he went missing. Now it's possible they could have hitched or cycled all that way, but let's face it, you wouldn't be able to do forty miles every day with a three-year-old in tow.

There is another sighting at a hotel in Nice, about four days earlier. Here she is seen talking to another guy, but he might just be a random stranger. I reckon she must have laid low somewhere between Bilbao and Nice for a while which gives me a massive range of possibilities. Like trying to find a needle in a haystack.

There are also a couple of sightings in Dubrovnik. Both are at ice cream parlours about a week after the Zurich sightings. Then, and I'm thinking of discounting these, just before Christmas, and also about ten days ago, a British couple on holiday in Goa reported seeing them, or what could be them, walking on a beach. That one, I think, is just too fanciful and both have black hair. The other sightings have people with red hair, blonde hair and brown hair. I'll look into the Indian sightings only if the European ones turn out to be incorrect.

Seems to me that Dubrovnik and Zurich are the strongest leads. I know that if I mention to Slobber that I want to go to either place, she'll just laugh in my face. I need to go above her or get other people to put pressure on her. Hmm.

The second half is about to kick off. It's 2–0 to Barca apparently.

Anna
Mobor Beach
19th January
03:00

I can't sleep. I have been awake for the past hour. For half an hour, I tried to get back to sleep, but even pleasuring myself did not work.

I made the mistake of opening my iPad. There is an exclusive story in one of the papers that Thomas has been seen in Zurich! There is not much else to go on, but I am very worried.

I need a new plan. I have been looking east. Thailand is a possibility. I could travel there as Anne-Laure and he would be Tomas Le Merre. The Thais have few restrictions in terms of visas and red tape. I have also thought of Canada. Travelling there as Jill Betts would be easy. Once in, we could slip into the US and eventually make our way to the Caribbean, maybe to Martinique as Anne-Laure and Tomas.

I know healthcare in Canada would be good for Thomas – the USA would be expensive. I suspect Thai healthcare will be cheap, but a bit basic, like here in India.

What is keeping me awake is that if they have traced us to Zurich, they will be able, eventually, to track us down here. Yet we are reasonably happy here. Nice home, good climate, good doctor. It has taken them four months to get to Zurich, so it may take them another four months to get to Dubrovnik and then years to get to Goa.

I feel better. I am feeling sleepy again. They are a long way behind us.

DCI John Hardcastle
Guardia Urbane
Barcelona
19th January
09:30

This is fucking stupid.

Slobber says I am not doing things by the book and I need to take a long hard look at myself. I retorted that if she means I am not behaving like a sleepy, lazy Portuguese plod, then she is right. If she means I am not trying to resolve the case, then she is way off beam. I also said that if she feels that strongly, it should be a disciplinary matter. She hit back that she was considering this and that I was to return to London.

I don't get it. I know, and so does she, that this is progress. Apparently, she is upset that I did my research with the airline companies alone, says we have colleagues who could have done that for us. I just wonder how long I would have to wait to get them to prioritise it. I've shared my results and methods with them anyway, so I don't see what the big problem is other than demarcation. I suppose I would be put on a disciplinary if I stumbled across Thomas and that bloody au pair and arrested her because I hadn't filled out some form in triplicate?

At least I did one thing right. I called that journo, Lisa Lagnoo, said she could use this, but not to quote me, just call me a 'police spokesman'. Anyway, I mentioned Zurich and left her to fill in the gaps. I've been recalled to London – got a meeting with Slobber at 10am tomorrow.

This job! A policeman's lot is absolutely not a happy one!

Anna
Mobor Beach
20th January
17:00

Today I took Thomas on a boat trip. We went out into the Indian Ocean. Me, him and a small crew on the boat. It was a sail boat. Big flapping sails, no motor, no sound, just us, the wind, the shouts of the crew and the water.

We saw dolphins and other ships and he giggled and chortled

and got really, really excited. We stopped in a bay and swam in the ocean. We had barbecued fish for lunch and then we sailed back.

I hope when he is older he will remember perfect days like this. We will not be here much longer and not be together as long as I'd hoped. I hope he realises that I was kind, that I loved him and that I did my best, even if my reasons were incorrect.

DCI John Hardcastle
New Scotland Yard
20th January
17:00

Slobber isn't going to put me on a disciplinary. But the meeting wasn't good.

She went through all her 'difficulties' with the way I have 'behaved', how I was not able to work in a structured or disciplined way. I listened and then I said, 'I think you have a problem with me. I think your behaviour comes close to bullying.'

She was taken aback.

'Bullying?' she said. 'I'm not sure what you mean.'

'Bullying,' I said, 'as defined in our staff code of conduct. That is: "Persistent, offensive, abusive, intimidating or insulting behaviour, abuse of power, or unfair punishment which upsets, threatens and/or humiliates the recipient(s), undermining their self-confidence, reputation and ability to perform."'

She swallowed hard.

'Exactly when have I done this?' she asked.

'It's been consistent. Since we first started working together. Any minor mistake is jumped on, which' – and I used bunny ears to hook around this part – 'undermines my self-confidence.'

'I'm sorry if you don't like being managed,' she said flatly.

'Oh,' I replied. 'I like being managed and I like good management. Remember, before you were my manager I'd had nine years in the force. Nobody had a problem with my conduct, the exact opposite.'

'That's not what I heard,' she said, sneering.

'Would you like to present the evidence then? Or shall I add that to the ever-growing list of "behaviour which threatens or undermines the individual"?'

She blushed crimson.

'Are we done?' she asked.

'You tell me. Tell me how you're going to stop this.'

She was silent.

'I'll reflect on what you've said,' she eventually replied with the weakest of smiles.

I got back to my work station. The walk must have been thirty seconds.

There was an e-mail from her. Already there – sent, it would seem, as I was entering her office.

'Please note that after today I will be re-assigning you to another investigation. I would be grateful if you could complete all your file notes by close of play tomorrow and add them to the case bundle. Thank you for the work you have undertaken thus far.'

Outrageous. Worse still, stupid.

Anna
Mobor Beach
21st January
12:30

We said goodbye to Neetha and little Ravi today.

Thomas will miss playing in the garden with Ravi. Neetha has given me an e-mail address. She said, 'Please keep in touch, Mrs Betts. Ravi is very fond of Thomas and I think they will be friends for life.'

I felt the tears welling up inside me and had to take a deep breath.

'Please don't be upset,' said Neetha. 'I am sure we will see you again after Thomas has had his operation in London.'

We hugged. Ravi and Thomas, in a strange formal way, shook hands as if they were grown-ups and then we waved them 'bye-bye' from the veranda.

Tomorrow, we leave. The game of hide and seek is coming to a close.

John Hardcastle
Kings Head, Victoria, London
21st January
13:00

I slept on it.

Overnight, I thought, *Why did I become a policeman?* Really, I put the uniform on to catch villains. I always carried a notion that there were good guys and bad guys. I knew some plods were bent, but also knew that most were doing their best. I never realised that, like in any other walk of life, you have your fair share of incompetent idiots. It's these people that make the job hardest to do. The bent ones you can deal with. It seems though that they just promote the useless ones.

So, with a heavy heart, this morning I resigned. I went straight to HR first thing. Said I was fed up with the constant bullying and with not being able to do my job. That being

181

moved off the Thomas Moore case was just about the last straw.

The woman in HR tried to persuade me not to go. Mentioned how I could put in for a transfer, work for another force, even look for a secondment overseas.

I explained that my heart was no longer in it. Sooner or later, I'd end up back in the same place.

Still, there is one thing left to do. I contacted that Lisa Lagnoo woman again. Thanked her for running the story, told her I had some more. We're due to have a sandwich and a pint together any minute now. Looking forward to meeting her. From what I've seen on the telly, she's a bit of alright. I'm hoping that leaking where I got to will kick Slobber up the arse, but more importantly, get Thomas home.

PART FIVE

Kieran
Biarritz
26th January
10:00

I'm looking at the Sunday papers online. I was actually looking to see how Brentford have got on and there it is.

It's big, it's got graphics and it shows a picture of Anna and the kid. It has lines on a map, drawn from Bilbao to Zurich, Zurich to Dubrovnik and then a dotted line from there to India.

The headline reads: THOMAS – IS HE IN INDIA?

The worry is, it fits with what I know. I know that she was in Dubrovnik at around about the time they claim. If they catch her they could catch me. This is not good. This is not good at all.

Anna
Stockholm Central Station
26th January
12:00

I am tired, Thomas is tired. We are looking for a hotel. We are going to check in as Anne-Laure and Tomas. We arrived as Jill Betts and Thomas from New Delhi two hours ago.

It is cold. Thomas is bad-tempered. We bought a few winter clothes when we stopped over in Dubai. We need more.

Tomorrow, we are going to Dubrovnik. I have told Thomas we are taking a long journey by train. I tried to make it sound exciting. It isn't. It will be boring and take about thirty hours.

We have sleeper accommodation from Cologne, which means we will be in a private carriage. Later today, I will cut my hair short. I will cut Thomas's hair short too, but keep it black. He looks like a little hippy at the minute. Quite cute.

The game is coming to an end. I have told Thomas this. He is excited. I am sad, but know that I am doing the right thing.

Kieran
Biarritz
27th January
14:00

Myself, Elena and Jorges are conferencing in the library. We're pulling together what we know is fact and what we believe is rumour.

The only fact we have is that Anna was in Dubrovnik with Thomas en route to Zagreb. From there, she could have gone anywhere. Zagreb has flights to London, New York, New Delhi and most other places. We agree it is conceivable she could have gone back to Zurich and from there she could have gone to India. Somehow, that doesn't work for me.

It is also possible she is still in Dubrovnik.

So we agree a plan. I will go to Dubrovnik, make some discreet enquiries. See what I can find out. Elena is going to go to Zurich in case she is there. She suspects that she will need to have changed her hair colour, so is going to make enquiries at high-end salons. It may not lead to much, but you never know.

Until this has blown over, I am putting my current projects on hold. I have e-mailed my live clients to explain that due to 'unavoidable business complications' I need to postpone my current projects for approximately eight weeks. This is pre-agreed code which they know about. I have thanked them for their patience and explained that I will advise them as to when projects can be reinstated. They know I am also protecting their interests. Suspending projects breaks our links, keeps them away from any mess that might develop.

The real question in my own mind is if projects can be reinstated.

Anna
Cologne Station
22:00
28th January

We are in our compartment. Thomas is excited, I am worried.

There was an article in an English paper which claimed we were in India. It was quite accurate, giving details of when we were in Zurich and Belgrade. The only good thing is that people think we are still in Goa. I am hoping that this means the hunt for us is outside Europe.

Thomas can see I am worried. He keeps on hugging me as if he can comfort me. He is not old enough to know I am evil; he is not old enough to know that I am selfish. Whether he will ever think these things about me, I do not know. Yet I think these things about myself. If I think this, then what must others think? Worse, I suspect!

Kieran
Bellevue Hotel
Dubrovnik
29th January
13:00

I've asked around. A few people have said that they may have seen her. Nobody really gives me any leads.

Not sure what I was expecting to find. Her waiting at the railway station with a bunch of flowers? A chain of restaurants called Anna and Thomas?

I'll give it a bit more time tomorrow, but I think this has been a waste. Oh, and getting away from here tomorrow, impossible. There is some sort of public transport strike. The airports, taxis, buses, all fucked. Me, I'm due to fly tomorrow. If it wasn't so cold, I'd stay. So I have to find a way out.

Anna
Hotel Bellevue
Dubrovnik
30th January
21:00

Oh my God! He didn't see me, but I saw him. He was walking away from the hotel just as we arrived.

I asked the girl on reception, 'That man, is he staying here?'

'Yes,' she said, 'until tomorrow.'

So Thomas and I, we have stayed in our room. I told the girl, 'My son is not well. We will just be ordering room service.'

Thomas was quite hyperactive and not behaving like a boy who is ill. She gave us an odd look, but then shrugged her shoulders.

So we have been here since we arrived. Ordering everything in. Thomas is really bad-tempered. He has so much energy. Three days on a train and then banged up in a hotel room with me. No life.

So we will wait until noon tomorrow. I am going to ask to

check out from my room. I will get the garage to send a car to collect us. We have very little baggage, but we need to get out quietly and quickly.

Fuck!

Kieran
Bellevue Hotel
1st February
01:00

I didn't think much of it, but when I just came back to the hotel, the girl on reception said, 'That picture you showed me yesterday, can I see it again?'

So I showed her.

She took a long look, then looked at me and said, 'No, sorry, I am mistaken.'

Well, at least somebody is paying attention. I slipped her a fifty-euro note for her troubles. She seemed happy.

'You're going tomorrow?'

'Yes,' I said.

'Give me a mobile number. I will keep my eyes glued. You are leaving tomorrow?' she asks again.

'Yes,' I reply.

'From the airport?'

I nod.

'There is a transport strike.'

'I know,' I say.

She looks sceptical.

'It means no taxis, a few buses, yes? A hard to travel.'

I nod again.

'You are a nice guy,' she says. 'I will arrange for hotel transport for you.'

This is what I call good service.

'We have more strikes now than when we were a communist country – what is the point?' She smiles at me.

I am tired, I need sleep, but I at least feel that I have a local ally.

Anna
Hotel Bellevue
03:00
1st February

Why is my alarm clock ringing? Very early.

Fuck! Fire alarm!

Kieran
Hotel Bellevue
1st February
3:05

Freezing out here and, to make matters worse, there is one stupid twat who won't leave their room. The staff say it is a false alarm, but they will be fined if people don't evacuate.

Selfish prat!

Anna
Hotel Bellevue
1st February
3:15

'It will be three thousand euros!' she is saying.

'I will pay,' I tell her through a crack in the door.

'You must love your beauty sleep!' she replies sarcastically.

'I'll see you in the morning,' I say and close the door.

It is worth it. Totally.

We have eaten breakfast in our room. Thomas is now, officially, I think, stare crazy!

The garage are delivering the car here in fifteen minutes.

We will drive. I am not sure what route to take or how long the journey will take. A week or so maybe? Thomas needs a break from travelling – maybe we will stop for a few days somewhere. Our only timetable is the one we set ourselves and I am keen to make this last a little longer. I love him, I just cannot give him what he needs. So I have to make a hard choice, which is sometimes, I tell myself, what real love is about. For me real love is not selfish, not about self-gratification, it is giving even if you know the gift will never be returned. That for me is real love, no?

Oh, for God's sake!

It was her.

I was stood in the foyer and, out of the corner of my eye, not that I am paying much attention, I see a cute ass. Then I see the hand from the woman with the cute ass is holding the hand of a little boy. My brain is moving too slowly to begin to piece things together quickly enough. A guy arrived in a sort of pair of overalls – posh overalls with a BMW insignia on them. He is leading the nice ass and the kid into a BMW 4X4. The cute ass climbs in, the kid gets into a seat in the back and then it clicked. It's fucking her.

I run out to the front of the hotel. She sees me. I hear the doors on the car lock. She puts the windows up. The guy is waving a form at her to be signed, but she floors it. The car roars off, up the hill, out of town. I run about in a panic, looking for a taxi, but there aren't any. I wave my hands at the guy in the BMW uniform.

'Follow her!' I say.

'With what? She was meant to drop me back!' He shrugs his shoulders.

I ran back into the reception, but there is a guy on duty, not the friendly girl from last night.

'I need transport!' I say.

'There is a strike – have you booked something?'

I become aware that every eye in the foyer is looking at me.

'Yes, but I need transport. Now!'

People laugh at me. This mad British guy, gesticulating, waving his arms, wanting transport on a strike day.

'You are?' he asks, looking down at a list.

I give him my name.

'Yes,' he says. 'You are down to go to the airport in twenty minutes.'

'I need a car now! Now!'

He smiles at me.

'Sir,' he says. 'Please be patient.'

His tone is gentle, but I want to hit him.

For no reason, I run back to the front of the hotel. The BMW guy is on a mobile, chatting and laughing. I tap him on the shoulder.

'Where has she gone?'

And he looks at me, dumbfounded.

'I deliver customers their cars. I am not responsible for their plans!'

So I end up back in the foyer, waiting for my lift to the airport. Furious. She has slipped through my fingers. I am stuck and she is free. Out-manoeuvred, outsmarted, out of luck.

Anna
1st February
Service Area
Solin
14:00

I don't think we have driven at less than 120kph for the past few hours. Thomas at times was screaming. When he wasn't screaming, he was shouting for me to slow down. I have only just stopped. I have taken him from the back seat and just hugged him.

'I am sorry, I am sorry,' I have been saying, over and over.

We have everything and he hasn't caught us. But how close does he have to get and how far behind us is he? How did he find us?

I am breathing deeply, I am slowly calmer. He does not know where we are or where we went. We are perhaps safe? Perhaps.

Kieran
Dubrovnik Airport
2nd February
01:00

Fucking strikers, fucking Anna, fucking life!

Been stuck here for nearly fourteen hours. Baggage handlers are out, air traffic controllers are out. Everything starts again at 2am. It means that the airport is like a refugee camp. Even in the lounges, it is jam-packed. Plus there are the suits who have been getting rat-arsed on cheap booze for the last ten hours. Not quite hell, but not far from it.

How did I let this happen? I don't just mean Anna slipping through my hands, I mean the whole bloody thing going wrong. I've had some breaks, the Romanian money came in handy, but to be honest they have been counter-balanced by the shit I have had to wade through. My dad used to say that when you're wading in poo, it will eventually get to your neck and that's when life starts to stink. Well, I feel like it is at the top of my chest and I don't like the bouquet around me. A stench of decay and failings.

For a few moments after she drove off, I tried to work out where she had gone. I suspected she would be heading for... and then I realised, she had the whole planet at her disposal with three false passports that she could have added to by now. She could have gone in any direction, taking that little boy with her. I had had my lucky chance, my moment of opportunity, but now it was gone.

I wish I wasn't feeling sorry for myself. In fact, it isn't really like me. I am a 'school of hard knocks' sort, dusting myself down after each fresh tumble. Yet this – it is like a slow-working poison, eating at me. I need to regain control, possibly get myself revenge, but I doubt that either of those things are possible. I keep asking myself as well, what does revenge amount to? I am just annoyed at being outsmarted. I got paid, I got my money, I don't have to be a spoilt brat forever.

Do I?

Anna
2nd February
Hotel Kolavare
Zadar
14:00

This morning we woke up and it was warm. Unusually warm. Spring is not quite here, but it is on the way.

Thomas needed a break. So we found this hotel, out of season, on the coast. There is a pool that is indoors, a play area and a nice seafront that we can walk along.

I want him to be happy over these next few weeks. I want him to know that I loved him. I have booked a big double bed for us. We will stay for three days and we will sleep, eat, bathe and be together. I do not know what I am hoping for. Will he forgive me? One day, it is possible. Will he love me anymore, now? He can't, he is a child. He only has a child's love to share with me and a child's words with which to share that love. I don't know the answer to these questions, but torture myself with them anyway.

Thomas has made me realise a truth, a truth I have ignored. One day, I want to be a mother. If I can feel this close to a child who is not mine, imagine how I will feel to one that is my own. I am quite shocked by this; it is an idea that has not previously been one that I have paid much attention to. I have focussed on enjoying my life and making money. Yet after this? I have done a bad thing which I am trying to compensate for. As a little Catholic Polish girl, I have been taught that we will be punished for our sins. I don't really believe this, but then sometimes I do. It is like my parents, they were never really communist, but they sometimes speak nostalgically about the past. They have been encouraged to do this, just as I have been encouraged to fear Jesus. We are both wrong, we know it, but you can't help thinking that one day the retribution will be visited upon you. What will mine be? A prison sentence? An inability to have children? A disabled child? A drunken husband? Cancer in later life? I suspect it will just be the worst one of all, a continuing sense of guilt. Very Catholic, no?

Kieran
3rd February
London
17:00

I am waiting for Uncle Tony. Feeling less self-destructive too. I am always better after sleep.

The place in St Albans is still rented out, so I crashed in a hotel near Covent Garden. Nothing flash because I think this is where I have been going wrong. Six months ago I was much more frugal. Recently, I have become too extravagant, as if I am taking my success for granted.

I am buying Tony lunch before he heads off to see Brentford play. I have to get back to France. To be honest, I am looking forward to a nice long train journey, Eurostar to Paris, sleeper down to the south.

I thought about nobbling Anna. Then I decided against it. The risks are too great. I could have gone to the police, but the danger is that the police would've eventually come to me and all my enterprise and hard work would be undone. Plus I hate snitches.

Too often they are the lowest of the low, the sort of person that sleeps with your wife, your daughter and then your daughter's best friend only to claim mistaken identity. I'm no snitch.

Tony arrives. He has a bundle of Brentford programmes for me. This is something he has done since childhood, bringing me match day souvenirs like treasure from the New World. I hardly ever read them, but their feel, their distinctive smell takes me back to a past where I was something more than the shitty failure I've become.

We talk; we talk about football, family and the weather.

'See you've rented your place in St Albans out,' he says. 'You need the money then?'

I laugh. I think Tony is one of the most frugal people I know.

'No,' I say with a laugh. 'I'm just never there. Makes sense to earn cash from it.'

'Oh, right,' he says. 'Just that if you're short of a bob or two, I can buy lunch, honest.'

I smile. Honest, indeed. Yet there is no way Tony will pay for lunch. He's a cheap date anyway, only ever ordering fish and chips.

'Maybe next time,' I say, with a smile.

That's the thing about Tony. He removes any malice you may carry. In his company, the world becomes a better, kinder place. I just wish the reality could be shaped by him and not by those of us who have so little to be proud of.

Without further debate, he is tucking into his fish, chips and mushy peas. The warmth of his sincerity melts me. We're relaxed, happy, chatting about the birds and the Bees – mostly the Bees and what a great season Brentford are having.

Then my phone rings. Like a baby, breaking the peace of our reverie. There's a sense that something is not right. I see the dialling code on my mobile: St Albans. A voice; firm, authoritative – Hertfordshire police. An incident, a tragic incident, at a property they understand I own. Suspicious circumstances – a fire and the death of a young man.

At the end of the call, I hang up. I don't give Tony the details, but explain I have to go. I know it's the Romanians. Catching up with me. Wreaking havoc. Not peace. War.

Anna
5th February
Hotel Kolavare
12:00

Today I asked little Thomas when he would like to leave.

'Not yet,' he said, quite firmly.

'Why?' I asked.

So he said, 'The swimming pool is nice, it is sunny and the ice cream is good.'

I smiled.

'So how many more days?' I asked.

'Two!' he shouted.

I am not so sure that letting him decide is a good thing. He is a child. Children don't really know how to make a judgement based upon perspective. I am comfortable with his choice – it delays our departure by a few days. Yet I know that I am allowing his want to obliterate any other considerations. He is not my conscience, I am his protector. I am giving myself an excuse for self-indulgence.

Yet, maybe he is right. As we get older our judgement becomes clouded. We think about money, we think about responsibility and we stop being in the moment. Ice cream, sunshine and swimming pools are not such a bad set of influences on decision making. They are much better than alcohol, earning potential or what other people will think of us. If Thomas has it right, is it possible that we all have it wrong? Either way, we are now staying for two more days.

Kieran
6th February
St Albans
16:30

There is red and white tape at the front of the drive. The officer on duty lets me through once I explain who I am.

There are the charred remains of what was my home and the air still smells of smouldering debris.

I have spoken to the police and they are working on the assumption that this has nothing to do with me, that the tenant must have got involved in some sort of dispute with somebody at work or in a local pub and that this was somehow or other the result. It seems that a petrol bomb was used, thrown in through the hallway window. The body is, apparently, too badly burnt for there to be an autopsy, but the important thing is that they do not see me or my business interests as having anything to do with this. They are happy that I am a businessman who runs a ticket agency – they have even hinted that they wouldn't mind tickets for a Spurs game at some point and I may oblige.

Now though, there is the mess. I've made some enquiries. Having the place rebuilt will cost about £200,000. Replacing all the furniture and so on, another £100K. The land value of the site is about £600,000, but you could probably get two properties on there, not one. I think I will sell it, get planning permission to put

199

two houses there and hope a developer shows some interest. If I rebuild, they will come back. They know where I am.

I have doubled security on the French property. Biarritz needs to be protected. New security cameras and an inner cordon have been installed. That is now my most valuable asset and I am determined that those Romanian bastards are not going to get their hands on it. The police might be right – it might not have been them – but I doubt it.

I do a cursory inspection of the site. I explain to the officer on duty that I will ask a structural engineer to come to establish if the place can be rebuilt.

'Probably going to be a week or so before forensics will release the site back,' he says.

I nod. I understand. There is no emotion here. It is an inconvenience. My bigger worry is what the Romanians will do next.

Anna
7th February
Hotel Kolavare
Zadar
11:00

We have checked out.

The open road beckons, but I am not sure which way. Heading north, through the Alps, will be quicker. There will be warmer weather if we stay south. I am thinking of a route through Venice to Avignon and then north. There is no rush. We will eventually get to London. I just need to think about what is the easiest route.

I am fed up with the life of a fugitive. This has only gone

on for five months. I could be OK on my own, but it is having Thomas in tow that makes it more difficult. He makes us more identifiable .

I am also thinking that going south will mean that we are retracing our steps. There is the possibility that somebody will recognise us. This is also exhausting. I am constantly checking places out for anybody who looks like they may be looking at us too closely. Of course, nobody does – all they see is a mother with an aggressive stare who fusses over her spoilt little boy.

He has been seizure-free for quite a few weeks now. I wonder was it the warmer climate that triggered his problems? Yes, I know there is the tumour, but how is it that he sometimes goes so long without anything happening? He is a very normal child. Happy, smiley, occasionally moody. Those Russians had the money to help him and yet they walked away. I wonder about these people with all their money wanting designer children, off-the-shelf perfection. How do they respond when things are not quite how they should be? Do they break down in tears on cloudy days? Are they so fragile that they cannot handle anything unless it is perfect?

All this, and I haven't even started the engine. West, I decide. I will head west. Towards the sunset.

Kieran
8th February
St Pancras Station
9:00

Enough of this. Crap happens, but I have to get focused back on the business element. Off to meet a client in Paris and catch PSG v Liverpool in the Champions League.

I've been looking at the accounts and I am way down on

where I need to be compared to two years ago. I need to start earning some serious wonga. All this inconvenience has been self-indulgent and expensive. Time for me to kick myself up my own rear end and get some cash flowing through the books.

The new client wants a little girl. Quite unusual in my line of work – it is normally boys people want. Yet the guy's wife has had three babies, all boys – rather than waste another pregnancy, they want a daughter.

I have three choices of targets for them, all in NW3. The usual profile: upper-middle-class professional couples. A barrister, a consultant oncologist and a stockbroker. I have started looking for a new recruit too. There are an awful lot of overseas students in London, running up debts and in need of cash. A Chinese or Indian student might fit the bill, I think.

After Paris, off to Biarritz for a team meeting, then back to London to recruit the new person.

Anna
11th February
Venice
Hotel Carlton
23:30

We arrived here yesterday. I thought Thomas might like to see a city where there are no cars, but boats instead. He seemed curious when I mentioned it to him.

'How do people get their shopping?' he asked.

'By boat,' I said, 'or they walk everywhere.'

He liked the sound of this and his eyes have been on stalks since we got here. We have wandered around, seen some of the sights.

At breakfast this morning, a rather handsome man struck

up conversation with me. He wasn't really that interested in Thomas.

'What brings you to Venice?' he asked.

'We're passing through,' I said, gesturing towards Thomas. 'We are tourists.'

Then, from nowhere, he asked, 'Would you have dinner with me tonight? I mean, the hotel can provide childminding services. This is too romantic a city for you to eat with him.'

This was strange; it came out as a single sentence with no pause for breath. For me though, I was thinking, 'An evening with an adult. That would be very different compared to a bedtime story and watching TV.' It was worth the risk.

I looked at Thomas.

'Thomas, are you OK if I get somebody new to look after you, just for tonight?'

Thomas gave me a big smile.

'Yes! Yes!'

I laughed at his enthusiasm and then turned to the guy.

'OK – shall we meet in the foyer at eight?'

He smiled. Seemed happy.

Thomas and I spent the day wandering around Venice. At about five, I took him for a pizza. Whilst he chomped away, I drank a glass of white wine. I was sort of nervous about whether this was a date. It had been over a year since I had been on one, in London. A Polish chef. That didn't end well. So tonight would be, well, the English would use the word 'interesting' in that very understated way that they have.

Back at the room, I got Thomas ready for bed. Another strange experience was dressing for a date. How long since I had done this? What should I wear? I settled on a black dress and heels, swept my hair back with an Alice band and applied some makeup. By the time the childminder arrived, Thomas was asleep and I looked pretty good. Not a million euros, but more than my over-extended credit card look that I had perfected over the past few months.

He was waiting in the foyer. A blue blazer, a white shirt, some chinos. He looked a bit like Tony Curtis in *Some Like it Hot*.

'Hello,' he said. 'You look amazing!'

I blushed and it was at this point we both realised that we didn't know each other's names.

'Jill,' I said, feeling sad that I couldn't tell him my real name.

'Oh,' he said, seeming surprised. 'I thought you would be Maria or Karolina.'

I smiled.

'And you are?'

'Stefan,' he said.

We established our credentials. He was Swiss, a rail man, quite senior, but in Venice for an international rail meeting.

We set off for the restaurant. I established that he lived in Zurich, was single, divorced, with no children from his last marriage.

'And you?' he asked, looking at me inquisitively.

'Oh,' I smiled. 'Not much to tell. Divorced. Thomas is my little boy. I am taking him to London to spend a few months with his father.'

I really didn't know where I got all this from, but he didn't seem too bothered.

The restaurant was a short stroll away. I had decided that whilst Stefan was charming, even quite handsome, tonight would only be about me enjoying being flirtatious. No sex.

So we were looking at the menu, trying to work out what to order, then I noticed, from the corner of my eye, a man eating alone. He was big, brutal- looking. I think, *He looks like one of those Romanian guys who were going to take Thomas.* Now the thought is in my head, I look at Stefan again and wonder if he is Romanian.

The thought cannot be shifted, it is stuck there. I can feel myself getting tenser. Has this all been a clever trick? Is the childminder not really a childminder?

I want to shout out, 'You are not Swiss, you are Romanian!' Instead, I try to keep my calm.

'Sorry,' I say. I can feel my insides turning over. 'I need the bathroom.' I pick my little clutch bag up, head for the toilets, but the door to the street is just beyond the entrance. I glance over my shoulder and head out.

Now another problem! I was not paying attention when I arrived, so I do not know which way the hotel is. I can see that there is a canal at the end of the street. So I run to it, but can't run fast. I take my heels off – this is better. I can run quicker now. Venice is a maze. I cannot find my way through the back alleys. In the end, I reach a gondola station. I bark the name at my hotel out to the gondolier. 'Quickly!' I say. He shrugs, probably thinking, *Who is this crazy bitch?* but I don't care.

We arrive across the piazza from my hotel. I pay him. He wants a tip – I tell him to fuck off and he starts shouting at me. I run off towards the hotel. I storm through reception, sensing people are alarmed by my speed. I run up the stairs, not risking waiting for a lift, and know I am close to exhaustion as I get to my floor. I feel sick, shocked that I could fall for such a trick.

I burst into the room. It is empty!

He is not here, nor is the childminder. They have him.

Then I hear the door opening and I twist around, convinced that they have come back to kill me. It is Thomas and the childminder.

I run to Thomas, scoop him into my arms and hug him.

'Where have you been?' I scream. He and the childminder look shocked, a little terrified even.

'Are you OK?' she asks with a concerned look on her face.

'I am fine. Just go please.'

'You are sure you are OK?' the girl asks.

I catch sight of myself in the mirror. I am sweaty, I have tears smearing my cheeks and my makeup makes me look a state.

'I am fine,' I say quietly. 'I will put him to bed.'

I hug and kiss Thomas. For one horrible moment, I was sure that he had been taken, that all my efforts had simply delayed the Romanians. I don't know what happened – how did I allow myself to be so stupid? A man chats to me and I become like a little school girl, giggling away? Stupid Anna! Stupid!

It's later now. I have a brandy, I have showered. I am calmer. He is sleeping. I am tired. Of everything. I need sleep too.

Kieran
Biarritz
12th February
15:00

I have been here for two days. It is calming, safe.

Jorges and Elena have been doing a good job. We have created an inner sanctum within the perimeter. We are also getting some Bull Mastiffs in. They will patrol the grounds, roaming free. They are trained to attack and will only be restrained upon command from either Elena or Jorges. We are hoping that this will act as an element of surprise for any intruders. New signs have also gone up, in French and English, warning that dogs patrol the grounds. I don't think it will have much effect – they will probably poison or shoot the dogs, but it may make them think twice.

We have just had lunch and I share a thought that has been lingering at the back of my mind for the past few days.

'I am thinking,' I say, not making eye contact with either of them, 'of selling this place.'

Neither Elena nor Jorges comment. They are my employees, why should they?

Eventually, Elena asks, 'Will you replace it?'

'Yes,' I say, 'somewhere further afield. Greece, perhaps.'

She nods.

'There will, of course, be jobs for you both, if you want them.'

Jorges speaks: 'We both like working for you – where we are based is irrelevant.'

Elena nods in agreement.

'So I could give you an assignment. Find me somewhere new. You know my requirements. Property is cheaper at the eastern end of the Med and the Greek economy is ruined.'

'That would be an interesting project,' Elena says. 'There are plenty of little islands off the Greek coast. The weather would be much better too.'

'You won't miss Biarritz?'

'I would miss working for you more.'

So we agree – Jorges will get the place valued, we will try to find somewhere in Greece that is even more protected and push through a sale as quickly as possible. I suspect that in the current market we will clear four million.

We are just finishing when Jorges looks at me and Elena.

'You know,' he says slowly, 'I don't think Greece will be any safer. From what I can see our Romanian friends will only be happy when they get their revenge or you make your peace.'

Elena and I glance at each other. Jorges normally doesn't express an opinion.

'OK,' I say, 'but they will have to track me down to a new place. The only two people who will know where that is will be you and Elena. I am sure that we will be harder to find and the place will be easier to secure.'

Jorges nods, thinking this through.

For a moment, I wonder whether Jorges could be working with them. Yet I dismiss the question almost as quickly as the thought occurred. He's loyal – he is not like that, is he?

That's the trouble with thoughts – once they get into your head, they're hard to shake off.

Anna
13th February
Hotel Carlton
Venice
09:15

We are checking out and leaving today.

I spent most of yesterday considering my options and decided that the obvious route back to London would be via Santander. The problem is that I would have to go back into Spain and that doesn't seem the wisest option. At the same time, I don't want to enter the UK via the Channel ports. So I am going to aim for Roscoff and take the ferry to Cork.

Today, we are heading for Geneva. If we leave now we should arrive early evening. It means that tomorrow morning I can transfer some money between accounts. I need to be sure I am solvent for the final part of our trip.

I have told Thomas he needs to be well-behaved as I am very

tired and have a long drive. His reward will be an ice cream and, if he is very good, a possible trip to Disneyland. Thomas likes the sound of this, although I am not sure if he really knows what Disneyland is. If it keeps him quiet though, I am happy.

I am looking forward to the drive through the Alps. We should see a lot of snow, but Thomas doesn't quite understand why he is expected to wrap up warm. It is mild in Venice, but it will be cold in Geneva by comparison. For him, he doesn't understand and probably thinks I am being typically Anna.

So that is our day ahead. Me driving, him sleeping, but not for much longer.

Kieran
14th February
University of London Student Union
16:00

I have seen three students today. All had responded to an advert I had placed on the Student Union website. None were suitable.

The first was a Chinese student. She was bright enough, but her English was simply not up to the job. The second one, a Malaysian student, was again very bright, but she asked too many questions, talked too much and was likely to draw attention to herself simply because she was so pretty. Then there was Sarb, a pretty Indian medical postgraduate, but she had the same problems as the Malaysian girl. Too attractive and she asked far too many difficult questions. Plus, all three were not on time. I specifically said sixteen minutes after the hour. Two turned up at a quarter past and one arrived at nineteen minutes past. Just not good enough.

At the end of the sessions, I checked my e-mails. We have started marketing Biarritz and there has already been interest. But there is another, worrying e-mail. An alert from my Jersey bank: 'Attention – your account is overdrawn.'

This can't be right. I know that there is at least £1.2 million in that account. It is my daily cash flow source. I phone the bank immediately. They take me through the last half dozen transactions. None of the payments are any I have made. They all relate to transactions in Bucharest. The Romanians.

I want to laugh, but I am furious. The bank explain that they will carry out a thorough investigation. They explain that they can get new account details to me as soon as possible and, as a matter of routine, they will for the moment issue me with new cards on a new account number. They will also refund half the monies that are missing straight away and the other half once they have completed their investigations.

The inconvenience is irritating, but worse still is the sense that the Romanians have tracked down my financial details. I have one other account with this particular bank and ask that they run through recent transactions. Everything seems in order, but, as an additional precaution, we agree that they will open up a new account for that money and transfer all that is in the old account to the new one.

The whole discussion takes much longer than I thought it would, leaving me annoyed, irritated and almost totally out of patience. As I hang up, a text message appears: *TX for your generosity*, it says. The Romanians again, taking the piss, but now I suspect that they have also hacked my e-mail account.

I should have realised that St Albans and everything else was a bit old-school – modern crime is conducted online. Quietly, effectively and for the maximum inconvenience for the victim. Now I will have to change a whole host of electronic passwords, update my firewalls and generally waste time doing the things I shouldn't have to.

A wasted day – a day when they have got the better of me.

Anna
15th February
Folder Grand
Zurich
06:00

I slept so badly last night. One of those nights when you are exhausted. You sleep for an hour, you are awake for an hour, you sleep for another twenty minutes, you are awake for forty more. I am churning over in my head what I should be doing. I have doubts.

All through this journey back I have been convinced that I should take Thomas all the way to Chiswick. Make sure he gets home OK. Yet I have now been wondering if a simpler solution would be to leave him at Disneyland in Paris. There is a certain logic to this and a total illogicality to me wanting to take him home all the way to London. Why am I making his safe return my problem? It is like I want to get caught. Is that what I really want? To be punished? I know that it isn't, so why do I think I need to deliver him back and put myself at risk?

I have done my duty. I have got him away from the Romanians, got his epilepsy diagnosed properly and I have a prognosis for how he can be made better. I have seen him safe, saved him and protected him. I have learned to love him – no, I have grown to love him – but I know that this cannot go on forever, so now it has become a chore and a risk to my freedom.

Today, we drive to Disneyland in Paris. We will stay overnight there and have two full days at the park. There will be ample opportunity to lose him on a ride. Leave him with a childminder, never to return. Is this a heartless end or the right end? That is why I am not sleeping.

The shock now, that we may only have forty-eight hours together. Is it really nearly over?

Kieran
Marylebone High Street
London
16th February
12:00

Estate agents are the lowest form of life, lower than any other lifeform. I need a place to rent, but London rents are exorbitant. I am willing to pay the full rental upfront, but won't spend more than fifty thousand. In the past, they would have bitten my hand off, now I'm just another punter.

I am also being forced further out. In my mind, and most other people's, Swiss Cottage is not central London, nor is Kilburn. Yet these bastards try to convince you otherwise. It's making me realise that I should invest some of my cash in one-bedroom flats. Not only will they accrue in value, but they will also give me a steady income. That's longer term though. At the minute, the bastards have got me over a barrel.

After much negotiation and searching, I've located a reasonable one-bedroom furnished place for £1,500 a week, just off the Edgware Road. It's north of Marylebone Road, so, at one point, it might have been called Maida Vale. Still, a base for six months. A nice mansion block where me and everybody else are anonymous. Just how I like it.

I'll pick up the keys later. I now have enough time to hop on the Tube to King Street, put an advert in a shop window and see who responds. The student route isn't right – bloody ridiculous really. Eastern European women are much more reliable. Much more precise too. So I'm sticking to what I know best.

Anna
16th February
Disneyworld Paris
17:30

Thomas is exhausted. Very happy, but exhausted. He has done most of the rides he is allowed on and still wants to do more. His face is a constant bright smile. He is gorgeous when he is like this. It makes me understand why parents spoil their children. Seeing them happy gives you an inner sense of calm that makes all their tantrums worthwhile. It is, at the same time, exhausting. My brain is aching with the constant minding of him, pleasuring of his wants, accommodation of his desires.

We are eating burgers. I am still wondering about leaving him here, rather than taking him all the way to Chiswick. It is an idea that appeals. All day today, I have been trying to identify where to leave him, seeing if there are places I can wander off to and then disappear into the crowd. There are, in fact, a surprising number. Food courts, enquiry points, rest areas. So it is possible. Will I do it? I will decide in the morning.

Kieran
17th February
Ellins Court
London
10:00

I have had over a dozen enquiries about the new opening. A very positive initial response. I have selected three to meet initially. All this afternoon. All are Polish.

The bank have e-mailed me confirming that the full amount that had gone missing has been credited back into my account. It seems that everything is slowly returning to an even keel.

Anna
17th February
Disneyworld Paris
11:00

I put Thomas to bed early last night. There was lots to do.

Yesterday we bought him a little Mickey Mouse backpack. It has Mickey's ears on it and pictures of Mickey playing different American sports. It is garish, but has numerous pockets. Handy for my purposes.

I also packed a small rucksack for myself. It had a blonde wig and a change of clothes. I packed my things and put them into the car. I packed Thomas's things, but left a tag on his case which I would leave at reception in the morning.

I also packed a small carrier bag with any possible evidence that would indicate where Thomas had been. I would dispose of this in the next few days as I wanted no trace of our trip from Dubrovnik. We had picked up a range of stuff, T-shirts and souvenirs that I'd bought to keep Thomas happy but if pieced together would form a neat pack of clues. I also put Thomas's fake passport in the bag and the Jill Betts passport. Jill was no longer needed. I would end my time as her later today.

I then wrote the two notes to go in the Mickey Mouse pack.

The first was simple. It said:

My name is Thomas. If you are reading this note please call my parents on 44-208-354-6189.

The second note is for his parents. On the envelope, I write: *Cathy and Graeme.*

Inside, I have written a letter addressed to Cathy:

Dear Cathy,

I want to assure you that no harm has come to Thomas over the past few months. He has been well looked after and has travelled a great deal, but he has not been harmed.

We have discovered that Thomas has a brain tumour. This is causing occasional epileptic seizures. Medical experts have told me that it can be operated on and that, once it is removed, he will be OK. There should be no more seizures.

I cannot begin to imagine the pain you have experienced since last September. I hope you never stopped believing that Thomas would eventually come back. I have managed to prevent him suffering a horrible fate and think it only right that he returns to you.

He is a lovely little boy with a bright and happy future. I don't think anything that has happened to him over the past few months will have done any harm. I suspect it may have given him a lifelong interest in travelling, but nothing bad.

I know that you will love him and cherish him now that he is back. I hope that you will see I acted in his best interest and have done as much as I can to protect him and return him to you safely.

I cried as I wrote this. I didn't sign my name. I left no clues. In about half an hour, I will take him into the theme park. I will leave him waiting for me near a rest room. I will get changed, put the wig on, plus dark glasses and head out of the theme park, alone. If I am lucky, I may have thirty-six hours to get away from here. After that, I am likely to be hunted by every police officer in Europe.

Kieran
17th February
Ellins Court
22:15

I was watching the ten o'clock news. The usual crap, politicians caught with their pants down, wars in faraway places, economic turbulence. Then the news was interrupted by one of those 'breaking news' banners. A picture of a kid flashed up on screen. It took me a moment, but I recognised it as Thomas.

Immediately, I turned the volume up. The reporter was explaining that Thomas had been found in Disneyland Paris. A graphic shot up on the screen which showed a map of France with Disneyland and Paris highlighted. He was alone, nobody had been apprehended and a full news conference would take place in the morning. They were all the details that had been released so far.

I switched the TV off, phoned Elena.

'They've found him,' I said.

She seemed sleepy. 'Who?'

'The kid, the one the Russians didn't want.'

Elena seemed to gain her composure.

'What does it mean?' she asked.

I considered this.

'I'm not sure,' I say. 'I doubt that they have anything to link him with us at this stage. I'm just alerting you so that you know. We are in unchartered territory.'

We finished the conversation. If they don't have Anna, they have nothing to link him to me. They will be looking for her, not me, and unless they catch her, which will take time, they will have nothing to link us to it. So, logically, I am in the clear. Yet, I have a sense, a deep and real sense, that the net is closing in.

PART SIX

Lisa Lagnoo
Breakfast TV Studios
17th March
08:45

So Lorraine is interviewing the parents, a month after Thomas has returned. It's the usual Lorraine interview. Lots of cooing, Thomas being made a fuss of. Bloody miracle, if you ask me. The parents look delighted, Thomas seems happy and there appears to be no long-term damage.

I'm on after as I've got the paper to start a campaign to tighten up the security around au pairs and childminders. It seems that the agency were not particularly attentive to the details of the workers they were placing. A further investigation suggested that three in five agencies were cutting corners when it comes to placing au pairs. I mean, we never claimed our research was scientific or anything, and we did, in fact, only contact five of the dodgiest agencies we could locate online, but hey, facts don't sell newspapers, they just get in the way of a good story. It's also the right campaign to run as it appeals to the market we're trying to reach. Dozy C-Class mums with more money than sense. These people need to be told how to run their lives and we're quite happy to do so. There's an opposition MP coming on to support the campaign and someone from the trade association that supports the agencies. They're in for a roasting.

So after the break, we are sitting on the sofas. Lorraine comes to me first, offers nods of agreement and positive looks as I explain the broad case. The MP is next up; she is passionate and makes all the right noises. Says she'll be asking her party to make

221

a commitment to legislate on the issue, blah, blah, blah. Then Lorraine turns to the person from the trade association. What does he think?

'Well, we've done some investigations of our own. It seems that Ms Lagnoo's paper only actually called five agencies, two of which are not our members and we would not endorse. So, whilst we share the general concerns, we don't think there is much basis for additional action or legislation.'

Lorraine turns to me.

'Was it really only five agencies?' she asks with a chuckle in her voice.

I try to wriggle out of the question.

'I don't think it really matters if it's five or five hundred, the important thing is that action is desperately needed in this area.'

Lorraine turns to the MP.

'So,' she asks, 'would your party be prepared to take action on such limited evidence?'

The MP isn't going to be caught out.

'No, of course not,' she says. 'It would be silly to legislate on the basis of such a small sample.' She throws me a look that suggests I am something she has trodden on in the street.

Lorraine turns to the trade association guy.

'So what should parents do when using an agency for au pairs?'

This gives the guy a chance to give a long answer and to talk about the initiatives he and his members are taking to tighten up self-regulation. He manages to keep talking and use up the allocated time and Lorraine comments to the effect that it is reassuring that work is already in hand to improve day-to-day practice and that the viewers at home have had some good advice on how to pick the right organisation for domestic support.

They go to the adverts.

'Are you a fucking lunatic?' The MP is straight into me. 'Five! How the fuck is that a representative sample?'

She storms off, leaving me and the guy from the trade association having our microphones removed.

'I know it won't have much impact,' he says with a smile, 'but we are taking this up with the press complaints people. Your paper has got away with peddling lies for far too long.'

He's not aggressive, not nasty, but has the air of a man who has won a famous victory.

Not a good morning. A pretty awful one.

Kieran
Ellins Court
17th March
9:00

I've just seen the parents on the news. Not much sign of any problems for Thomas. They seem happy, said it has brought them closer together in their marriage. I wonder what that actually means. I have heard it said before by couples and just wonder how it works. Anyway, a positive – my work, it seems, helps to save couples in trouble. An unexpected bonus and side-effect.

A month on, there has been nothing linking me to Anna. No badly drawn photofit picture of a man resembling a vague likeness of any number of people, from Lord Lucan to Simon Cowell, and no mention of an accomplice. Just an assumption that Anna was somehow slightly warped, the au pair from hell. There was also a media interview with the mother where she seemed to suggest that she was always wary of Anna, but pushed her doubts to the back of her mind.

Anna's picture was, for a couple of weeks, all over the media, but without any particular effect. She was last sighted with Thomas on CCTV inside Disneyland. Then, nothing. She appears to have disappeared. A car she was thought to be using was found at Orly Airport. That was three or four days after police announced that Thomas had been found.

The media interest has slowly dissipated – in Anna at least. People are more engaged with the heart-warming story of a bright little boy being reunited with his parents. Anna is incidental to the story, whereas Thomas has become a bit of a media star. In one interview, he was asked, 'If you could say something to Anna now, what would you say?' And his response? 'Thank you for all the ice cream.'

Meanwhile our plans for the new project are developing. I have a new girl, Sonya. She is good and we are about to place her with the host family. Now, like you, I would expect people to be more careful at times like this. They're not. They are like motorists – they rubberneck when they see an accident on the motorway, but within a few minutes, they are flooring the pedal, driving too close to the car in front. You see, like everybody, we think shit happens to other people, not us.

Things are moving in France too. Biarritz is proceeding to sale. Sold within two weeks. Elena and Jorges are in Greece now, drawing up a shortlist of properties. We are looking at the islands around Patras. I figure the area worked for Aristotle Onassis, so it should be OK for me.

Suddenly, the world is a good place, where everything fits.

John Hardcastle
18th March
Croydon
14:00

I've thought about it, yeah. Thought about contacting Slobber. No hard feelings and all that. Seems that the girl who took him was the au pair, after all. All my work was along the right lines.

Whether or not Slobber would agree I was doing the right thing is neither here nor there. I'm no longer a copper now. I reckon if the little fella had been found dead, there would've had to be a formal enquiry, an investigation into what was missed. As it is, by some sheer fluke, the kid is back with his parents. End of. Case closed. One au pair being searched for but, to all intents and purposes, case shut. Of course, there is the possibility she will strike again, but I don't think that'll happen. More chance of Palace winning the Champions League!

Me? Teaching. History, as it happens. Got myself a licensed teacher role, so I do the quals as I go through. Yeah, young minds, free from cynicism. That's what I need. It will be a tonic; cathartic, a cleansing of the soul.

Anna
19th March
Protea President Hotel
Cape Town
17:00

Of course, I am not Anna anymore. I am Anne-Laure. Anna is just a friend from the past.

Here I am not known. A European woman, a white woman,

225

hanging out with all the other sun-worshippers and hedonists in the shadow of Table Mountain. Nobody worth noting, just another guest at the Protea President Hotel.

It has been a hectic month. Ever since I left Disneyland, I have been at a high state of alert, even higher than when Thomas was with me. In the past I was just a woman travelling with a little boy who might have been Thomas. Now I am a woman wanted for abduction. My picture has been in newspapers. I am a public enemy, a non-person.

I am intrigued. I have followed the story online. No mention has been made of the epilepsy or the brain tumour. I wonder why? Is the truth somewhat inconvenient? A criminal with a conscience or a sense of guilt? Never mind grief.

Yes, I grieved. From the moment I left the rest room, I longed for Thomas. I wanted to hear him asking for ice cream, to look in my rear view mirror and to see him, as he always was, looking out of the window, intrigued and fascinated by the world around him. I wanted to hear him laugh, to hear him cry, to hear his tantrums and his breathing grow deeper as he fell asleep. There were tears in my eyes as I drove away. For days and days, there was an ache in my chest, a pain that I think can only really be described as heartbreak. That pain is still there, still real, still raw, gnawing at me.

I took the car to the airport at Orly. Still in disguise, I left it in a multi-storey car park. I boarded a train for Paris and from there I travelled to Geneva. At that point, there was no other plan.

Instead of the swanky hotels, I went down-market. Guest houses, pensions. Checking in as Anne-Laure Le Merre, nobody seemed that bothered. There are plenty of single French women who pass through the city.

I was, in the few days I was there, able to sort out a few

things. I have over €1.2 million left in my accounts. I have spent a lot of money, but I am still relatively wealthy. The bank was helpful. The accounts have been amalgamated into one. No questions asked – this is how people live when you are privileged. Money talks.

Then, having secured my finances, I sat down and planned what to do. I quickly came to two conclusions. Firstly, that staying in Europe, at least for now, would be a mistake. Secondly, that I needed to really think about what comes next. I knew that I was in a kind of mental refugee status. I had survived the turmoil and, without recognising it, all of my energy had been consumed by the need to survive. Beyond that, I was running on empty. Me, Anna, had been pushed into the margins, a non-person with no rights because I existed so that Thomas survived.

Yet, in the darker recesses of the recent past, there was me, who had lost all sense of direction, all sense of there being a world that I could occupy and take my place on my own terms. I knew that I had to reach inside and find the new me.

The trouble was, I was really just a kid. A kid with a shed load of cash and an even bigger sense of guilt. I had stolen a child, to order. What sort of person had I become? I knew that inside me, somewhere, there was a good person fighting to getting out, yet even if I knew this, the world saw me as a mad, warped au pair who had gone weird and stolen a little boy. How sick can you get?

I think the English term is 'an existential crisis'. I had no idea about the place or space I occupied. I just knew whatever I did was bad. So, as time went on in Zurich, I just grew more and more exhausted.

That's how I ended up here. I was through with self-examination, through with the guilt. I needed a place to be. A place to be me. Right now, I have no clever answers, no easy solutions – just a need to discover me again. If I tell you the truth, if I am honest, I don't think that is such a bad space to occupy. You may disagree – you may think I should be thinking about a form of penance, a sort of apology. If the truth be told, in all honesty, I would say, 'Screw you,' because you know nothing.

So my days here have developed a pattern. I get up early, go for a run along the seafront, I come back, swim in the ice-cold pool. Then I have a light lunch. I sleep. Late afternoon, I head off to a beach bar. Talk to people, sometimes let guys pick me up. I have even let a couple of women hit on me, but nothing happened. I am usually back here by midnight. Throughout it all, I am looking at the people and things around me. Do I want to become that person? Is that the sort of car I want to drive? Are they the clothes I would like to wear? When you can be anyone, the choices are infinite. It is not like being a child again – you are already shaped, totally formed, you just have to look for the clues and act on them.

I know that I have exhausted Cape Town. Winter is coming anyway. I have to leave soon. I just don't know where I will arrive next.

Kieran
23rd March
Ellins Court
London
12:30

The new girl, Sonya, is placed with the family. I won't bore you with the details now, you know them. Win the trust of the family. Find a route into their lives, befriend the mother, let the dad fuck you if you have to, that sort of stuff. You are building a domestic alliance. Simple.

I've taken a precaution this time. I have suggested that she mention she has noticed something funny about the kid, have they checked she is OK? This way we won't repeat the mistakes of the last lift.

Tomorrow, I go to Paris. Meeting the client for an update. He and his wife are excited by the idea of a daughter. It feels great to be making people happy. We are going to a match and then having dinner. After that, I have to go to Biarritz, sign some documents, organise the storage of things from the house. Then I am off to Greece. There are four properties to look at – all quite good, all in the right price range. Elena will meet me in Athens, a total shithole of a city, and then we will travel down to the coast and look at various properties.

It feels good to be working properly again and moving forward.

Lisa Lagnoo
24th March
Canary Wharf Station
08:45

Unbelievable! I have been suspended – on full pay, but suspended nonetheless. The boss called me into his office first thing. He claimed that my methods of investigation had fallen below the standards of integrity demanded by the paper. This from someone who was implicated for phone tapping in the past, but still kept his job. He offered me an alternative of publishing a full apology about the childminding story, but I rejected that out of hand. So, there will be a further investigation and I may be sacked, at worst, or be fined.

I really wonder about resigning. Last September, I got plenty of praise for my on-air stuff. Channel 5 are rumoured to be keen to talk to me as the anchor for their early evening news programme. The story I heard was that they like my feistiness and the fact that I am not afraid of being assertive. I am growing bored of print journalism anyway. Any fool can string together copy from press releases – it's like being a glorified photocopier operative if you ask me. If they dare to either discipline me or fine me, I'll walk. In fact, I might walk anyway. Bastards!

Kieran
25th March
Charles De Gaulle Airport
12:30

Waiting for my flight. Just had a text off Sonya. Apparently the parents weren't too happy about her suggestion that there may be something amiss with their daughter. In fact, they were quite angry. Told her that she was only there to look after the kid, not to give medical advice. She said she had managed to calm things down, but it's not good that she has got off to a bad start. Texted her back to tell her to hang on in there, maybe to buy the mum some flowers by way of apology. She thinks this is a 'cool idea'.

Interesting that she uses words like 'cool' and 'fab' quite frequently. She seems to be a walking dictionary of 60s buzz phrases. Maybe her parents were hippies? Not that it matters, but it strikes me as curious that her turn of phrase feels dated.

So, Athens. Overnight in Plaka and then on to look at the new places. Should be tolerable for one night. After that, back to London. Tony has tickets for a Bees match at the weekend. Be nice to buy him lunch, sink a few beers and catch up.

Lisa Lagnoo
27th March
Home House London
18:30

I am waiting to meet the Managing Editor from Channel 5 News. This is his club. Great place, not how I imagine a London club to be. Laid back, lots of women, very unstuffy.

They have yet to make any decision at the paper. There is an HR review meeting next week and it will be discussed there. They like to string things out, a bit like the execution of Anne Boleyn.

Must ease off on these cocktails. They are very quaffable and I don't want to be pissed by the time he arrives. I checked online – the place has rooms upstairs. I've decided if I have to screw him to get the job, I will. Be worth it, in every sense.

Anna
29th March
Dubai International Airport
01:00

I am on the move again. Cape Town was starting to get a bit cold for me. So I looked online to try and find inspiration. I wanted somewhere that I could blend in as a female traveller that would not arouse suspicion. I ruled out Australia, for no reason other than winter was approaching there too. I am not ready to return to Europe and don't really have a plan as to when I will. If I go back, it will not be to London, but it could be somewhere else in the UK.

Looking at maps, and seeing what the weather is doing, I

have decided to head for Thailand. I may also travel to Cambodia and Laos, but I want to see how things go. The other advantage is that Thailand is relatively cheap to travel in and blending in won't be a problem.

I am feeling a little less sad about Thomas. I miss him still, long for news about him, but the pain is gradually fading. I think about him continuously. I wonder if he is having his operation soon. I hope so. If he can be cured or stabilised, then he should be. I would love to phone him, just to hear his voice, but I don't want to give my location away. A few days ago, I watched a TV interview with him online. He seemed happy, and I liked that the only thing he said about me was, 'Thank you for all the ice cream.' I am hoping that there is no lasting damage.

Thailand. I am going to Bangkok, first of all. Then to Chiang Mai and then maybe Phuket or one of the other islands. I have also read about a women's Buddhist retreat where I would like to spend time at. I do not know if I have the courage to spend time there as I am scared that it will be a little bit too introspective. Yet I also know that I need it. Maybe I will go there after I have been to a few full moon parties. I am in no hurry to become a nun and already feel very alone. I need contact with people. Happy people, sad people and normal people. Mostly normal people, I think.

Kieran
30th March
Ellins Court
17:30

I am worried. I have had no contact with Sonya for seventy-two hours. I have texted, but she has not responded. I wonder if she is ill?

I will give it another forty-eight hours and then I will see if I can go to the house. I have done this once before. I put a shirt and tie on and posed as a Jehovah's Witness. It meant that I got to see the girl who was working for me at the time, although she had trouble not laughing out loud when she saw me looking so square. Needs must.

We have found a place in Greece. It is on its own island, a half mile off the coast. Jorges thinks it is perfect. It needs some updating and we need to get the security right but, subject to some further negotiations, we can start development after Easter. I am concerned that there is only a jetty – we need a helipad for some of my clients. I have asked Elena to investigate this with the relevant authorities. I don't think it will be too problematic.

Things look good and they are very good if Sonya is OK.

Lisa Lagnoo
31st March
Pimlico
10:00

I have been in bed for a week.

I haven't been out. I have ordered food online or lived off takeaways. I am looking to get away for a few weeks soon too.

Home House should be renamed Humiliation House.

The Managing Editor turns up, but he has another colleague with him who was introduced as his deputy. It kind of threw me for a few moments, but I recovered my composure. I didn't realise it was going to be an informal panel interview, but what the hell?

We had a round of cocktails and things seemed to be going well. Then his deputy asked me about what some people had described as my 'unconventional journalistic methods'. I asked him what he meant and he said, 'Well, there was the recent story you did about au pair agencies – I mean the figures were exaggerated.'

I laughed and said, 'Look, darling, you know as well as I do that boring statistics don't sell a story, but exciting numbers grab the attention.'

So we discussed how I have used dodgy data in the past. They even brought up the stupid Thomas Moore case asking where I had got the first thirty-six hours stuff from?

I was now – and there is no other way to describe it – well on the way to being pissed. Totally stupid.

'Well, everybody believed it!' I said with a laugh.

'So it was made up?' he asked.

'Absolutely! Yet look at the traction it got on the story and it got the useless Diegos to pull their fingers out, didn't it?'

'You mean the Portuguese police?' he said.

Well, anyway, by now I wasn't quite liking his angle and just said something like, 'We've all done stuff like that, love. Stop being so pompous.'

Anyway, his boss changes the subject and he gets up and goes to the loo.

A few minutes later, he comes back with a camera crew, sound man, lighting guy and a microphone in his hand.

His first words are, 'Lisa Lagnoo, we have just been secretly filming you because we think your methods bring journalism into disrepute.'

I think my jaw hit the floor and, because of the alcohol, I just swore at him. I didn't quite realise how much until I saw the piece on the following evening's news, but it required almost continuous bleeping. Jesus!

Well, needless to say the rest of our competitors have

been having a field day. The paper have sacked me for 'gross misconduct', claiming I talked to another media outlet without their permission and, more importantly, that my standards weren't consistent with their ethical code of practice.

By the morning after Home House, every fucking broadcast crew you could imagine was outside. Just waiting to fucking doorstep me. Luckily, I am a member of the NUJ and got the union to supply me with a lawyer, but there is even talk of me being expelled from there, so fuck knows where that leaves me.

Disaster. Total bloody disaster!

Anna
Bangkok International Airport
1st April
14:00

Two days. That's all I could stand the place for. I am off. Bangkok is smelly, noisy and aggressive – in fact it's just horrible. I don't find high rise buildings exciting and dislike the fumes from vehicles. Whilst some of the temples and palaces are fantastic, stepping back outside is too unpleasant.

I am heading for Chiang Mai. This city is wrong, horrible and wrong.

Kieran
Belsize Park Tube Station
1st April
15:25

This is not good.

Just returned from a visit to Sonya – well an attempted visit to Sonya.

I did the right thing, decided to recce the area before approaching the house. First thing I noticed was two blokes opposite sat in a 4X4. At first, I thought they were Romanians, but closer inspection suggested otherwise. Short hair, dark suits – they were obviously coppers. This suspicion was confirmed when I noticed a uniformed plod on the doorstep.

Now, there are two things you can do in these circumstances – either run like fuck, which draws attention to yourself, or behave normally. So I chose to act normally – in fact, ultra-normal.

I stopped and got a small pocket *London A-Z* out. Then I approached the car.

'Excuse me,' I said, tapping on the car window, 'which way is Belsize Park Tube?' I was putting on a French accent; not too Inspector Clouseau, but still reasonably authentic.

The plod in the passenger seat leant across.

'Back that way, mate. Go to the main road and turn right, about eight hundred metres.'

'*D'accord*,' I said. 'Thank you, you 'ave been very 'elpful.'

The guy smiled, probably thinking something vaguely racist about this bloody foreigner. You see, no matter how many diversity courses you send plods on, they're still racist bastards. I wasn't going to hang around though. As far as I was concerned, it was time to get away as quickly as I could.

So now I am about to go back into the Tube system. I have taken a new SIM card from my wallet. It is one that is kept for such purposes.

I send a seventeen-character text to Elena. *Operation Vanish.*

Time is now of the essence.

Anna
Chiang Mai
1st April
19:00

This is much better. Much nearer to what I need, albeit not perfect.

Things move slower here. There is some traffic, but none compared to Bangkok. There are people, but not too many and the air is clean.

I have a reasonable hotel on the edge of the old city. Now I am feeling exhausted and just need to close my eyes. I will eat later, but first I need sleep.

Kieran
Ellins Court
1st April
20:00

Everything is packed into two holdalls. Tonight, I will travel to Ebbsfleet, then tomorrow on into Europe.

Operation Vanish has been developed over a number of years. You plan these things in the hope that, like nuclear weapons, you will never have to use them. Once activated though, I felt incredibly calm.

Elena and I had discussed and refined how the plan would be implemented in a great deal of detail. We had come up with a method that meant that once I had received the first instructions, everything else would become self-sustaining. So for the first night, I was told to go to the Crown Plaza Hotel in Lille and check in as Mark Garvey. There would be a fax waiting for me

237

and I was to travel on a false passport in the same name. In truth, I would be totally in Elena's hands. Only she knew the full details and all I was aware of were the general principles. We had worked on the basis that the less I knew the better, largely because this would maintain my heightened concentration.

Now that we don't have Biarritz I am intrigued to see how the plan will work, but I am not overly concerned. Elena is thorough and I implicitly trust her.

The financial aspects are more complex. We have had up our sleeve a sales agreement for the ticket agency which means that effectively it will disappear, along with all associated business accounts. Of course, the sale is not a real sale, but it means that, as of tonight, my business and all its assets are transferred to a third party. The proceeds from the sale have been transferred to an offshore account in the Cayman Islands. In terms of liquidity, there is money stored in various accounts which will be activated tomorrow morning. This means that we have approximately three years of cash flow, based upon a decent standard of living. If I choose to live more frugally, the money could probably last seven years.

Ellins Court will shortly be a place I used to live. I've left the keys in the kitchen drawer and advised the agents that I no longer need the property. There is a train to catch to Ebbsfleet in twenty minutes. I will go by taxi to St. Pancras. Taxi avoids anyone seeing me and, unusually for me, I will not engage the driver in a conversation about how Spurs are underachieving again, Labour is the cause of all the country's problems or how foreigners have ruined the place. Another time, but not tonight.

Everything is in place. I'm confident, but not complacent.

Anna
New Tearooms
Chiang Mai
14:00
2nd April

I slept for fourteen hours! I don't know how that is possible. I was woken when a cleaner wanted to service my room. Otherwise, I think I would still be sleeping now.

It is good here. Peaceful. People are friendly, calm, welcoming. I do not ever want to go back to Bangkok – it was like a nightmare for me.

Earlier, I was speaking to some Australians. They told me about an island, Samui, which sounds perfect. I will go there, but after I have been to Udon to a retreat. I have not found an all-women's retreat, but in this one there is strict segregation. Some days are silent – I will find that interesting.

In the meantime, I need to get some energy stored and hope that this tiredness passes.

Kieran
2nd April
Crowne Plaza Hotel
Lille
15:00

There is no note, no fax, no e-mail.

I checked in an hour ago. What is wrong?

The rule is that I cannot move on until I have her instruction. Yet there is no rule about what to do in the absence of a note from Elena. Am I to wait?

I will give it until 18.00 and then work out what to do next. Infuriating!

Anna
New Temple Guest House
Chiang Mai
22:00
2nd April

Still very tired and I have just realised that my period is a week late. I am normally like clockwork. Does this explain why I am so tired? I am hoping that it is simply my body clock out of sync and not one of the two or five nights of passion I had in Cape Town.

I had a fantastic meal tonight – all amazing Thai food in a chic riverside restaurant. I never expected to find this sort of place here. The wine was delicious too. I wonder if I should be drinking, but I am not pregnant – I cannot be pregnant. I took precautions and I think I only had sex a few times. It cannot be possible, no.

Kieran
Crowne Plaza Hotel
Lille
2nd April
18:15

About twenty minutes ago, there was a knock on my hotel door.

I opened it and there was a uniformed member of hotel staff, a young woman in her late twenties, quite pretty.

'I am very sorry,' she said. 'I 'ave a document for you which 'as been in our business centre all day. I think you have been quite anxious to receive it, no?'

She handed me a fax. The sense of relief was amazing. I felt like a crew member on Apollo 13, realising that my mission wasn't to crash and burn, but that I might just possibly make it back to the little blue planet called home.

I asked her to wait and returned, thrusting a twenty-euro note into her hand. She seemed taken aback.

'No,' she said, raising both her hands. 'I am sorry, I am doing my job, that is all.' She handed the money back.

So I went and sat down on the bed and read the fax she had given me.

'Tickets booked Lille to Cologne. Collect at Lille Europe from ticket machine tomorrow morning by 09.15. Second set of tickets will be at DB customer services office, Cologne Bahnhof.'

That was all.

I decided to pop down to the bar for a celebratory drink. As I went to leave the room, I picked up the TV remote control to switch off the television. On screen was a picture of Sonya and a caption: NEW THOMAS KIDNAP FOILED?

I dropped the remote.

I quickly picked it up again and turned up the volume.

Within a few seconds, a photo-fit picture also appeared. Whilst not flattering, it was clear who it was. It was me. Underneath the scrolling text read: 'Last seen yesterday at Belsize Park station. Police appeal for more information.'

This was worrying. Whilst I have always worked on the assumption that photo-fit pictures could almost be anyone, the likeness to me was clear. Would one of my neighbours at Ellins Court or someone from the letting agency recognise the picture as me? What clues could the police pick up?

I locked the hotel room door. I was not going anywhere, not until checkout tomorrow morning.

Anna

3rd April

Chiang Mai Bus Station

09:30

I am feeling dreadful. I have been sick a few times this morning. Maybe the food was too rich last night. I would have to be sick on the morning I am leaving.

I have thought about flying to Udon, but part of me wants to see Thailand from the ground. It is a long coach journey and feeling the way I am, it is probably the worst thing for me. I think I may have to sleep for some of the way. We shall see.

At least the coach is air-conditioned and not too busy. So I have a seat near the front, on my own. This is fine. It is raining, but very hot. My clothes are sticking to me which isn't helping how I am feeling, but hopefully, once we leave, I will feel OK.

There are lots of thoughts that are crashing through my head. One is that running is tiring. I no longer want to keep moving, I want to stand still. I feel I have been moving all the time since I left Poland. Perhaps that is why I am unwell, perhaps I have perpetual motion sickness?

Little Thomas – he comes to me in my dreams. It is only then that I see his face clearly, only at that point I am able to properly capture his face. I spent so long with him, but, when I am conscious, he is a shape – in my dreams, I can see every detail of his hands, his face, hear him giggle and smell him, that little boy smell. This worries me. How long before he is not even in my dreams?

Now I am going to try and sleep. At least he may join me for my coach journey?

There are a couple of policemen standing by the entrance to the customer service centre. It could be nothing or it could be they know of my plans. I sit on the platform nearby. I am agitated. What if my connecting service is leaving soon?

I decide to take a chance. I walk straight to the front door and enter. They don't even notice me – presumably they are just bored cops, killing the hours on their shift.

Inside, I speak to the girl behind the counter.

'Good afternoon,' I say. 'I believe you have a ticket for me to collect?'

They ask for my name, key it into the computer and then continue the conversation.

'Ah, yes, Herr Garvey, a First Class ticket for you. Oh, and there is a note on the system to let you know you are booked into the Hotel Munchen Palace. Your train is at 15.44 from Platform 5. Is there anything else I can help you with?'

'No, I don't think so,' I say with a smile.

'Very good,' she says. 'You are welcome to use our First Class lounge.'

'May I leave my bag with you?' I ask.

'Of course,' she says. She gives me a ticket for my bag. 'I will keep it safe for you.' She smiles. She is the nearest I have to a guardian angel.

I have an hour or so. I head towards the enormous cathedral that dominates the city centre – it is like a vast alien spaceship, dumped into the middle of Germany. I have no desire or intention to go inside. God is not a presence I need.

Instead, I wander through the streets on the other side of the cathedral and finally find a beer hall selling *Bratwurst*. It is sometime since I have had a *Currywurst*, maybe not since my last visit to Berlin. With time to kill, it seems appealing, not to mention a cold beer too. Surprisingly, the day is warm, unusually warm for April. So a big beer, a *Currywurst* and chips has an appeal that excels the Gothic monstrosity that is the big cathedral. At the back, there is a garden with some trees with apple blossom and I am struck by how, in the strangest of situations, perfection suddenly emerges from nowhere.

The staff are all male, friendly, tolerating my suspect German and my brave attempts to engage them in conversation. So, in all of this, I am suddenly aware of the vastness of my freedom. I can go where I want when I want. I feel foolish that my desire for money, for material gain, has, one way or another, put all this at risk. The simple things, beer and *Bratwurst*, choosing where I sit, who I hang out with. I imagine that incarceration would be intolerable by comparison.

I spend maybe thirty minutes here. Then I call for my bill. As I do so, I reach to my inside pocket for my wallet. Then I realise it is back in the bag at the station. I have everything else. Mobile, two passports, rail ticket, but not my wallet. I contemplate doing a runner. It is possible that I could go outside and just run back to the station. The staff are busy – there aren't enough of them to notice, but it feels stupid.

There is a guy sat at a table a few metres away. I decide to chance my luck.

'Excuse me,' I say. He looks up.

'Do you speak English?'

'Yes,' he says flatly.

'Might you be able to help me? You see I have left my bag at the station and it has my wallet in it. Here is my ticket for the train to Munich in thirty minutes' time. If you would be kind enough to pay for my meal, I will pay you double my bill if you accompany me back to the First Class lounge at the station.'

The man looks at me – he has a slightly amused smile playing across lips.

'You will pay me double?' he asks.

'Of course!' I nod.

'Well – that is appealing but you might be some sort of vagabond, no? What proof do I have that you will not just run off?'

'I have my ticket,' I tell him. 'It is in my name.' I show him the ticket.

'How do I know you have not stolen that ticket? Maybe it is a trick you have used before?'

I am almost irritated with him now. Why on earth would I do such a thing?

'I have my passport,' I say.

'Show me,' he says.

I hand him my passport but, a moment too late, I realise it is my real passport, not the Mark Garvey one.

'You have two passports in different names. Why do you have these?' he asks.

He calls across to one of the waiters. He is speaking very quickly in a local dialect which isn't quite German.

'I will pay for your food and drink,' he says, 'but you have some explaining to do as to why you possess two passports.'

I am kicking myself now.

By now, he has paid the bill.

'OK,' he says. 'I want double my money – thirty-two euros.'

We walk across to the station together. He stays very close to me. I suspect he is worried that any moment now I might run.

We approach the First Class lounge. The two cops have moved away a little. I ask him to wait. I go in, collect my bag. I retrieve my wallet and come back outside with thirty-five euros.

He is waiting.

'One moment,' he says and holds up his hand. My train is due to go in seven minutes.

He shouts across to the police officers. I hear '*Zwei*' mentioned and they come ambling across and then the phrase, '*Ein Englanders – Ja?*'

Then the younger of the two men speaks.

'May I see your passport please?'

I hand him my passport.

He examines it.

'This gentleman says you have two.'

'I am afraid he is mistaken. He has been demanding money off me, even when I was eating my lunch. Look, I don't want to make a scene, but I have a train to catch in just a few minutes.'

The man looks at me and at the Mark Garvey Passport, then speaks.

'Very well, Herr Garvey. We will deal with him. You must hurry. Your train leaves soon.'

He is polite, courteous. I take my leave and, as I grab my bag, racing across the station, I can see the old guy remonstrating with them. I wander past a rubbish cart and drop my real passport in there. I will have just enough time to catch my train. I hurry away, determined, but not unduly hasty – if I make it to my seat, I will rename it the 'Freedom Express'.

PART SEVEN

Anna
10th September
Full Moon Retreat
Udon
14:00

Did I intend spending so long here? I don't think so. I think when I stepped off the bus, I thought it would be maybe two or three weeks. Not the months I have spent here.

Within a couple of days, I realised that this was the space I had been searching for. My quest was to find peace and some sort of reconciliation. Here nobody questioned me, there were no intrusive interrogations about why I was in Thailand – it was enough for me to be here, to have made the journey.

The daily rituals also gave me a structure. A morning sit, some stretching and yoga. Communal living and the exclusion of alcohol, fish, meat and caffeine. If you had asked me if I could imagine this ever happening to me I would have said a very clear 'no'. In fact, I think I would have assumed that you were mad – Anna was a wilder child than this, Anna was a party animal, not a woman who could enjoy silence, who could enjoy the stillness of the moment. That was not me. Yet as the time went on, the kinder, gentler me began to emerge. A me that had deeper insights into other people, that could sit and watch the rain falling and see the link between the rain as it fell and the jungle that grew around me. The me that would, each morning after breakfast, take two bananas into the undergrowth and delight as the monkeys I fed began to be gentler with me and to eventually take things so gently from my hand that I was almost accepted as one of them.

Then there are the people. Women from all over the globe. America, Australia, Chile, England, Ireland, France and India. They have become more than friends, they have become my sisters who care for me and I care for them. Of course, they know nothing of my past, but here I am judged in the moment and in the moment I am caring, giving and attentive.

These sisters have helped me. As my shape has changed, both mentally and physically, they have been there by my side. They know me as Anne-Laure, the pregnant French girl. They have shared my fascination as my belly has become distended and I let them listen as the new life inside me moves around, occasionally kicking, but seemingly healthy and content. I will give birth in six weeks.

That has forced another decision upon me. I do not want to have the baby here. I want to have the baby in Europe. Jennifer, a girl from Manchester in England, has suggested I travel back with her. She has told me that there is a Buddhist centre in the city where there is space for me to live. She has also said that the National Health Service will look after me – it feels the right thing to do even though the risks of my past catching up with me are a distinct possibility. I have to do what is right for the life inside me. We leave in a few days – any later, I will not be able to fly.

I am sad to be leaving. This place has been fantastic. I am a little afraid, but leaving is what I must do for the baby, not what I must do for myself.

Kieran
11th September
Hohenasperg
09:45

Not long left now – I have been lucky.

I hate the Germans now. I hate this place and I hate the way I am spoken to. I hate it when in the morning they shout my name, '*Garvey! Wo ist zu, Garvey?*' It always cuts through me like a knife.

A few more paces was all it should have taken. I should have run faster, but instead I tried not to be too suspicious. That gave them time to catch up with me. The stupid fart was running behind the two policemen. He was yelling in German, '*Halten sie! Englander, halten!*' They literally collared me within a step of boarding the ICE. Even then, I may have got away with it, but the stupid, officious kraut comes barging into me and, as a reaction really, I somehow swung a punch at him. As soon as it connected, I knew it was a mistake; he fell, grazing his head against the side of the train. That was it. They were on me. Cuffs, frogmarched away. Taken to the police station and detained. My bag was searched, but, to all intents and purposes I was Mark Garvey, a social worker from Birmingham.

It was still hellish. I was convinced that this was going to be it, that gradually my story would unravel and that I would be unmasked as the real me. As I say though, I have been lucky.

German justice does not take kindly to acts of physical violence. I was sentenced to 150 days' imprisonment. My sentence was later extended when I got into a couple of fights inside, so my release is not due until ten days. Yet they never unmasked me. Someone from the British consulate came to see me. He explained that my offence was not too serious, that I could, if I wished, transfer to a British prison and that, in all probability I would be tagged and would only have to serve a third of my sentence. Yet that seemed too risky. In Britain, the authorities would ask more questions than here, there were greater risks. At least from here, I will be able to continue on my way once I am released. I am not convinced that would have been the case if I had ended up in a UK jail.

We had a contingency anyway. Elena and I had worked out that if there was radio silence for forty-eight hours, any plans would be abandoned.

Most of the time, being incarcerated has not been so bad. Some of the other inmates are fucking scary, evil, but they leave me alone. I suspect that prisons here are not as brutal and the emphasis is upon rehabilitation, not punishment. We get by, to a fashion. Some speak OK English; we can discuss football, food, the weather, but it is limited and boring. At times, I have been desperate for a deeper, more meaningful discourse – cinema, art, theatre, anything really. It just never happens. Most criminals are not particularly bright, so most simply communicate in their native language.

Now autumn is coming. I will be out before the nights close in, hopefully in Greece. Just a few more days. The objective, the only one that matters, is survival.

Anna
Manchester Buddhist Centre
17th September
07:30

The rain, it always falls here. Somebody told me that the wealth of this city was built on rain. The rain gave the city the right conditions for working a particular type of cloth and the cloth meant they built mills and the mills meant that trade came.

When I arrived at the airport, I was very worried. I was concerned that maybe the passport would not work, but I was waved through Passport Control without a hitch. We were met by a monk – not that he was dressed as a monk – called Lalitavajra. He is pleasant, gentle, smiling.

252

He hugged Jennifer and then turned to me. He spoke in French.

I didn't understand what he said.

'I am sorry,' I explained. 'I am French, but I do not speak the language.'

He looked puzzled. Which meant I had to explain my back story. I had got used to this by now.

'My Father was French. He left my mother when I was small. She came to England with me and I grew up here. I am French, but I have lived everywhere. And now, I am living in Manchester.'

I smiled. It was a learnt smile, the Buddhist smile. It is meant to tell the questioner that they do not need to ask too much more. It worked. Lalitavajra got the message. He just embraced me and my swollen, life-filled belly.

'Well, welcome to Manchester,' he said, using the Buddhist smile to indicate a thought like, *This goes against my instincts, but my teachings tell me to see the good in everyone.* This is why Buddhists are like small children who want to believe in Santa Claus – even if they have found Christmas presents in their parents' cupboard.

Then there was the journey in a little car with all our things crammed in around us and me in the front. We edged our way through the traffic, through rain-filled streets and, finally, right in the centre of the city is the Manchester Buddhist Centre. A place of peace, of tranquillity, in a sea of noise and people.

Once inside, it was like being back at the retreat in Thailand. There are eight apartments on the top floor. I have been told I can have mine for as long as I need which could be years. This generosity is easy to exploit, yet I know I will resist that temptation. I may not always tell the purest of truths, but will not take the not-given.

On my second day here, I went to see Lalitavajra.

'The rent here, how much is it?'

He smiled.

'We ask you to pay what you can afford and if you cannot afford one penny, you can still stay.'

'But what,' I asked, 'do people usually pay?'

'Comparisons are odious,' he said, with a beatific smile.

This man was driving me mad.

'I want to stay for at least six months,' I tell him. 'I want to stay until after the baby arrives.'

He nodded and was still smiling.

'So if I pay you seven and a half thousand, will that be enough?'

'That would be very generous indeed.' He nodded.

'Then I will pay eight thousand. That way I will help someone with a little less than me.'

He does not applaud, but nods again.

I am now standing in a small one-room apartment with a bed, a bathroom and an old but very comfortable armchair. There is a floor-to-ceiling window that looks over the surrounding buildings. My baby kicks. Maybe he or she is happy, maybe they are showing that they could play for Manchester United. More importantly, whatever baby is saying, I know that we are safe.

Kieran
18th September
Munich Hauptbahnhof
08:30

Am I free? Not as me. I am free as Mark Garvey.

In the plan, there were three stages to my re-entry. So I now have to find an Internet café so that I can complete stage one. I have €130 euros on me, plus a travel warrant that will take me to any station outside of Germany.

I have nowhere to live and nowhere to stay – just the bag I was travelling with when I was arrested, some clothes and a few toiletries.

Phase One involves contacting a charity in London that we gave some money to. It is a charity for homeless people and, five years ago, I gave them £100,000 on condition that they agreed to forward e-mails sent to their Chief Executive. It was all above board, but also underhand and a bit dishonest. Charities though – they are money-grabbing, not altruistic, building their empires so that they can become fat and bloated and the competition dies. You shouldn't believe their cute leaflets.

Once Elena gets the e-mail, she will put Phase Two of the plan into place. I will be told to go to a hotel and, from there, a driver will eventually collect me. If the plan works, I should be in a decent hotel by lunchtime and then away by tomorrow morning.

Typing the e-mail feels difficult. I have only been in prison for a short time, but I feel a bit overwhelmed by even the simplest of tasks. Buying train tickets, coffee and the like is far too complicated. Inside, everything was organised for me. Meals were cooked, laundry cleaned, my lack of choice became a kind of freedom. Now all these new choices are oppressive. Freedom will take getting used to.

Anna
06:45
19th September
Manchester Buddhist Centre

Lalitavajra is in my room. He came in about twenty minutes ago, even though I explained that I was getting ready for my morning sit.

'Anne-Laure,' he begins, 'why do I think that you are not truthful with me?'

This is his opening comment. I'm unsure how to respond. Thinking like a Buddhist, I choose silence.

He continues, 'You are an intelligent woman. You are about to become a mother. I am worried that the truth is outside and around you, but not within you.'

He is calm as he says this, tilting his head to show curiosity at the end of the last statement.

I still choose silence.

His response is silence.

I can feel the baby moving inside me. This child is not entirely comfortable with the concept of stillness. He or she moves, he or she expresses herself through that movement, but seems less comfortable when there is silence.

In the end, I respond with a question.

'Why do you question my truth?' I ask. 'Why my truth and not all truth?'

He smiles benignly at that question.

'A fair observation,' he says. 'Let us suppose all truth is here with us now, in this room, everywhere. Would it recognise us as being true? Or would it see a falsity? A stinging hornet?'

I go back to being silent, but eventually respond.

'Often, the truth stings or bites,' I say. 'It is neither a hornet, nor a wasp, but has the presence of a baby's kick inside a mother's stomach.'

He nods. I wonder if he nods because he realises I can talk this shit for hours. Hornets, babies kicking – it is like breakfast cereal wisdom.

We are silent for a while longer. Then he speaks again.

'I need you to leave soon,' he says. 'I don't feel your presence is conducive to positive energy within the sangha.' He smiles at the end of this.

I nod.

'So will I be able to stay until after the baby is born? At least for a few months?'

He looks at me impassively.

'I am concerned for your child's welfare. I would not, of course, ask you to leave straight away. I think the longest I would like you to stay is for six weeks after the child arrives.'

He pauses.

'Of course, you have given me far too much money, so some will be returned to you when you eventually leave.'

I nod. I am thinking, *So, you're giving me a refund. I bet it won't be anywhere near what I should get, but doubtless you will console yourself with the fucking convenient refrain that 'all life is suffering'. We shall see.*

He has been seated, but now stands. He walks to the door and then turns.

'Anne-Laure, there are no ultimatums. I am simply asking you to think about the right actions that you may need to take.'

He really is annoying.

'The stinging hornet,' I say, 'may be the elephant in the room.'

He looks shocked. Whereas me? I have simply spoken a riddle that I myself cannot understand, but which, in the warped world of the sangha, appears deep and philosophical. No wonder the world is fucked.

My money has nearly run out, but I'm keeping twenty euros spare in case something has gone wrong with our plan. Twenty euros isn't much, but it gives me the chance to keep communications open. Twenty minutes at an Internet café is €1.50. I have to keep six euros spare so that I can keep checking my e-mails.

There is nothing at the moment. No reply. Has the charity sent the mail on or conveniently forgotten about our arrangement? It's possible that they may not have sent an e-mail to Elena. Worse still, it's possible they have and Elena has ignored it.

I have always had faith in the plan, so never thought about a contingency. Now I am wondering what I should do if Elena fails to make contact. She may have decided that she could make more money by selling the Greek place, banking the cash and simply vanishing. She knows how to become untraceable and she also knows that I would have no money to pursue her. Money gives me access to all the resources of a criminal. There is nothing that money can't get you. Guns, drugs, women, revenge murders. All come at a price. In criminal terms, fourteen euros doesn't even get you a wrap of coke. If I really have nothing, I am pretty much finished.

I decide to use eight minutes of the eleven I have left to check out what has happened. I google Fish, initially getting lots of images of fish, thus wasting valuable seconds. I type his name in fully: Dr Steve Fish.

The first item that comes up is a news story, about three months old, from the *Evening Standard*:

Police were today widening their investigations following the discovery of a man in a West London suburb. Well-respected GP, Dr Steve Fish, was found badly beaten not far from his home in Isleworth. Police suspect that he had been attacked by two Eastern European men, thought to be Romanian, who were seen involved in heated exchanges with Dr Fish near to his home.

Despite the efforts of medical staff at Ealing Southall Hospital, Dr Fish never recovered from his injuries. Doctors turned off his life-support machine yesterday afternoon and he passed away a few hours later. Police confirmed that they are now conducting a murder enquiry into the GP's death.

I stare at the screen. I feel myself shaking, I have started crying. Fish didn't deserve that, but the Romanian bastards must have linked him to me. The thought occurs that, if they have got to Fish, they may have also got to Elena. Could this explain the lack of response?

I spend so much time looking at the Fish article that I use up all my minutes. I will come back later today. I wonder how far those bastards have penetrated into my team.

Anna
19th September
Royal Infirmary
Manchester
17:30

I have heard more Polish voices in here than in the last six months. They seem everywhere. In the ambulance, in the outpatients, on the ward. Am I in Krakow or am I in England? It is impossible to say. All I know is I am in labour.

I came by taxi. Everything seemed to happen very quickly. One moment, I was helping prepare our evening meal in the communal kitchen, the next my waters were breaking and there was fuss all around me. Then I was bundled into a taxi and sent to hospital alone. Nobody came with me – I was a bit surprised by that, but why would they? I am a stranger, an unwanted presence, perhaps. A French girl who speaks no French. They do not intend to take me to their bosom.

Now I must wait. There is a midwife who keeps on offering me drugs and checking what's happening, but I feel OK. I want to experience childbirth as naturally as I can.

Yet I am also thinking how I am alone, with nobody here, no fixed place to live and no place to go. They will ask awkward questions once the baby is here. I need a plan. The trouble is, how can you plan with so much fucking pain! Argh! I tell you, Catholic childhood or Jewish one, in future I never have sex without a condom!

Kieran
19th September
Café Cyber
Munich
19:30

This place closes in thirty minutes. I have come in as late as possible. I have eight euros to my name. I have not eaten and I am starving hungry. I have a large water bottle with me and the guy who works here, a bearded hippy, has refilled it for me from the kitchen tap.

I log on with trepidation, hands shaking, possibly due to my hunger. Then, in my inbox, there is an e-mail:

Kieran,
We have to be quick. I will be in Munich in the next few hours. Please meet me near Platform 7 at the main station at 23:16 tonight. Don't arrive early, don't arrive late. I will be there. I will explain more when I see you. Do not reply to this e-mail
E

The tone is disturbing. Elena is normally calm. This was not a calm e-mail, not by her standards. Something is up.

I have time left but it is raining in the street outside. I search some more around Fishy. There is nothing – not even a mention of a funeral or a will. Just a few snippets about the police investigation, then the trail goes cold. He was just another middle-class bloke attacked for a random reason in London. Nobody links his death to a bigger picture because, unless you knew, nobody would link his death to a bigger picture. There's a link though. There's a link between the tone of Elena's e-mail and the murder of a doctor in London. Yet the police can't seem to piece together the jigsaw because the pieces are scattered across Europe, not in a neat box in a London suburb. The only distinct advantage is that they can't also see a piece with my name on it, with my ID.

A warning message appears on screen in German. My time is up, my fate hangs between the platforms at Munich Station.

Anna
19th September
21:30
Royal Infirmary
Stoke-on-Trent

People said to me, 'When you hold new life in your arms, the past nine months are worth it.' They said that the baby taking its first mouthful of milk from your breast or falling to sleep in your arms melts you like nothing can. They told me that life becomes explained. You are no longer alone in the world; there is you and your baby, you and the billion possibilities that now exist. There is a joyfulness; you are at last at peace and the world becomes beautiful.

I don't feel this. I don't have a sense of excitement for the future. I am too tired. I don't have anything that enraptures me or makes me want to burst into song. I ache, my body hurts and the nursing staff gathered around my bed cannot heal my sense of despair. My baby, the thing I have nurtured for nine months, cannot have plans. My baby was stillborn. The phrase is so English. Not dead, stillborn. The word 'dead' cannot be mentioned. Just as my grief is not allowed to be vocalised, but instead I must 'get some rest'. Not wail, not cry out, but sleep. They have pumped so many drugs into me anyway that now I cannot stay awake. I just wish that it was my baby's cries disturbing me, not the relentless background humming of an air-conditioning machine.

Kieran
Munich Hauptbahnhof
19th September
23:15

I am pretending to study train timetables, looking studiously at the listed services on the wall. From where I am standing, I can see onto the main concourse. I can see platforms 5 and 6. Platform 7 is to the right.

Killing time when you have no money is a thankless task. I spent an hour in a church, sat quietly with only a few people coming in for confession. I wondered how long my confession would take. I even wondered if I had that much to confess to, other than making a dishonest living. I haven't done much else to cause me regret and I don't particularly regret what I have done. In Moscow, Abu Dhabi, Damascus, Leningrad and many other cities, there are children who are having a very good life. They will receive the best education, have holidays to exotic destinations and want for nothing. I know that they all came from comfortable middle-class backgrounds, not from poverty, but the life I've given them is so much better than the life they would have had. That can't be a bad thing.

I look at the station clock. It is time.

I make my way across the concourse. At precisely the right moment, Elena appears. She has a wheeled pilot's case with her. She doesn't wave and she doesn't smile.

'We have to be quick,' she says, glancing around. 'Everything you need is in the case. There is a blue Mercedes at the front of the station. Go to it. The driver will take you to the airport, to a private jet. We can't stay around here talking. With luck, I will see you in a few days. Now hurry!'

'The Romanians?' I ask.

She nods. 'No time now, just go!'

So I do as she says. I move quickly across the concourse. Just before I leave the station, I glance back. Two men are talking to Elena; something about their gait suggests that the conversation is not a timetable enquiry. I have no time to interfere.

Moments later, I am in the back of the Mercedes. As soon as the door is shut the driver floors the engine and we shoot off through the city streets. This guy has no regard for the basic rules of the road.

'Relax, sir,' he says.

Then I realise the driver is Jorges.

I smile.

'Thank you, Jorges. I've always trusted your driving.'

The Mercedes, travelling at 140km per hour, is a cocoon. Secure, almost silent, perfect.

As the journey progresses, I notice that the signs for the airport are pointing in the opposite direction to the way we are travelling.

'Jorges,' I say, trying not to sound tense, 'we are heading away from the airport.'

'Relax, sir,' he says. 'This is a diversionary tactic.'

Yet it doesn't feel right. I can sense that something is wrong.

Then, without warning, the car is spinning. A very loud bang behind me. I can see Jorges struggling to control the car. As we hit the crash barrier, airbags inflate all around us. I am not thinking of survival, but about how many airbags there are – there seems a ridiculous amount. Then there is the sound of metal scraping against something hard and, very soon after, silence.

It is dark; there is a strong smell of petrol. The driver's door opens and I hear a gunshot. I am next.

The door opens beside me.

It is Elena.

'Get out! Get out now!'

She has a gun, but she is pointing it away from me, keeping us covered.

I step into the night air. Cars rush past us on the autobahn. Elena bundles me and the pilot case into a big 4X4. She throws me in the back, jumps into the driver's seat and we head off again. I don't care to where, I just want this to be over.

FINAL PART

A doctor is sat with me.

'Sir,' he says very firmly, 'from what I understand, you are far from a well man. You have been through a great deal recently.'

Elena is beside him, nodding.

I have been here for nearly two weeks and slowly the story is emerging.

Jorges apparently switched sides just after handing in his notice. He went to the Romanians because, by his calculations, I was finished. In his mind, he felt he was backing the wrong horse. He compromised Elena, led the Romanians to her and, in return for not killing her, demanded that she led them to me.

They underestimated her. Elena is loyal, Elena is shrewd. Elena would not betray me. So she designed a scheme whereby the Romanians were led to believe that she was with them but, once she knew I was safe, she could plan our escape. She knew the route Jorges would take. She also made plans – first to kill the Romanians and then Jorges. She did not think for one minute that I was a spent force, that our business was over. Elena made the right choices.

Now she is concerned. She thinks I have made some poor choices. That I have trusted the wrong people. She agrees that she wants the business to continue, but she needs me to be stronger. There is nothing physical between us, nothing that hints at romance, but she and I are now equal partners. I owe her my life. She has earned her place as my equal.

And Villa Spyros is perfect. It can only reached by boat or by air. It is in an acre of grounds with a private beach. The villa itself is grand, spread over three floors with an annexe. We need to add to the security, but we are already recruiting a replacement for Jorges. Now, in late September, the day is hot, there is the smell of fresh pine and the sea. Birds sing, the sea laps against the shore just metres away from me. This is a place of peace.

The doctor is gathering his things.

'Lots of rest, you take time. Then you may be able to work again.'

I smile, nod wryly. He is a good man.

I am alone whilst Elena takes him to the jetty. I am lucky. Some people aren't. Some people get all the crap, whereas people like me glide our way through it. There's no God, no justice, there is simply life. I know you wish you had my luck, my chances, and I know that you never have and that you will never get it. Which is why I'm in a villa in Greece, on an island, and you? Let me guess, you're grateful when you open the credit card statement and you can just about pay the minimum amount and you go into raptures if you get a seat on the Tube or manage to find a free parking space for your eight-year-old Ford Focus. 'The god of small things,' you tell yourself, but deep down it eats at you. Life is not fair, particularly if you are virtuous and conscientious like you. The most you get is a holiday to the Algarve, sex every third Friday and a few friends posting on your Facebook page on your birthday. You know life is not fair and you hate that my life is better. Well, here's the rub, I hate yours. I hate your limited ambition, your flaying ability and your pathetic pretence that you are a success. You have failed. Haven't you realised it yet?

Elena
Villa Spyros
Spetses
30th September
06:45

I adore the mornings here. Something about the light on the water and the mountains in the background, they make the place even more magical than it really is. I give myself my one self-indulgence of the day at this time. I smoke a single cigarette watching the sun rise, luxuriating in the sense of it in my mouth. Sometimes, if the mood takes me, I blow smoke rings into the cool morning air, but mostly I just sit and smoke. The moment is mine.

He is not strong. He is weak. I am a little concerned. I have always found him hard to read, hard to gauge. Recently, he has started talking about moving away from his 'current business model'. I am astounded! He only knows crime and he only knows criminality. It pays him well, delivers beautiful homes like this, with occasional inconveniences. It would be ironic if his time in a German prison has rehabilitated his thinking, but I don't think it has.

He will, for the time being, remain weak. I need to make some additional arrangements. He thinks I am loyal to him. Well, let him. I have one loyalty and one faith – myself. Perhaps he will eventually realise this, but if he doesn't, well, it is hardly my problem.

Anna
Krakow
1st October
09:30

It is a risk. I know it is a risk. Yet this country is mine, where I am from, with a language I understand and a people that are like me.

I decided to take a flight here. Ryanair. It is to flying what McDonalds is to wiping your arse. Even so, I spent some time last night in the city square where I had spent my childhood. Nobody knows me here anymore, I am anonymous. It is to me like a distant former lover, an ex, who I fondly remember and may even have the odd shower fantasy about, but who will ever remain exactly that. A part of my misspent past – not me in the current or in the present.

In ninety minutes I catch a flight to Zurich. I am going up in the world. This one is EasyJet. When I leave, the place is dead to me and Anna is dead to it. I was just making a fleeting appearance, not at my own funeral, but at my rebirth.

And you know, I haven't even begun to explain how heavy my heart feels. A mother without a child, a heart with no companion, a soul without a choice.

Kieran
Villa Spyros
Spetses
3rd October
Noon

Something is very wrong. I am not getting stronger; I am getting weaker. The doctor has been back, and he looked concerned. He took my pulse, some blood, spoke to Elena in Greek and then gave me a beatific half-smile.

He shrugged his shoulders. 'I will do tests. Something is not right, but I will sort it.'

I have noticed that speaking is becoming harder. I want to say, 'Thank you,' but it comes out as, 'Fa kew' – neither polite nor comprehensible. The doctor looks at me, nods. I think he understands.

When he is gone, Elena and I are left alone. She begins talking.

'I have been thinking,' she says. 'I have been thinking it might make sense if, on a temporary basis, you transfer the business side over to me.' She tilts her head inquisitively.

Everything is such an effort. I think what she is proposing makes sense. I nod my agreement.

She looks at me inquisitively.

'This is only a short-term thing – you know that, don't you?'

I nod again. I understand.

'OK,' she says. 'I will have some papers drawn up over the next day or so. All right?'

Our eyes meet. She is strangely beautiful and beautifully strange. I agree with her. We are doing the right thing. This is comfortable, despite the effort required.

Anna
Zurich
3rd October
11:30

It is surprising, but not so in a way. I have spent lots of money. Maybe three hundred thousand euros in total, but I seem to have lots of money left. Is this the point about being wealthy? Once you are rich, it is hard to become poor.

I am feeling empty. The world seems a long way from me. Yet I have decided certain things. When I headed for Manchester, I was drifting, in a trance. I had convinced myself that the Buddhist love would protect me. Yet once I was away from the warmth of Thailand, back in the rain and greyness that is England, I realised that this was only a place where unhappy things have taken place. Thomas, losing the baby, they are not positive moments in my

271

life. So my decision is that I will keep away from that place. A tiny part of me wonders about Wales or Scotland, but it does not wonder enough for me to actively do much about it. It will still be cold, wet and grey there. So I do not want to waste my time.

I need warmth. I need sunshine. I have thought about the Caribbean but there are too many Americans there and I do not like Americans. I have also wondered about Mozambique. There are memories of a snatched conversation with a couple of spaced-out women in Cape Town who were describing how amazing it was. It's only a fragment though, not a real want or a desire.

The bank people have said that, providing I am in Europe, there is no problem getting money to me. Outside of Europe, it is OK, but the costs mount up. I want somewhere where I can be warm most of the year and where I will blend in. It doesn't have to be picture postcard, just warm and friendly and not grey.

Time. I must take some time to consider.

Elena
Villa Spyros
Spetses
17:00
5th October

I want to tell him the truth, but he is a man who has lived his life through a lie for so long. So the truth is a luxury he has lived without, an inessential item in his list of moral needs. I just wonder if he knows.

The doctor you see – well, he isn't a real doctor. He is just some sozzled local who has agreed to pretend to be a doctor. If he thought about it, he would realise that aside from taking his pulse and blood pressure, which any fool can do, and looking concerned, he has never actually done anything a doctor would do. He has been receiving injections, but I am administering these.

When the doctor came today, he explained that he thought Kieran had a rare blood disease. As of yet they were unable to locate the cause. He also explained that he had a colleague in Switzerland who he had been talking to who specialises in these things. Now wasn't the time to travel but, if he became much worse, then we would see about chartering a plane to take him there.

At one level, it is sad. His eyes have become sunken, he has become thinner and speech has become much more difficult for him. He is not always easy to understand and I can see he is becoming upset.

I will keep administering the injections. I only have my best interests at heart.

Kieran
Villa Spyros
Spetses
3:40am

I am awake. These dreams. These dreams are strange. Two nights running. Explicit.

I see Zie first. She is crying, she is looking at me and she is crying. When she speaks, I cannot hear her. But she keeps gesticulating, pointing outside of the room, getting more and more agitated.

Then Fishy walks in. He speaks to Zie and then he sees me. He looks shocked, very upset. They are both shouting at me, but I can't hear them. They are pointing at the door, encouraging me to leave. I can't. I am unable to move. They come closer and closer to the bed; they reach out to pull me and, as they do so, I wake.

When I wake though, I know I cannot move, I know that I cannot speak. This sickness is making me a cripple. I am not getting better, but worse. Speaking, breathing, eating – it is all becoming too much. I wish the doctor would hurry up and make me better. Life is becoming hell.

Anna
Limone Café
Larnaca
7th October
10:20

No, I didn't expect to be here either. I was browsing the Internet, looking for businesses for sale when I came across this place. A café with accommodation. It is nice, but I do not find Larnaca to my liking. Too cheap as well.

I like Cyprus though. It has enough here. There is some bustle, some beauty and there is the warmth of the island. Tomorrow, I am driving up to Polis, to see a place called the Love Apartments. It has a small bar, a restaurant, pool and twelve self-catering apartments. Three hundred thousand seems a good price and the season runs from May to mid-October. Even today, the temperature is set to be 23°C, the sky is blue and people are smiling.

I want to stop. I want to stop running and start building my life again. This feels like the place. This feels like a possible new beginning.

He looked at me, just a few minutes ago, and I wondered if he knew. Has he worked out what is happening?

I don't really care. I see a man who is unable to control his speech, his limbs and even his bowels. Do I care? Not so much. Do I feel guilt? In no way whatsoever. He has caused far more pain and suffering in others than I in him. It is not that the end justifies the means – that kind of logic is too cheap and too linear for me – it is that this is his fate, the price he must pay for the things he has done.

I sometimes ask myself, *What do I get from this?* Well, clearly there is the financial gain. More than that though, there is an absolution. I have earned a living from a false morality – if I can draw a halt to that maybe, in my own mind, everything will be all right. I am not sure if this is fair, but it seems appropriate. That to me is OK.

Let me reassure you. I am not a psychopath. I am not somebody who is doing this without any sense of pain. I have shared meals and wine with this man. I have learnt so much about him and I don't hate him. Yet, and this is my point, I don't pretend he is anything other than a man of the lowest morals, a cockroach, vermin. When I was a student, I lived in a house with a mouse. I didn't hate that mouse. In fact, sometimes I looked forward to hearing it scuttle across the floorboards while I lay in bed. The sound was, if not reassuring, at least a sort of comfort. Yet the day I fished its bloodied and decapitated body from the mousetrap was a day of celebration, a moment when I realised the bad things in life can be put to one side – they are not permanent.

He is not permanent. When he is gone, I will do more constructive things with his wealth.

Anna
Nicosia
Café Anette
12th October
11:30

It is done. I have signed. I have bought the hotel in Polis. I am changing the name. The Anna Love Apartments.

My life now is sorted. I have money, I have a business, I have put all those things that I am ashamed of behind me. Thomas, my dead baby, they are gone. The future is different – the future is not muddy, stained or cracked glass, it is a clear champagne flute where the bubbles rise to the surface and tickle your senses. I am a better person than Anne-Laure or Jill Betts or whoever else I was pretending to be. I am decent, I am honest. In my new world, all that I have been does not matter. All that drives me is who I can now become.

You? Don't steal this from me – we have made this journey together.

Kieran
Villa Spyros
Spetses
13th October
04:00

Awake. Again.

Everything is so much effort. Breathing, swallowing, toilet, moving. Too much.

Fish and Zie there in my dreams again. The same routine. Trying to get my attention, pointing to get me out. In the last dream, Zie actually touched my hand. I woke up when she came to pull me out of bed and it was as real as if she was there in the room with me.

Now, here in the darkness, I can hear the crickets singing, the night. In the distance, there is the sound of a ship's horn, perhaps there is fog? I wish I could be better, but I have wished that all my life.

Elena
15th October
Villa Spyros
Spetses
16:45

The time has come.

His eyes are dead, there is not much life in them, but he still expresses his feelings through them. He always looks happy to see me, but this is ridiculous. In a few minutes, I will tell him why.

I pour myself a glass of water, pull up a chair at his bedside and sit down.

'I have some news,' I tell him. 'It is not good – there is no other way to explain it.'

He looks interested, not worried, but I have his attention.

'We are going to Zurich tomorrow. A plane will arrive and you and I will fly there together. All your affairs are taken care of, the business is in my name, I have control over all of your finances. You have done the right thing. The truth is, you are not going to get better, but it was always going to be this way, once I had decided.'

He flutters his eyelashes quite quickly; this may be a sign that he is angry or could just be a side-effect of the last injection I gave him.

'You will find it strange,' I explain. 'It's not that I hate you, although I have never found much to like beyond a certain arrogant self-confidence. I liked that. No, I don't hate you. It's just that I don't respect you, don't see how I can be expected to either.'

I swear that there could be a tear in his eye now. Rather pathetic, but there you go.

'You have caused many people pain and suffering and fear. Life is full of suffering, we know that, but, in my own mind, it is the fear that is the worst thing. You probably don't understand. To a woman, fear is a constant. Fear that you will get pregnant when you don't want to, fear that you will get attacked if you take the wrong turning in the city streets and fear that once your looks fade, you will not amount to much because the men have taken all the best jobs and you have been kept subordinate to them. So, because we earn less and have your children, we end up worrying that all we have to look forward to is poverty in old age. It was after Dubrovnik. I think it was then I started to see that you could be made afraid. The panic getting away from the scene, the worry that you had. It was then that I started wondering, could I turn this to my advantage?'

I pause, take a sip of my water and brush my fringe back.

'The fire at your place in Hertfordshire' – and now I am looking right at him – 'that was me.'

His eyes flutter rapidly at this.

278

'It was so easy to make you think that it had been the Romanians. It wasn't them. So you ran around afraid and fearful, but you were scared at people who did not have the guile or ability to harm you. You looked for enemies abroad, not at home. When you ran off into exile I was able to track where you were. I knew you were in prison. I knew what had happened. When you came out, I sat on that e-mail for seventy-two hours. You see, I wanted your gratitude. At the station, it was easy to hire two heavies to come and look menacing. The funny thing is that they were bouncers from a local gay bar, one of the wisest uses of two hundred euros I have ever made, don't you agree?'

I smile to myself about this, looking across at him again. Yes, he is angry now. I can see that.

'Jorges? Well, I am genuinely sorry about him. But, you see, if he had lived he wouldn't have allowed me to bring my plan to fruition. You'll understand that sometimes in business there are people who, even if you like them, have to be let go, purely for business reasons. Now I have everything. Your money, your property and your future. You have, by the way, taught me so much. Obviously, as you will appreciate, the business will change. I mean, seriously? Stealing children? Is that the only pathetic way you could find to make a living? Couldn't you have, I don't know, been a teacher or a civil servant or even worked in something ridiculous, like Human Resources?'

I take a deep breath. I am getting a bit emotional. I sip some water.

'So, tomorrow. A plane, Zurich, a doctor, then peace.'

I nearly forgot.

'Ah, yes, that reminds me, in case you're wondering. Dr Fish. That wasn't me – that was purely bad luck on his part. You know how London is, not the safest of cities anymore. He was unlucky. OK?'

He looks drained by all this. I lean across, wipe the hair from off his forehead and plant a gentle kiss there. I think he has probably always wanted me to kiss him. I will now leave him to his fears and torture.

Elena
Zurich Airport
Swiss Airways Executive Lounge
17th October
16:45

I am waiting for my flight back to Greece.

They say these things are dignified. I am not so sure. Even the name, Dignitas, points in that direction.

Luckily, we had Dr Parlour on hand. I had kept in touch since Biarritz. It is, in my experience, always good to have a broad professional network, particularly as far as specialists are concerned. He was able to supply all the relevant supporting documents and ensure that there were no awkward problems on the day. For this he was paid half a million, but he will not, by the way, get to spend this. It is too dangerous having him around, so, through my network, I have arranged for him to be taken out in the next forty-eight hours. I never liked him, but besides, business is business.

As for the last few hours? He was so drugged up by the time he got on the plane, he was a virtual vegetable anyway. Not recognisable as the person who he was. I say this as a statement of fact – it is neither good nor bad.

Afterwards, there was nothing to do. The clinic would arrange for his cremation and the ashes would not be collected. A death certificate was issued there and then – as his loyal personal assistant, I was issued with the necessary documentation to sort out his legal affairs.

I have a small glass of champagne in front of me. I am not one for extravagant celebration. It is not my style, it is not the basis of my success. I am quiet, I am dignified; I could pass for a successful corporate lawyer or financial adviser. Look around you, maybe you'll realise, there are many like me preying on people like you.

EPILOGUE

Anna
Anna Love Apartments
Polis
April – 18 months later
13:00

Easter here has been warm and bright. The smell of spring is everywhere and bookings are looking very, very good. I love this place. I love the smell, the warmth, the people. Life is a joy – a blissful and complete joy.

I have been in the office, tidying up the accounts and the books. One of our first improvements was to add a taverna at the side of the development. We serve breakfast, lunch and dinner there; trade is good, but today, it being so early in the season, we only have a handful of guests.

Kris enters. He comes across and kisses me. He is the most loving man I have ever known; we have been together for about a year. Yes, he is older, but he is gentle and kind and sincere.

'You have a visitor,' he says.

This is OK – over time I have grown used to guests wanting to discuss something with me or locals enquiring about weddings.

'Who?' I ask, smiling, feeling the happiness inside of me.

'A French woman, I think, blonde, says she knows you from a while back.'

A while back worries me. A while back makes me tense.

Kris guides me out into the taverna, to the terrace at the side.

Under the table beneath the big olive tree, there is a well-dressed woman. She is drinking a glass of wine, wearing a big sun hat, huge sunglasses and a black dress.

'Hello,' I say. 'You wanted to see me?'

She smiles, looks up, and then removes her sunglasses and I recognise her. She stands and leans across and kisses me on each cheek.

'What do you want?' I hiss at her.

She speaks to me in that same calm, measured tone she always used.

'There is no need to be afraid,' she says. 'I just have some news.'

I am not sure, but I am unable to throw her out. Kris knows nothing of my past, but this woman – she could spoil everything.

'Please,' she says, 'sit down.'

I sit and look at her. I am not comfortable, but know that strange behaviour could lead to Kris asking too many questions. Elena has not been rude, has not been aggressive – if I throw her out, he will want to know why.

'You will want to hear this news,' she says. 'He is dead.'

I blink.

'Sorry?' I say.

'He is dead and you are safe. He will not harm you. Nor will I. I just want you to know that you are free. You don't need to be afraid.'

It has been so long since I thought about him, but the fear has been ever-present.

'When?' I ask.

She shakes her head.

'You don't need to know. Nobody else was involved. You just need to know that you are safe.'

We sit in silence. Eventually, she places a hand on mine.

'He made good people bad,' she says and then squeezes my hand.

Kris approaches our table.

'Ladies,' he asks with a broad smile. 'Can I get you anything else?'

'No,' Elena responds. 'I have to be going.'

He looks to Elena. 'I will get you your bill,' he says.

'No,' I tell Kris and smile at Elena. 'This one is on the house.'

She stands; we hug.

'Thank you,' I whisper into her ear.

'It was my pleasure entirely,' she whispers back.

I stand and watch her make her way to a black BMW. Kris puts his arm around my waist and I turn to him, looking up at his curly dark hair and his rich hazel eyes.

'Who was that?' he asks.

'An angel,' I say.

'So angels look like accountants now?' he asks with a laugh.

I don't answer. Perhaps they do. All I know is that the future is safe – for all of us.